THESE PERFECTLY CARELESS THINGS

A NOVEL

TASH DOHERTY

///BookBaby

It is [...] up with you and [...] hear about how you are [...] thing in Park Slope! This story can represent the travels to london you never had, lol. The flattip will take you right there! Hope you enjoy it

Love Tash

ISBN: 979-8-9892407-0-8 (PDF)

ISBN: 979-8-9892407-1-5 (Paperback Print)

ISBN: 979-8-9892407-2-2 (Audiobook)

ISBN: 979-8-9892407-3-9 (eBook / Kindle)

Front cover image by Tash Doherty.

Book design by Vellum.

Printed by BookBaby.

First edition printing 2023.

Disclaimer: Some characters and events in this book are fictitious. Any similarity to real persons, living or dead, is coincidental and not intended by the author.

www.tashdoherty.com

To the teenage dreamer in us all.

Courage is the most important of all the virtues.

Because without courage, you can't practice any other virtue consistently.

— MAYA ANGELOU

1

"Have we met before?" Max Fritz-Galloway said to her from across the garden table.

Half-full ashtrays, bottles, and beer caps lay strewn between them. Max was wearing a black T-shirt and a crisp dinner jacket. He had that strange kind of male beauty where none of his facial features made sense individually. There was nothing particularly attractive about his short nose or his hollowed cheeks. Yet when Abbie took in the complete picture of him, her insides began to tingle.

"With the other Etonians at Capital VIP," Abbie said. Fond memories of that night at the Ministry of Sound club arose in her mind. The club had multiple levels and a foam room, where students from England's elite public schools had paid to network with tongues. The hefty £40 entry ticket had been more than worth it.

"Of course." Max gulped, evidently trying to remember if he was one of the eight boys Abbie had pulled on the sweaty dance floor. He hadn't been, but at least now he was desperate to remember her and obviously trying to chirpse her. His attention gave her a brief yet energizing sense of power.

The sky above them was cloudy and tinted a pastel orange with the light pollution of London at night. Cars and double-decker buses hummed in the distance. The pounding dubstep music of Horace Bermond's house party wailed over the chatter coming from indoors. Across from them at the garden table sat Charles Barry. Charles's blond curls were smoothed back, gently dusting the collar of his velvet blazer. His angular face was attractive enough, but his large nose was heightened in the reflection of his phone screen. He had been texting incessantly on his BlackBerry all evening. The tip of Charles's lit cigarette glowed deep amber in the chilled night air. Did she have a better chance of getting with him or Max? Abbie didn't know. Either way, she needed to loosen herself up—and fast.

Abbie reached for the bottle of gin. She was about to take a swig when she saw a snail skulking along an ashtray. The snail's path glistened along the rim as its antenna circled the air helplessly. Abbie gazed at the snail for a moment before she picked it up by its shell. She sucked in her stomach as she stood up and brought the snail over to a rosebush in the corner of the patio. There she nestled it safely in the soil.

Returning to the table, Abbie heard drunken lips smacking together just beyond the rosebushes. The sounds made her nauseous. Before the party, she had shoveled McDonald's Chicken Selects and salted chips (with extra ketchup) into her mouth on the way up the hill, rushing to Horace's house to be sure she wouldn't be late. Now the excess fat and salt came back to haunt her, churning in her stomach. Puking that all up, Abbie thought, would be better than listening to the girl's moaning and the boy's grunting for a second longer.

She turned her attention back to the table. Charles and Max were in such high demand these days. Abbie had hardly expected them to show up at the party. She had to keep the conversation going for the sake of her reputation. She pointed subtly towards the couple in the bushes. At last, Charles looked up from his phone.

"Moe and Horace," Abbie whispered.

"I thought you were shagging him?" Charles said.

"We never shagged—"

"So he parred you off for your best friend?" Charles said, loud enough for the entire street to hear.

Abbie glared at him. She had forgotten how much of a rude prick Charles was, playing with other people's gossip like it was a game. With his attractiveness and social relevance, Charles could get away with an awful lot. But still, had he no tact?

"M-Moe can have my sloppy seconds," Abbie said. "Horace's knob is tiny, anyway."

Max sniggered. Abbie tried to laugh along with him. Yes, she had seen Horace's knob. And yes, it was nowhere near as big as Danny Watson's. But she still felt guilty for spewing such private, damning information.

"I have no idea what he sees in her," Charles continued. "I mean, Moe's got nice tits, but apart from that, she's munters. Her teeth are so fucked up."

"Oh, completely," Abbie said, swallowing her viciousness. She had never imagined that one day she would be siding with Charles Barry and throwing Moe, her best friend at Agerton Hall School, under the bus.

"Hos before bros," Moe had pinkie-promised her early last summer at a gathering in Hyde Park. As Horace's girlfriend at the time, Abbie had been a fool for believing her. Abbie's strongest memory of going out with him had been one cringeworthy Sunday afternoon. They had kissed for hours to the same La Roux songs on repeat because those were the only songs Horace had bought on iTunes. Eventually, Abbie succumbed and gave Horace a poor excuse for a hand job, from which he did not come.

All had been well until Horace dumped her and started going out with Moe the next day. Horace had wanted to have sex, and Moe had quickly risen to the occasion. Like in *Mario Kart*, Moe's roads were thick and sturdy, christened with rainbows and booster pads that would send Horace well into first place. And according to the noises coming from the bushes, Moe was about to lose her virginity to Horace any day now, if she hadn't already.

The rustling beyond the rosebushes subsided. There were a

couple of quiet footsteps. Abbie glanced at Max for backup, but he had started texting on his BlackBerry. There was no one to shield her now. The couple emerged into the dimly lit patio. Horace's long-sleeved shirt was unbuttoned, revealing his hairless chest, blank like a sheet of paper. He had his arm around Moe, who giggled and swayed. A large chunk of her mousy-brown hair had come loose from her ponytail. Beneath her American Apparel dress, her laced, purple bra was on show to everyone. Abbie squirmed at the sight of it. She recognized that bra. She had been with Moe when she bought it from Ann Summers, a lingerie shop in Chiswick. Now her memories of that day were ruined.

"Good to see you, Abbie," Horace said. Moe clung to his side, barely able to stand up with his help. "Charles! Max! Chuffed you could make it."

"Hi," Abbie said. She felt a hollow ache in the right side of her chest.

"Mate," Charles said, looking up from his phone, "Bugger off and enjoy the gash. She's an easy one."

"Ch-Charles, fuck off," Moe spat.

"Ignore him," Horace said.

"We were just leaving, anyway," Moe said, dragging Horace away. Her kitten heels clacked on the concrete as she zigzagged towards the house. Horace steadied her against his shoulder.

Charles paused for a moment. He put down his phone and winked at Abbie from across the table. Abbie grinned in a guilt-ridden way, basking in the knowledge that Charles was admiring her. Abbie checked that he was still watching and took a swig from the gin bottle. Her eyes watered from the scorching in her throat, but she didn't wince. She tried to lure the boys in.

"So, the election's coming up. Who would you guys vote for—"

"Why are all these Agerton Hall girls so easy?" Max said.

"My thoughts exactly," Charles said, glancing at her playfully. "They're banging about, practically begging to be shagged."

"I dunno," Abbie said.

She sighed. She wished, for once, that the boys might value her as more than just a virgin dartboard they could take a jab at. In that department, she was still performing terribly. It was late April, months after she and Horace had broken up, yet Horace was the last person she had pulled. Abbie had to get off with someone soon. Perhaps if she just had one more shot of gin, she could head into the house and hunt down an Etonian or a boy from St. Peter's Collegiate School (a.k.a. Collegiate) to shack up with for the rest of the evening.

The back door creaked open and was quickly slammed shut. Emily Watson strode towards the table. Her dark blond hair was tangled. The ruby of her belly button piercing glowed between her crop top and miniskirt. Emily was the third member of Abbie's former girl group with Moe and the sister of her repulsive ex, Danny. More annoyingly, Emily had been obsessed with Max Fritz-Galloway for years. She had reserved him like a parking spot, even though she didn't have a car and was far too young to take driving lessons.

"There you are, Maxie!"

"This one can't leave me alone," Max muttered to Charles.

Emily squeezed his shoulder. "You know, everyone says you're the fittest boy in the whole of Eton. And you—"

She locked eyes with Charles.

"Isn't your dad running for prime minister?"

"Someone put a muzzle on the one with daddy issues," Charles smirked.

Abbie giggled. It was a blissful moment of respite, watching Emily sink deeper into her demise. She sensed an opportunity for easy revenge.

"What's your pin?" Abbie asked Max, holding out her Black-Berry. It was the gin speaking, giving her strength. Emily's stare burned into her.

"Sure," Max said, taking Abbie's phone with ease. He typed his BBM pin into Abbie's phone like he was signing an autograph for a fan. Abbie caught a glimpse of Max's hands as he passed the phone back to her. She imagined him typing diligently, texting her back.

She almost melted at the thought of it. She smirked as she read the screen name of her new BBM contact:

Max

At once, Emily sprang up from the table, waving a cigarette at Charles.

"Light it for me, Charlesy," Emily commanded. Charles pulled a box of long matches out of his pocket and struck one.

"Don't call me that—"

"Thanks, babe," Emily said.

Emily made her way to Abbie's side of the table. As she folded her arms, her lit cigarette grazed Abbie's arm. It brushed up against her bare skin. It felt like the stab of a fatal injection. Abbie could almost hear her skin crackling and smell the odor of her blood vaporizing. Abbie shrank away from her in less than half a split second.

"Ouch!" she said, glaring at Emily. Her arm throbbed in agony.

"Oopsy daisies." Emily shrugged.

Abbie scoffed, aghast. She looked up at the boys, but neither of them had noticed. Abbie bit her tongue through the pain. The last thing she needed was Charles calling her a wimp for crying.

2

After Horace's party, Abbie walked home to Clarendon Road. The street was quiet, away from the midnight bustle of Notting Hill Gate. A thin mist hung between the white houses and the Victorian streetlamps, which hazed deep and golden, like honey, along the shadowed street. The windows of number 173, where her family had always lived, looked strangely foreign and vacant. The only lights inside came from the basement, where a single lamp was interrupted by the jagged lights of a TV screen.

Abbie opened the black iron gate at the side of the house and descended the narrow staircase. She peered in through the basement window. Yolly, her housekeeper from the Philippines, was hunched over in a soft slumber in the worn armchair. Yolly's long, greying hair was braided, and she was bundled up in her nightgown and slippers. Abbie smiled as an image of a couple cascaded outwards from the TV. Korean dramas were Yolly's favorite.

A soft blue rug stretched out in front of Yolly's feet. As a child, Abbie had played there with her dollhouse and Barbies while Yolly stood over her, ironing endless cocktail dresses and suits for Charlotte and Richard Chesterton, her mother and father. Freddie, her older brother, had been sent to boarding school at six in preparation for Eton, leaving Yolly and Abbie alone together. Even on journeys to Harpburgh House, where Charlotte's parents lived in the country-side, Yolly sat alone with Abbie; they had read princess fairy books and played I spy and peekaboo.

Abbie kicked up the corner of the wiry doormat. A small key was hidden in the layer of muck beneath it. It was a minor miracle that Yolly had left it out for her. Abbie could almost see the rules she was breaking right under Charlotte's nose in the glint of the key's silver edges. She entered the basement and slipped the key under Yolly's door. As she reached for the light switch, Abbie heard her heartbeat thumping in her ears. Light flooded the corridor. The whining of the laundry spinning in the dryer descended slowly before coming to a complete stop and buzzing loudly. Even now, at the age of fifteen, the basement terrified her. For most of her childhood, Abbie had pictured armies of daemons trying to joust her as she ran up the stairs to the security of the living room, where Charlotte could often be found talking on the house phone. Not to mention when Abbie had gotten physically stuck in the small gap between the washing machine and the closet that enclosed it. She had been only six years old and trying to surprise Yolly, except that Yolly was utterly distraught and had to call the firemen to help pry her free. She remembered Yolly crying, the fear swelling like poison in her eyes and her voice. Seeing that horror on Yolly's face made Abbie feel like the world was ending. It had shaken her to her very core.

Abbie took a deep breath and continued down the corridor. Here, in Yolly's quarters of the house, a plastic crucifix hung in the middle of the wall. The surrounding stucco surface was covered with Abbie's creations. Yolly had framed the colorful paintings Abbie had made as a toddler, with photos of them having ice cream together in Holland Park and Yolly pushing her in a swing as a baby. There was another photo of Abbie asleep in her pushchair, wearing her pompom hat in the winter with Yolly's younger, smiling face beside her. There were her scribbles from kindergarten decorated with dried pieces of macaroni. There were the mutant animals she had put so much effort into drawing in Year 1. Shell necklaces hung like prayer beads from shiny blue ribbons. There were the Christmas ornaments of dried white bread, cut into stars and hearts with cookie cutters that she had splashed with green and yellow paint. Pages were carefully laminated from her first spelling books, where Abbie had learned to write her name. There was a Happy Birthday card that she had spent hours painting for Yolly, of a dove and a cross in watercolors.

"So beautiful! Thank you, my wonderful girl," Yolly had said to her, her hands shaking with delight as she had taken the card out of the envelope and hugged her. Abbie remembered Yolly beaming and the creases of the wrinkles around her eyes deepening. At the time, Abbie had hardly realized that painting something small yet lovely could have such a powerful effect on another person. It had made her try harder in her Art lessons for a month or so afterwards. But since then, Abbie had never been able to re-create the shading on the bird, or the joy on Yolly's face.

Yolly had savored the relics of Abbie's childhood like little pieces of treasure, but they were a little discolored now. Their importance only seemed to fade more with time. Of course, Abbie still needed Yolly to cook dinner and clean her room. Yet she was glad that Yolly did not look after her anymore. She shuddered at the memory of when Yolly had picked her up from primary school and taken her to evening mass. Every time Father Michael addressed the congregation at Our Ladies of Victories Church, he said,

"If you can love your friends and family with a grateful heart, no matter their imperfections, you will know the full glory of the life God has given you."

Abbie had no idea what Father Michael meant. In mass, she had always been more preoccupied with drinking the last drop of her Eucharist wine after the paperlike token had dissolved on her tongue.

Abbie climbed the stairs into the safer realms of the house. The grandfather clock outside her parents' room struck once as she passed it. She jumped and almost tripped over a pile of her school uniform that Yolly had tucked aside neatly on the stairs. In her bathroom on the top floor of the house, Abbie turned on the light and saw her face in the mirror.

"Urgh!" she said.

Black mascara and eyeliner hung from her eyes, dripping like leaking bags of moldy cake batter. Had Max or Charles really thought she was fit? Abbie couldn't stand her forced celibacy any longer. She rehearsed her upcoming BBM message as she brushed her teeth. Then she typed it into her phone and sent it.

Abbie Chesterton: Hey, Max. It's Abbie. How are you? Xx

3

"Was that you coming home at that ghastly hour on Sunday morning?" Charlotte asked, glancing at Abbie over the top of her floral reading glasses. "Were you not at Moe's house for a sleepover?"

They were sitting at the breakfast table in the back corner of the kitchen. The tablecloth was covered with a smattering of teacups and toast, interior design magazines, and samples of silk fabrics. Water gargled down the kitchen sink drain, where Yolly stood washing the dishes. Above them, the slanted windows of the conservatory were speckled with rain. A robin sang intermittently from the tall, ivy-clad tree that took up most of the garden.

Abbie took a long, nervous sip from her teacup. The tea was warm in a comforting way. She peered into the garden, searching amongst the leaves just starting to grow across the broad branches. She prayed their tiny bursts of green might suddenly inspire her with a reasonable answer to her mother's questions. The branches hid much of the patchwork of pipes and windows at the backs of the neighbors' houses. Abbie wondered what the neighbors discussed at their breakfast tables. Had any of them ever lied to their mothers?

"Of course, I went to Moe's," Abbie found herself saying, "but just as we were about to go to sleep, some boys came over. And they were drinking. And I didn't want to have any, so I came home. Luckily, Yolly let me in."

"Heavens, Abigail!" Charlotte said. "Gosh, you are such a good girl. And you too, Yolly."

"Of course, madam."

"Next time, please, just go to the cellar and take any bottles of red after 2000. Darling, I simply cannot have you ending up in hospital."

"Certainly, Mummy," Abbie said, trying to hide her excitement as she dabbed a teaspoon of marmalade onto her buttered toast. Abbie had spent the last two years buying cheap Gordon's Dry Gin from a creepy man in Hammersmith who had gold crowns on his teeth. She had had to use her fake ID, obviously. The prospect of drinking her parents' alcohol and never having to return to that off-license was like music to her ears.

Charlotte opened her copy of *The Spectator*; her reading glasses eased down her nose as she began to read. Abbie noticed the title of the issue.

"Britain on the Brink: Allister Heath Says a Hung Parliament Could Send the Country Spiraling into Disaster. 6th March 2010."

Below the title was a giant red picture of the UK being sucked into a vortex. *The Spectator* always blamed other people for the country's problems: immigrants, America, and trees imported from France that disrupted the natural order of old-growth forests. Charlotte loved to read it. Everything about her mother screamed very classic, very English, and very dull. Her dyed-blond hair was fading into a mousy grey. Her navy cashmere cardigan was buttoned neatly over her ironed, collared shirt. Her knife balanced perfectly on the edge of her tea plate. She chewed with her mouth closed as the light wrinkles on her upper lip bent silently. Her elbows were nowhere near the table while she was eating. Charlotte was a master of manners. It made Abbie want to snort lines of ketamine off of Max Fritz-Galloway's chest and never look back. How could she have almost forgotten?

Abbie checked her BlackBerry. She reread the BBM.

Abbie Chesterton: Hey, Max. It's Abbie. How are you? Xx

Abbie had sent it thirty-one hours ago, and it still had not been delivered. She was beginning to think the worst. Had Max given her a pin to a phone he no longer used? This was a new low for her. She was far too embarrassed to tell anyone about it.

"Darling, no phones at the table," Charlotte said.

Abbie glared at her mother. She smacked her phone down in front of them. The cutlery rattled. Tea sloshed over the side of Charlotte's teacup, staining the tablecloth.

"Children are not invited to the Chelsea Flower Show. Or to go dress shopping at LK Bennett—"

"I don't want to go to the stupid flower show with you and Aunt Belinda!" Abbie said. "And how many times do I have to tell you? LK Bennett is for old people. I won't wear it again until I'm a hundred years old."

"With that kind of ingratitude, Abigail, I will be canceling our ladies' lunch at the Ledbury and our hair appointments. You can telephone Tarquin and schedule a cut yourself."

"Fine!"

Abbie grabbed her phone and stormed out of the room. The food at the Ledbury was delicious. She was furious to miss it. But she would rather cut off her left hand than inspect nauseating garden scenes with Aunt Belinda ever again. Aunt Belinda, Charlotte's closest friend, had an ample bosom and too many hairy moles on her face. She had seen Abbie in her most humiliating childhood moments, like the time when Abbie had stepped in a giant dog poo outside her primary school. If only Abbie could have been more like her more prim, well-behaved classmates, who always colored inside the lines with their coloring pencils.

"Have a blessed day," Yolly called out to her as she cleared Abbie's dishes away. Abbie pretended not to hear. She grabbed her schoolbag at the bottom of the stairs. She stomped through the entryway, passed the weathered prints of the English gentry, who sported black velvet top hats and coattails, hanging on the dark green walls.

She shoved the new letters addressed to her father into the mountain of post that had accumulated by the front door. Then she stepped outside into the brisk air.

Morning swelled in the windows of Clarendon Road. The sky was unforgivingly grey. Abbie walked past some of Notting Hill's finest houses. Glorious, curtained, tasseled-filled windows hid the residents within. The brick rooftops clung together between the church steeples, wrapping around them like spiral staircases. The distant clang of a church bell striking the hour became inaudible over the hum of red double-decker buses and the rattle of black taxis.

Abbie turned down Abbotsbury Road, still grumbling to herself. She was on her way to meet Julie, her friend and loyal bus buddy, just south of Holland Park. From there, they would head to school together. But this morning, for the sake of her sanity, Abbie decided to take a detour. She turned left through an open gate and entered Holland Park.

The morning light peeked through in small diamond shapes between the awkwardly twisted branches of the trees. Ivy grew freely behind the fences of the path, acting like a wild carpet on the forest floor. It wound around the ebony wood of the trunks, veined with vibrant moss. The narrow, darkened path tunneled through the trees. The air was damp with dew and mud. Along the edges of the trodden earth sprang bright stems and bluebells, like lanterns on the tables of a fairy's restaurant.

As Abbie gazed out into grassy clearings, she took a deep breath of fresh air. She tried to calm herself, but the same anxious thoughts looped through her mind. Thanks to her parents, Abbie had attended private schools her entire life. She had even been on family safari trips to South Africa, apparently a once-in-a-lifetime experience. But something important was missing. If anything, Abbie had been given too much in her life so far. Too many rules. Too much of a sense of what polite, well-mannered young ladies did or were supposed to do. The voices and the pressures seeped into her mind like a stream of word vomit. For years, Abbie had exhausted herself trying to be a "good girl." Charlotte had forced her to play with Barbies even when she wanted to build a tree fort with Freddie in the garden or mobilize his Playmobil as they battled with the Action Men. But things had only worsened as Abbie got older and grew bigger and spottier with puberty. She laughed too loudly. She mumbled her words. She desperately wanted to be one of those girls, or one of those grown-ups, who could pour a glass of Pimm's from a large pitcher in the summer without spilling it. Or who could write a thank-you letter perfectly the first time around. And yet, aged fifteen, she was still as unladylike as ever.

"What am I going to do with my life?" Abbie whispered to herself. "What do I even want to study?"

She was allergic to the idea of becoming a lady who lunches. That was basically what Charlotte did, sprinkled in with a bit of yoga, tennis competitions, and renovations of Harpburgh House. Abbie was tired of being a doll in her mother's dollhouse. And she was sick of playing the petty, social-climbing games of the people who were supposed to be her friends. It was all a distraction, and because of them, Abbie had lost sight of everything that mattered to her.

A year ago, when Abbie was secretly going out with Danny Watson, she had first dreamt of what her life could be. She dreamt of seeing her work displayed in a gallery. She imagined one of her large, abstract collages framed on a wall. A collage of layered, colorful cutouts from graphic design magazines that she loved. Collaging was the only thing that brought her peace in this world. She felt drawn to the bold, fantastical images in *Vogue* magazine. But rather than reading the magazine from cover to cover as a young lady would, Abbie felt an insatiable urge to tear out pages as she went, combining, cutting, sticking, and folding until all the different colors sang together. A franken-creation of her own. She had asked her mother for a subscription to the magazine, but Charlotte had promptly rejected it. Since age thirteen, Abbie had spent most of her extra pocket money on *Vogue* instead of sweets at the corner shop. She stashed her cutouts in a nondescript blue folder under her bed, where she collected the images of alternative universes, salt flats in

Bolivia, and the mirrored walls of Château de Versailles. These worlds were new and vibrant to her. They brought her joy, but they also terrified her.

"What if I'm not good enough to be an artist?" Abbie mumbled, "What if I spend my whole life doing something, and it turns out I'm terrible at it?"

She bit her nails as she continued through the park. The trees around her gradually evolved into rose gardens and tennis courts. Abbie walked under a wide brick arch at the exit and checked the time on her phone. It was 8:23 a.m. Gosh, she was so late. On her phone's screen, she caught sight of a small yellow envelope with a 1 next to it. A new message. Her throat ached at the sight of it. She clicked through to read it.

4

A bbie glanced up from her phone. Julie stood ahead of her, leaning against the brick wall of a neighbor's house on the corner. No matter how much she tried to tame it, Julie's thick, dark brown hair was always lopsided when put in a ponytail. She was still learning how to pluck her monobrow. Julie had survived her first full-body wax, which she had gotten the last time her family went to their house in Saint-Tropez.

"Where have you been?" Julie asked. They set off for the bus stop on Kensington High Street. Abbie said nothing. Her attention diverted towards her phone. The possibility that Max Fritz-Galloway had texted her revived the butterflies in her stomach. But her excitement quickly fell flat. Instead, she had a BBM from Finlay Thorpton, a short, insecure boy from Collegiate.

Finlay T: Gathering at Griff's house on Saturday night. Can you bring Moe and Emily?

Abbie groaned. Alfie Griff lived in Angel, North London. It was a trek and a half away from Abbie's usual stomping grounds of Notting Hill and Chiswick. Still, she wanted to hang out with the boys. The Collegiate boys were an intellectual group with snarky, multileveled humor. They were a bit too intelligent and a bit too anxious to pull any girls. Finlay's groveling text was a disappointing example of that. Clearly, to him, Abbie was nothing more than a gateway to her super attractive former girl group. She quickly messaged him back,

Abbie Chesterton: I'm up for it.

"Who's that?" Julie asked.

"Finlay Thorpton."

"You're not really going to hang out with the Collegiates, are you?"

"Maybe."

Julie rolled her eyes.

"Come on," Abbie said as they got to the bus stop, "I've got nothing better to do." Now that she thought about it, Griff's gathering was her only chance to regain her former social glory.

"I can't believe you're still trying to be friends with Moe and Emily after everything they've done to you," Julie said. "I mean, I just hope one day you'll appreciate who your real friends are."

Abbie ignored her. Julie just didn't get it. Julie's parents had raised her on world-class wines so she would never chug vodka at a house party. An aggressively room-temperature bottle of Smirnoff was beneath her. But to Abbie, there were people to meet and places to go. Abbie's network was important for her future. And she had invested so much time and effort into her social standing. She wasn't about to throw it all away.

"What are your plans for the weekend?" Abbie asked, changing the subject.

"Flying to Geneva with my parents again," Julie sighed.

"Won't that be fun?"

"No. I've got to go to Arnaud's grandma's château near Lausanne. She has a rabbit problem."

"That sucks," Abbie said, feigning disappointment. Secretly, she was glad that Julie was busy that weekend. Julie was a good friend but far too goofy to deserve an invite to Griff's house. Julie would probably embarrass her if she ever found herself there.

"I guess we've missed Pig," Julie said, her eyes downcast.

"Yeah," Abbie said. They liked to gossip together in code names. It made the world of riding the bus to school a far more enrapturing place. Pig was Marco Pigatelli, a fit Italian boy who went to The Barnes School, who Julie had been on holiday with (but never managed to kiss).

"Maybe we'll see him tomorrow."

They boarded a red double-decker bus headed for Hammersmith and sat on the top deck. As they rode the bus to school, Julie tried to flatten the poof of her ponytail and dig a piece of porridge out of her braces. Abbie felt a pang of guilt as she watched her. She had ruined one of Julie's only chances of interacting with a boy that week. Julie was a late bloomer and had not gotten her period. Abbie imagined her as one of those magnolia trees that didn't know what season it was and randomly flowered for two weeks in the middle of winter. Yet the sad reality was that Julie was light-years behind her. Julie talked a big game about Pig, but Abbie knew that Julie's prospects with him were little more than an overhyped fantasy.

"So?" Julie said to her in an excited whisper. "Did you go snorkeling this weekend?"

"Snorkeling" was their other code word.

"The reef is dead," Abbie said blandly.

Julie snorted a bit as she giggled. "Weren't there plenty of Etonians to fish from?"

"Not really," Abbie said. "Just Moe and Horace sucking face again."

"Ew, gross. Some things never change," Julie said.

Abbie frowned as she saw her fugly reflection in the dirty bus window. She missed getting smashed at Moe's house in Chiswick while her parents were home and skateboarding with the bad boys from the local comprehensive school. And convincing the homeless man who slept on the bench by Turnham Green tube station to buy them more booze. And laughing at the ridiculousness of it all with that deep, belly-aching laugh that brought tears to her eyes. Abbie wished she could return to that time when her life had been so carefree. If only she had settled with one of Horace's less-than-intelligent friends from Charter House to secure her social position. Then her popularity might not have died over the winter.

They got off the bus at Hammersmith Broadway. The latest shop boarded up at the station was a Chicken Cottage, which had also been graffitied. Police dotted about the area. Stabbings happened in Hammersmith a couple of times a year. Still, the only violence Abbie had ever experienced was the death stares from the older Agerton Hall girls. They were like piranhas, swarming to compete for a single Barnes boy. As she stepped onto the escalators, Abbie recalled a phrase Charles Barry had once said to her:

"Agerton Hall girls are like double cream. Thick, white, and rich."

They passed groups of Agerton Hall girls, Barnes boys, and other teenagers whose school uniforms Abbie didn't recognize. The state school teens and their uniforms were so foreign to her. They wore ties as short as possible and small, black Nike backpacks that made Abbie wonder how they ever fit any books in them. The girls pulled their hair back flat and tight and wore chunky gold jewelry that almost ripped their ears. They spoke of *wastemen* who did *mad* things, *innit.* They flicked their knuckles in a way Abbie had never been able to do while they laughed about *bruvs* and *mandems.* A couple of them were huddled around a lighter, burning gum wrappers.

Abbie was minding her own business as they approached "The Statue," a giant statue of a mermaid and a merman, where Barnes boys would come to meet Agerton Hall girls after school. She stood next to Julie, using her as a human shield so she didn't have to face this battleground alone.

"Don't look now," Julie said. "It's Evil."

But it was too late. Suddenly a scene of utter repulsion unfolded in front of their eyes. Abbie gagged at the sight of them.

"Fuck," she said before Julie could pull her away.

It was Danny Watson, with a new girl. A glimpse of his brown buzz cut, earring, and cheekbones brought her back to the time she had gotten on her knees in his bedroom, and he had pulled down his trousers, and she had seen his penis for the first time.

"Go on, babe," Danny had said to her, closing his eyes as he braced himself. Abbie had been utterly unsure of what to do next. "Touch it."

A dollop of puke bubbled up and stung the back of Abbie's throat. When she had gone out with Danny last year, behind Emily's back, their relationship had been the talk of the century. Abbie had ridden the wave of his popularity as a Barnes boy in the year above her until it ended in disaster when he dumped her via voicemail on her old Nokia flip phone. She had listened to it one morning with Julie on the bus to school:

"Hey, Abbie, um, so I've been thinking...haha. Posey, bugger off. Stop it, lads! Hey, so yeah, this isn't going to work for me. No can do...haha. Good day to you...salutations...au revoir—"

Then everyone thought Abbie was a complete sket and a back-stabber. Unsurprisingly, it had ruined her relationship with Emily. In a way, Abbie knew she kind of deserved it after all the terrible things she had done. That was why Julie had nicknamed him Evil. Because of the things Danny had done to her and the person he had turned her into.

From the way Danny was enticing this new Agerton Hall girl, who Abbie did not recognize, it was clear that he was still up to his old, sleazy tricks: conning girls into getting with him just because he was very well-endowed and had an insatiable libido. Danny liked the challenge of trying to get with every new fit girl in his path, like another password to a bank account that he had to crack.

"It's the lock and key analogy," Danny once told her. "A lock opened by many keys is a bad lock, but a key that opens a lot of locks is a good key."

As Abbie watched him grope the girl's leg, she felt a squeezing in her chest that could only mean one thing. Part of her wished Danny still pretended to love her. Part of her still craved his lustful manhandling. She could not decide who she was angrier at. Danny, for being a generally selfish bastard, or herself, for falling for him. It hurt her to look at him because it reminded her of a time when she had been so paralyzingly naïve. She was desperate to run up to Danny's new girl and shake her by the shoulders. The girl was about to be used if she wasn't being used already.

Abbie trudged away from them. Nothing could have prepared her to see Danny so captivated by another girl. Meanwhile, she was destined to be alone forever. She might end up like Aunt Belinda, childless or, even worse, unmarried. And she would have three cats and live in Somerset, with only the bleating of sheep and the smell of cow pat to keep her company. Her eyes stung with tears.

"Oy vey," Julie said, patting her on the back. "Next time, I'll poke his eyes out with a pencil." Abbie smiled at her and tried to blink back her tears, but her throat kept aching. She needed something to distract her. What would she wear to Griff's that weekend? None of the Collegiate boys were that fit, but at least she could flirt with Finlay and try to get his attention.

5

That Saturday evening, Abbie climbed the gentle hill towards Notting Hill Gate station. There was an earthy smell of stone and Gulf Stream mist. Baubles of pollen tumbled from the branches of the plane trees. They broke apart silently on the ancient pavement, draped in leadlike damp. The last of the pink cherry blossom petals gathered in the gutters. The chill of winter had gradually thawed, revealing the aged city's beating heart.

Abbie held her head high, trying to muster a sense of confidence. She wore dark blue leggings with a white stripe down either side. She had bought them for £5 from Portobello Market and had never worn them. Even now, she didn't feel edgy enough to pull them off. At least she was covered up by the black faux-fur coat she wore over her white crop top. Her coat was thick and causing her to overheat, but she had to keep it on. She was already sweating so much that she worried that if she took it off, everyone at Griff's party would see her draping sweat patches.

With her silver hoop earrings, Abbie's outfit felt aspirational. She wanted to run into one of Charlotte's friends on the street just to see what they would say. She had tried to copy the cool girls in the years above her at Agerton Hall, the ones who wore thick, black eyeliner

and smoked outside school, who waited for their boyfriends to pick
them up on their motorcycles. Abbie wanted to be them, yet she had
struggled in front of the mirror. She had rubbed her eyes red raw, and
puffy, as she tried to put on her makeup. Now that she had finally left
the house, she felt very misaligned. It was a heavy kind of discomfort. This outfit was not very "her." She was trying to accomplish too
much too soon, and she was sure that all the strangers she passed
could tell.

She felt apprehensive about the journey to Griff's house. What
would she talk about with Finlay for the next forty-five minutes? He
was bound to share endless details about how his growth spurt was
just around the corner. Abbie decided to follow her mother's advice.
On more than one occasion, Charlotte had whined to her,

"Abigail, must you talk for England? Perhaps you could ask
someone else about themselves once in a blue moon."

As Abbie neared the station, she searched for Finlay's curly,
ginger hair in the crowd of commuters. She saw him wearing a thick,
brown leather jacket, probably supposed to make him look bulkier.
He nodded as she approached. To Finlay's left stood a familiar face.
It was Jonah Wood. Jonah was slightly taller than her and a bit overweight, a stark contrast to Finlay. Jonah's black hair was shaved
short on either side and longer on top. He was wearing a dark purple
cashmere jumper. The collar of his shirt was tinted with light purple
pinstripes and was folded unevenly. The legs of his black trousers
were too long. Trapped between his brown suede boots and the pavement, they were gradually getting ruined. Jonah frowned as he
smoked a cigarette.

Abbie was not sure what to make of Jonah's style. He was well-
dressed in a way that Charlotte would approve of. From his stance,
he looked more than a decade older than her, yet she had to remind
herself that he was in her year at Collegiate, so he was probably the
same age.

"Sup?" Finlay said, hugging her.

"Not much," Abbie said. She looked at Jonah. He looked away
and took another drag of his cigarette before stubbing it out on the

ground. Abbie had kind of forgotten that Jonah Wood even existed. He rarely came to parties, even though she knew he was part of Griff and Finlay's friend group from Collegiate. She wondered why he wasn't more social and why he had chosen to join them for tonight's gathering.

"Moe's not with you?" Finlay asked.

"No."

"But she's coming, right?"

"I don't know."

"Fine. Well, I guess let's get going?" Finlay huffed.

Abbie felt a sense of dread as they set off into the station. The boys were barely settling for her as their strict Plan B. Now they had this extra-long tube journey ahead of them, and she didn't have as much of a drop of alcohol in her bloodstream. They descended multiple sets of escalators. The thin, cylindrical tunnels dropped relentlessly deeper under the ground. The air was stifling, thick with perspiration. Abbie sped ahead of them as she heard the familiar, slowing rhythm of a train pulling into the station. She followed signs for Central line trains heading eastbound. Jonah and Finlay hurried behind her. They boarded the train just in time.

"The next station is Queensway," the automated woman's voice sounded over the train's loudspeaker. Abbie sat down, relieved. Jonah and Finlay sat across from her. The train accelerated, slamming deafeningly against the tracks. She could hardly hear what the boys were saying. She felt disconnected from them. They made no effort to include her, so she leaned towards them, trying to pick up more of their conversation.

Jonah's accent had mellowed tones. That's right, Abbie remembered. His family was from New York. Jonah's fingers were chubby, and when he gestured with his hands as he talked to Finlay, they curved slightly upwards. His neck was thick and reddening along the sides. Jonah pulled at his purple cashmere jumper as he spoke. He was probably overheating, too. His jumper was baggy. He rested his hands in his lap, revealing the roundedness of his lower belly. He was out of shape, undoubtedly. Still, he seemed confident and relaxed. His feet were firm, just more than hip-width apart.

Abbie tried to remember how they had crossed paths over the years. She wasn't sure exactly where the Woods lived. It was somewhere down Elgin Crescent, on the other side of the communal garden from where her primary school friend, Amber Rutterdown, used to live. She and Amber had been friends during their tomboy phase in Year 6 when they were eleven. They had worn bandanas and jeans with holes in the knees. They had listened to Christina Aguilera's new album on Amber's CD player. Abbie was glad that this phase had happened before people got digital cameras for Christmas. Without photo evidence, the world would forget that that phase of her life had ever happened.

Abbie remembered that one summer afternoon, she had been at Amber's house, and they had been playing in the playground. She could only have been about nine at the time. There, she had come across Jonah and his younger brother, who were eating enormous ice lollies. Their giant, black Labrador, Moonshine, had been asleep on the picnic blanket beside them.

"Popsicles," Jonah's little brother had said as red and yellow food coloring dripped from his face onto his T-shirt. Abbie remembered feeling embarrassed for them but also very envious. Their *mom* had allowed them to have ice lollies, perhaps the biggest ones in the entire world. It could only mean one thing: Jonah's mother had brought them from America, and there was no way that Abbie could ever have one. Everything from the States was bigger and better. These details were enough to set the Woods apart, like oil from the crisp, clean water of the people of Notting Hill. They were not the only Americans, but they were by far the least integrated, with the strongest accents and the strangest habits. Even though Jonah's dad was probably a banker who was generously paid, Abbie knew that any mention of popsicles instead of ice lollies would be enough to give Charlotte a migraine.

Abbie leaned in again, hoping to catch a couple more words of the boys' conversation. She was desperate to say anything to make them acknowledge that she existed.

"So, I should buy Apple stocks then because I like Apple?" Finlay said.

"N-not necessarily," Abbie butted in. She swallowed hard, speaking loudly over the whirring of the train as it sped through the tunnel, "because if you only invest in one stock, then if the stock goes down, then you lose all your money."

Jonah glanced at her enigmatically. Was he judging her? Whatever he was thinking, he wasn't happy about it.

"Exactly," Jonah said with a tight lip.

"But what could go wrong for Apple? They're about to come out with the new iPhone. That stock price can only go up," Finlay said.

"What if their manufacturing plant breaks down in China?" Abbie said. She gave examples to a perplexed Finlay from the 1929 stock market crash that she was learning about in History. And how it was similar to the crash in 2008 because of a bubble in stock prices. Abbie glanced at Jonah again. Now that she was saying vaguely intelligent things, Jonah seemed intrigued.

"Who are you supporting in the election?" Jonah asked her.

"I don't like Gordon Brown because he looks like a basset hound—"

"So, it's all about looks to you, then?"

"No," Abbie insisted, "David Cameron is a bit sleazy, and I don't like most of his policies. I agree more with the Lib Dems and getting rid of university fees."

"Is your house worth more than £2 million?"

"Probably."

"Then your daddy's going to suffer with their mansion tax. Don't you want to be able to drink champagne whenever you want it?" Jonah teased. He seemed so pleased with himself.

"I mean, my dad doesn't buy champagne. He buys wine."

"Oh, well, you're off the hook then," Jonah said. "Still, you didn't answer my question."

Abbie looked at him, puzzled. It didn't matter that her parents had survived the financial crash or that Richard had a more extensive collection of wine in the annexes of Harpburgh House than in London. Charlotte had often told her they were struggling and didn't have enough money to renovate Harpburgh.

"What does it mean to buy wine?" Finlay asked with all the innocence of a kindergartner trying to spell their first words.

Jonah and Abbie took turns explaining it to him, as well as the differences between owning your own business and having a salary and paying taxes. Jonah's dad worked at J.P. Morgan in New York and had to pay capital gains tax on his dividends, whatever those were. Jonah had a slight lisp when he said things like "stockbrokers" and "safe investments." It made him sound grittier and nerdier like one day he might be suited up with black leather loafers, a briefcase, and a fedora hat, catching the subway in Manhattan. His light brown eyes were fixed in a clear gaze when he spoke.

Finlay struggled to keep up with their discussion. Somehow, Abbie riffed off Jonah as they talked about wealth, power, economies, and the big, bad world out there. The more Abbie spoke, the more she felt her points of view were being pulled back from behind a veiled curtain she hadn't known was there. Abbie said what she thought. Jonah listened. He must have thought she was at least smart enough to talk to.

They got off the train at Islington and headed out into the darkened streets. The rows of houses were slightly less majestic in Angel than in Notting Hill, but each brick doorway was framed with the same white columns. The streetlamps illuminated the worn, cracked pavements on their way to a corner shop. There, Jonah managed to purchase a cheap bottle of vodka while Abbie and Finlay waited outside. Onwards they went to Griff's house.

Finlay soon switched the conversation to something he was far more interested in: Moe, Emily, and the other girls. Agerton Hall girls weren't that bright, he repeated. Moe hadn't even known that the Eurostar train went under the Channel, connecting London with Paris and Brussels. Abbie rolled her eyes as Finlay talked them down, partly because her old friends were taking up so much of

Finlay's attention and partly because these girls were as fake as imitation crab. She didn't find Finlay attractive, but she still wanted him to rate her and talk about her, only saying nice things, of course.

"Why do you like them so much if they're so dumb and wear so much makeup?" Abbie interrupted him.

"Because they're fit," Finlay said.

"Even Moe's fake teeth and everything?"

"My grandma's got fake teeth, and I'd still fuck her," Finlay said.

Abbie glanced at Jonah. They burst out laughing. Finlay smiled. He seemed to think his joke was funny and was unaware they were laughing at him.

Jonah turned left into a small front garden and rang the doorbell. Griff opened the door, his thin frame towering over them in the doorway. Griff had a large gap between his front teeth, and his hair was long and erratic. He clapped Jonah on the back,

"You look like a right twat. Who dressed you? The vicar?"

"Fuck off," Jonah snapped. Abbie giggled at his grumpiness.

They shuffled into Griff's house. The entryway smelt like lavender, and the sounds of low voices were muffled through the walls. They walked into the main room on the ground floor. It had a combined dining room and kitchen, the same layout as her house on Clarendon Road. Abbie's heart sank. Collegiate boys sat around the dining table, no other girl in sight. The table was awash with irrelevant faces. The boys tucked into their greasy dinner, probably from a chippie nearby. The smell of vinegar mixed with battered cod and sizzling oil wafted around the room.

"Want some?" Griff asked, thrusting a foam plate of chips and a wooden chip fork towards her.

"No thanks," Abbie said, patting her stomach.

"Don't be ridiculous. You're really skinny," Finlay said, pinching her forearm.

"I wouldn't be a proper teenage girl if I wasn't trying to lose weight," Abbie said proudly.

"Whatever," Finlay said, grabbing the plate of chips. He lathered them with more vinegar and shoveled a couple into his mouth.

"Fuck you and your high metabolism," Jonah snapped at him, "I need a cigarette." He motioned to Finlay to finish eating. Finlay gulped down an extra chip, and they left the room.

Abbie found herself alone, a couple of meters away from the boys sitting around the table. There was no space for her, and they were talking about football. She didn't want to scrape into their conversation and risk looking like an idiot. The boys' eyes skated over her, checking out her leggings and her coat and her crop top. After years at single-sex schools, seeing anyone of the opposite sex was still an awkward novelty. And being the only girl left her looking like a total loner.

Abbie wandered away from them into the kitchen. The white SMEG fridge had curved edges as if it belonged on a spaceship in the 1960s. The mantelpiece was covered in knickknacks and figurines draped in textured patterns. It was the kind of décor Charlotte would enjoy in a travel magazine but would never have bought herself. Hanging off the wall was a large pinboard covered in family photos. There was one of Griff standing outside his house in his school uniform, his long-sleeved white shirt basically down to his knees. All the boys were getting taller these days. Most of their voices had dropped, and they were growing embarrassing, limp hairs on their chins. Even Finlay was almost as tall as her.

Abbie headed out onto the balcony at the back of the house. It had started to rain, and she was glad to see Jonah and Finlay huddled under umbrellas.

"I don't usually smoke around girls," Jonah said as he made space for her. "Want one?"

"No, I don't smoke."

The garden beyond the balcony was cold and empty. The rain dripped like notes on a scale along every angle of the ironwork. The wind shook the wooden fencing that separated the neighbors' gardens. The lit ends of the boys' cigarettes stood out like beacons. Abbie huddled under an umbrella, slightly closer to Jonah.

"I'm on my third pack of Camel Blues today," Jonah said in her left ear. A tingling feeling grew in Abbie's stomach. It was the same sensation she had felt when she first bumped into Horace at Capital VIP. But Horace was so much better looking than Jonah. But Jonah's arm was so close to hers. Jonah exhaled and tried to blow the cigarette smoke away from her. Was he doing it to be courteous?

"Do you normally smoke that much?" Abbie asked.

"We went to Thorpe Park today. I had to have one before and after every ride," Jonah said.

"You were such a pussy, though. You didn't even go on Stealth or Saw," Finlay said.

"I hate roller coasters too," Abbie said, "Maybe Jonah wasn't scared. He just had better things to do, like smoking cigarettes. Probably getting ready to *die*." She looked at him, hoping to get a reaction. Jonah took another drag of his cigarette.

"Did you hear what I said?" she pressed him. "You're probably going to die from smoking."

"No, you're going to die," Jonah said, his face lighting up.

"No, you're going to—"

"No, you are going to die!" he shouted. Abbie burst out laughing. A moment later, Griff came out onto the balcony, scolding them,

"Guys, can you shut up? The neighbors are going to flip."

"Griffy, don't fret," Jonah teased. Griff shook his head and went back inside.

Abbie was still giggling, hardly able to contain herself.

"What's gotten into you?" Jonah said.

"Nothing."

The rain started to pick up. It trickled down her arm. Abbie shuffled slightly to the left, and Jonah moved the umbrella to better cover her.

"Fuck this," Finlay said in a huff, holding his hand out to measure the rain, "I'm going inside."

Jonah flicked his cigarette away, a gesture that seemed so casual to him that he might have done it a million times. Abbie waited for him to light another with his red-tinted plastic lighter. Then, her confidence came out of nowhere.

"Please, shake my hand," she said, "I'm getting drunk tonight, and when I do, you better have my back. I don't want to make a fool of myself."

"All right," Jonah said, briefly taking her hand in his. His palm was coarse and a little sweaty. "But you have to do the same for me."

"Deal. Let's drink to it."

Abbie turned to go inside.

"Let me finish this," he said.

"No, let's go inside now."

Jonah groaned. He took two deep drags. Then he flicked it way off into the garden.

"Come on!"

Back in the room full of boys, Abbie found two shot glasses. She poured a healthy amount of vodka into each and added a little orange juice to hers. Then she thrust the glass into Jonah's hand. The bottles of spirits were passed around the table.

"What are we drinking to?"

"To tomfoolery!" she announced.

"To tomfoolery! Cheers!" the room toasted with her, laughing.

Abbie grinned, relishing in her success. It was by far her coolest moment of the night so far. She made a note of it to herself. She would relive this later to remind herself she was super confident and secure. The vodka hit her throat like liquid fire. She almost choked, but she pushed through the pain and downed it in one. She smacked her empty glass down on the dining table.

"What's wrong with you guys? Can't handle your drink?"

"N-no fair. You didn't drink it straight," Finlay said, spluttering.

The doorbell rang. Abbie's bliss evaporated in an instant. Before she could catch her breath, she was hugging each of the girls, kissing them on both cheeks, breathing in some cheap, floral perfume Moe had probably picked up on sale from Superdrug.

"OMG, hey, babe! How are you?" Moe shouted in her ear. Abbie found herself trapped between the soaking sleeve of Moe's coat and her cleavage. Once she loosened her grip, Moe took off her jacket and handed it to Horace, who followed behind her. Underneath, Moe was wearing a very low-cut black tank top with a baby blue cardigan and a jean miniskirt. Abbie felt the energy in the room slowly gravitate towards Moe.

"Babes, I haven't seen you in ages," Emily chimed in as Abbie hugged her. Emily's eyes were caked in eyeliner. Her face was covered in a vibrant orange foundation. It looked powdered and was far too dark for her skin color. Not to mention that Emily was wearing a white, floral-patterned dress. White was a dangerous color, especially given Emily's history of getting completely plastered and rolling around in every boy's lap. Emily shoaled like a fish behind Moe, wondering which direction she was about to go in. Drinking more vodka helped Abbie stifle the forcefield of new energy in the room. The girls were all soaking, their makeup melting down their faces. There were so many people now. Abbie felt the oxygen depleting from the air. She didn't know who, if anyone, she could hang out with. She could hardly attach herself to the girls who had just arrived. But that seemed like a better option than sitting down with a couple of boys she didn't know as they ate greasy chips. Those boys had not even figured out how to shave their light mustaches. Abbie felt less cool just looking at them.

"Griff, turn on some music," Moe said. "This party is so boring. I want to dance."

Griff hastily obeyed. He plugged a shiny silver iPod into the speaker jack. The wheel of the iPod clicked as he selected a song. Soon, the electro-pop beats and Kesha's groovy voice bounced around the room. "TiK ToK" was the hottest tune in town. Moe immediately started grinding on Emily, who took a large swig from a bottle of whiskey.

"Pass it over." Abbie motioned to her. Emily handed her the bottle. Abbie needed her sobriety to evaporate and fast. As she took a swig, she glanced across the room. Finlay had his eyes on Moe now. It was all so unfair. Abbie wanted him to look at her in the way he looked at Moe. She wanted Horace, even, to look at her that way too. Like he had done earlier that year. Abbie took another large gulp from the bottle. She fake-smiled at Emily and took her by the hand. Emily's fingers were dainty. Abbie twirled her. This was the only

way. A couple more swigs of the whiskey bottle. A couple more
sloppy twirls with Emily. Abbie grabbed Emily by the hips and
shimmied against her. She tried to move her butt and body like she
had seen Shakira do in the "Hips Don't Lie" music video.

"Abbie!" Emily giggled as Abbie leaned in and pretended to
kiss her.

Abbie felt the boys look over at her again. Their attention lifted
her spirits. For a moment, Abbie felt at peace. She caressed Emily's
cheek. She grabbed the back of Emily's wet hair, strawlike and
knotty. Maybe Abbie would kiss her for real this time. The smell of
fish and chips was making her nauseous. A large dollop of sick
sprang up from her stomach, stinging the back of her throat. Her
insides swelled with pride as she brought Emily's face inches away.
Abbie felt the boys' attention sparkle across her shoulders. Emily
closed her eyes, ready for her.

"Ahem." Someone probed her gently in the back.

Abbie turned around. It was Jonah.

"W-what do you want?"

"We shook hands on it."

"Well, th-thank you, but I'm dancing with my friends."

"You're making a fool of yourself—"

"L-let me dance!" Abbie said. She wanted to grab the whiskey
bottle from Emily and grind on her again. But Jonah had raised an
eyebrow at her. He was tutting, looking down on her like he was a
wise prince on a high horse. Jonah beckoned for her to follow him.
Abbie grumbled. She trudged behind him, away from the girls. They
left the room. The music, the swelling chatter, and the calls for
another round of vodka shots became indecipherable as Jonah shut
the kitchen door behind them.

"Urgh!" Abbie said. "Y-you're no fun at all."

"After you," Jonah replied. He motioned for her to walk in front
of him up the stairs. She lunged for the banister, steadying herself.
Her limbs were heavy. They walked up the stairs forever, it seemed.
Eventually, Jonah pointed to a room on the right.

"This one?"

"Yeah."

"Jesus fucking bollocks!" Abbie cried as she pushed the door open. It was Griff's bedroom. His desk was piled high with books of German and Latin translations and squiggles of gibberish paper. She gawked. "God. How can teachers read this shit?"

"Mine's much worse," Jonah said. Obviously, he thought that everything was a competition.

Abbie stumbled a little. Suddenly, her desire to sit down became overwhelming. Griff's bed was covered with a fuzzy, dark blue blanket, which did not seem very clean. She didn't want to sit on it with Jonah; her uneven steps in a wide circle around the bed told her that much. Instead, she collapsed onto a beanbag in the corner of the room. Jonah got onto his knees cautiously before he sat down across from her, resting against the bed.

"Collegiate accepts girls for Sixth Form. You should apply, you know," Jonah said.

Abbie startled awake. St. Peter's Collegiate School was so academic, so much better than Agerton Hall. The schools were in entirely different leagues. Collegiate was for geniuses. Collegiate was for politicians and famous people.

"But I'd have to be smart to go there," Abbie said.

"I think you could do it," Jonah said.

"W-won't I have to pretend to be a completely arrogant ponce in the interviews?"

"No. You could just be yourself."

"We got a plan, then." She smiled, zoning out. In her drunkenness, she had to keep it together. But she felt like she had dropped a bag of marbles that kept rolling away from her. And she was tripping all over them, trying to pick them up.

"Urgh, I fucking hate her so much," Abbie began.

"Who?" Jonah said.

"Th-the whole lot of them, really."

"Why?"

"Th-they just have no respect for themselves. Like they just show up here with their boobs hanging out. Then they go straight for the boys and the whiskey. And they're so *butterz*. They just wear tons of makeup."

"What makes you so much better?" Jonah said, looking her up and down.

"I actually have things that I want to do in my life," Abbie protested, "I—I have ambitions. I don't want to end up as a house-wife in Chiswick." Was she shouting? Why couldn't she control herself? Jonah was going to think she was crazy.

Instead, Jonah sighed. Then he looked her straight in the eye and said,

"What do you want to be, then?"

The dim glow of the bedroom light reflected in the strength of Jonah's gaze. His lip was firm and sure. Abbie peered at him, shaking a little. She felt her heartbeat thumping in her ears. No one had ever asked her that question before. No one had ever paused with her and said something that daring. And that earnest as well. Abbie blinked hard as her eyes began to water. It was like a messy stream of all her feelings were rushing into a river, tangling into one. She remembered the sound of paper tearing smoothly from the spine of a magazine. She remembered the vibrancy of the images as she cut them out, forming new shapes and visions. How the pinched corners of the cutouts felt so jagged and sharp compared to the glossy, smooth pages. Watching the watercolors flow from the end of a fine-tipped brush, creating color. Yolly's gleeful smile at the sight of the birthday card.

A tear formed at the corner of Abbie's eye. Her throat tingled.

"I think…I…I want to be an artist," she said. The weight of the words heaved like lead, tripping out of her mouth.

Jonah gazed at her, his expression unchanged. "I've wanted to be a screenwriter ever since I was a kid," he said.

Abbie's breath was cut short. There were those American words again, with that twang. She pictured Jonah surrounded by famous actresses at the Oscars in a paisley bow tie and a tuxedo. She imag-ined Jonah sitting at a desk lit by a reading lamp in some studio in

Los Angeles, like a craftsman of words, as he chiseled them into screenplays and set directions and lighting fixtures.

"R-really?"

"That's my dream," Jonah said.

"I want to make something of my life!" Abbie said.

"I know." Jonah nodded. "I mean, we're just a couple of fifteen-year-old kids. But I have no doubt. The world's never seen anything like you."

"You mean it?"

"Cross my heart—"

"Hope to die—"

"Stick a needle in my eye," Jonah said.

Abbie chuckled. Her eyelids felt heavy. She looked into the depths of his brown eyes. Jonah seemed open and grounded but nervous. Perhaps he had never been alone in a room with a girl before. That didn't matter much to her. All she could feel was the pureness of his soul radiating out at her.

"My whole life," she said, "I've never known anyone with big dreams like me. My family, my school...I...Everyone is just so against the idea of standing out and doing something different."

"I feel the same way," he said, "and I get it. It's about purpose, or destiny, or whatever you want to call it."

"I don't want to be forgotten," Abbie said. "I want to live forever!"

"You won't be forgotten," Jonah said. "That's the plight of the lone genius, the artist. It's all about creating a legacy."

"To live on after we're gone?"

"Exactly," Jonah said.

Abbie was beaming. She was no longer alone in this universe, in this life. It was this thought that uplifted her, carried her, cradled her. The heat of the alcohol burning in her chest seemed to lift her upwards.

"I've never told anyone about this before," she said.

"Me neither," Jonah said. He smiled a little and winked at her. He seemed to understand her essence. And knowing this about each other, she was sure, would make them great friends. "But you know, it's better not to conform. We're on a different level. I know it."

"Maybe," Abbie said. She was starting to believe him. A single tear rolled down her cheek. She wiped it away, confused as to why it had formed in the first place.

Suddenly footsteps were thumping loudly on the stairs. Seconds later, Emily burst into the room, her white dress stained with splodges of mango-colored foundation.

"Abbie! There you are! I sucked Griffy off."

Jonah looked down at his feet.

Abbie felt herself seething. "Why didn't you fuck in his parents' bed, then?"

"I don't know, I just swallowed. Griffy's spunk tastes so clammy. Did you ever swallow?"

"G-go wash your fucking mouth out with soap, then," Abbie commanded, pointing out the door.

"But—"

"Go on!"

Emily left the room.

Abbie looked at Jonah, hoping to read him. Was he disappointed? Was he jealous?

"Let me get your pin," Jonah said, passing his BlackBerry to her.

Abbie mistyped it, deleted it, started over again, then checked it twice. She handed his phone back to him. She wondered if this was her window into a new world. A world where she could leave Emily's egregious sex acts behind her.

"Everyone out!" Griff called up the stairs. He burst into the room. He looked from Jonah to Abbie and back again. "Come on, poppet, time to go."

Abbie started, "What if I don't want to—"

"The neighbors called the council. Apparently, people were shouting racist comments in the garden. Sarah's cut her hand, and Finlay's crying because Emily sucked me off and not him," Griff chuckled with a bantering tone.

Abbie groaned. She would have complained more, but she didn't want to look like a whiny brat in front of Jonah.

"I'll call you a cab," Jonah said. "I've got my dad's Addison Lee account anyway."

"W-would you?"

"Yeah, of course."

Abbie steadied herself to her feet. She checked for her phone and money and keys. Bugger! She had left her coat downstairs in the kitchen. She stumbled downstairs to find it. Jonah was on the phone, calling the taxi, ambling behind her. She entered the kitchen. It was dark, except for a single lamp that hung over the dining table. Horace sat there alone, looking glum. His arms were folded.

"W-where's Moe?" Abbie asked him, grabbing her coat.

"She got a cab back to Chiswick with those girls," Horace said. He hadn't bothered to remember any of their names.

"So h-how's it going, being Moe's boyfriend?" Abbie spat.

Horace's face reddened. "Fine. Why do you ask?"

"J-just wondering."

"Moe told me you used to be good friends," Horace said. "Why's that?"

"We have our differences."

"I hope it's not because of me."

"Nah, it's nothing to do with you," Abbie lied. It seemed like centuries had passed since Horace had broken up with her in Holland Park. Yet this time, she was determined to rewrite her tragic ending. "C-congrats on getting with Moe, though. And taking her virginity. That's a real accomplishment."

"Shut up," Horace said. He wouldn't let her make fun of him.

Abbie smiled at him smugly. She put on her coat and left the room. Jonah was probably waiting for her, and she had far more important things to discuss with him anyway. She found him by the front door.

"The cab will be here in five minutes—"

"W-why do you smoke so much if you know it'll kill you?" she pressed him.

"My uncle is seventy-five, and he's been smoking since he was ten," Jonah said.

"So?"

"I like smoking. Maybe I'll regret it later. But for now, I'm fine."

His words infuriated her.

"B-but what if you die at the age of thirty-five before any of your films come out? And then you're just dead?"

Jonah paused for a minute.

"I don't know you that well. But if you wanted me to stop, I would."

"Th-that's so dumb," Abbie said. "I know you're not going to quit. All the damage to your lungs has already been done. You can't undo it." She was arguing with him already in a way that upset her.

Jonah shrugged. He opened the front door. She heard the car pull up outside. She looked into the darkest corner of Jonah's brown eyes. Not in a loving way. In a way that she hoped, drunkenly, she could show him that she was scared for him. Jonah gazed back at her, acknowledging it in a way.

Out on the street, Abbie got into the taxi. The scent of industrial car air freshener and bleach was overpowering. She closed her eyes and leaned her head on her seat belt, desperate to be home in her bed and for it to all be over. The taxi driver said nothing to her, and she was glad for it. Her stomach felt like it was being torn in two and squished back together again every time the car turned a corner. She had to fight herself not to chunder everywhere.

6

The following morning, Abbie crouched on the floor and looked underneath her bed. Just beyond the odd hair tie on the beige carpet, she saw the perforated sides of a thick blue plastic folder. The carpet lightly burned her knees as she reached for it. The dividers within it squeaked as she pulled it out. She sat down against her bed.

The folder was covered with a thin layer of grey dust. Abbie sighed, looking at the particles that had accumulated around the name tag, appropriately labeled "Art" in bubbly handwriting. It irked her to think of all the projects she had started with it. All the compositions she had never finished and all the ideas she had accumulated that had never come to be. She had ideas for grand collages that spanned enormous walls in the Louvre or the Met. But she couldn't make something now. A hangover of homework awaited her. Sunday was a pittance to her, barely counting as the weekend. The thought of sitting down in her double Biology lesson by 9:30 a.m. on Monday loomed large. It ate away most of her day. Outside, the sun was high in the sky, tucked behind the house. She had woken up too late.

Her neat Longchamp schoolbag, with its mauve material and crisp leather handles, sat in its regular place underneath her desk below the window in her bedroom. She had discarded her schoolbag haphazardly in the entryway on Friday afternoon after a terribly long day at school. Yolly had faithfully carried it upstairs. The sight of it was a like a shadow Abbie could not escape from. Her Physics textbook peeked out of it. She had made big plans to get ahead. She had a test on electromagnetic forces in two weeks. Yet she was burdened by an English essay on five chapters of *Journey's End*, which she hadn't read. This essay was the real obstacle standing in the way of her freedom.

"But maybe I'll always have homework to do," Abbie said to herself aloud.

She paused. Applying to Collegiate. Becoming an artist. Finding her purpose. With Jonah alongside her, crafting the way with his creations. Of course, that had just been the alcohol speaking. A single Latin phrase came to mind, the only one she remembered from three years of studying it.

"In vino veritas." Under the influence of alcohol, a person tells the truth.

Abbie frowned at the folder. She pressed its clasp. The front of it popped open. Her fingers picked up a slight edge of the dirt. She sneezed. Which cutouts had she saved again? Were they from *Vogue* or from that graphic design magazine that she loved? She could already hear her parents' words binding her mind like masking tape.

"Artists never make any money," Richard had told her when they had attended an Old Masters auction at Sotheby's, "but collectors do. And as Chestertons, we've got the eye for collecting." Her parents only liked art that had been painted by someone who had died a long time ago. The porcelain in the drawing room had to match the tartan upholstery, which had to match the portrait of her distant ancestor in his admiral's coat, painted by Gainsborough, which hung above the fireplace.

"History of Art is a real academic subject. You could always study that at Oxford," Charlotte had said to Abbie more than once over a Sunday roast. Both Charlotte and Richard had gone to Oxford. Charlotte might have a heart attack if Abbie didn't get accepted.

Getting into Collegiate would be challenging, but it would considerably improve her chances of going to Oxford. And though they might never let her study Art there, that would make her parents happy. All subjects at Oxford were on the cards for Freddie; he could study something competitive, like Economics and Management, but Abbie had to be realistic. Charlotte would want her to pick something straightforward and dull, like Geography.

What would happen if Abbie did make a collage, but then Miss Hewitt, her Art teacher, hated it? Everyone at Agerton Hall was so allergic to the idea of breaking the mold. Abbie was sure to ruffle their feathers. No one in her class had ever made *bold* art. Many of them had mentioned that they couldn't wait to have babies and be housewives in Chiswick, doing the same things that Charlotte wanted Abbie to do, except at less fancy parties, drinking less expensive wine. The more she thought about it, the more Abbie was sure that Moe and Emily were destined for second-rate universities and societal mediocrity once their powerful days in secondary school were over. Abbie felt lost, but at least she had class, and they did not. The prospect of becoming more successful than her friends was enough to push her in a new direction. If Abbie got accepted to Collegiate and could leave Agerton Hall, that would show them.

Abbie stretched the folder open. Lush magazine pages slipped out onto the carpet. Their colors came alive in front of her eyes. Vibrant greens and midnight blues. Annie Leibovitz, re-creating *Alice in Wonderland* for a shoot in *Vogue*. Natalia Vodianova, young, skinny, the size of the room. None of it was believable. Yet Abbie wanted to exist in a fairyland world like this. Where she would be the central focus of an editorial shoot. But the closest thing she had gotten to it was being cast as a tree in *The Wizard of Oz* in Year 6. Just the sight of Natalia Vodianova sprawled across the forest floor in a ball gown was enough to make Abbie want to skip dinner and breakfast the next day.

A sinking anxiety crept over her. Abbie was not pretty enough to be a model. She would never jet-set off to Paris and Milan to hang around with the most beautiful people in the world. She would never command the catwalk, the attention of men, or the envy of women like those young models did. She could never be a successful child actress, starring in commercials before she could walk or talk. It pained her to face it all. How would she survive being unfamous forever? What was the point of living in this world when she wasn't beautiful enough? What if she never made it into Oxford? Then all those hours she had spent studying for exams would be a complete waste, too. She had already wasted her whole life. She was destined to die a nobody.

Abbie shivered all over.

"Who cares about Natalia Vodianova?" she pleaded to herself. She was going to do Art for the colors, for the impact her work, if she ever made anything again, would have on people. And she would make a collage again. Just not now. She simply had to get her more pressing homework out of the way first. If she wanted to get into Collegiate, her marks in all her other subjects still mattered a lot. She simply had to pick herself up and get this essay done. And she was so behind. She was long past the point of getting a top mark. Now her only goal was to avoid making a complete fool of herself in front of her English class on Wednesday. She could already see the beaded strings of Dr. Edmonton's reading glasses dangling with disappointment. She imagined her English teacher shaking her head as the class erupted into nervous whispers.

Abbie got up and reached for her schoolbag. She found her bent, hardback copy of *Journey's End* and slapped it on her desk. She plugged in Charlotte's old ThinkPad laptop. She searched her ring binder for the pitiful scribbled notes she had made in the lesson.

As Abbie found the notes and the rustling of papers subsided, she heard her phone vibrate twice. Her ears perked up. Was it Finlay? Or Charles? Or, finally, Max? Was he inviting her to an exclusive underground gig in Brixton next weekend? She lunged over the side of her bed. She opened her messages. The BBM was from a number she hadn't saved.

Jonah M. Wood: Want to get coffee this afternoon?

~

AN HOUR LATER, they sat at a small wooden table for two at Le Pain Quotidien. The café had a fake, aged feel to it. Classical music trickled in the background. Jonah sat across from her, frowning at the menu. The folds of his black hair looked cleaner than they had been last night. He wore a dark blue jumper and a light red, long-sleeved shirt that poked out at the collar and the cuffs. He put down the menu and cracked his knuckles.

Abbie had managed to shower and was wearing a black chiffon dress, draping an elegant U-shape across her shoulders. Abbie had carefully dabbed Dream Matte Mousse foundation on the bottom of her chin. It covered a tiny but painful patch of acne that had sprung up out of nowhere like a troop of mushrooms.

They sat close. Abbie caught a trace of Jonah's smell for the first time. Cigarettes, definitely. That was the initial thread of his scent that hit her. But it was infused with notes of deodorant and cologne, corrupted by tones of his family's laundry detergent. This combination brought out more of a sweetness to the cigarettes. For the first time in her life, Abbie distinguished between cigarette smoke and the tobacco itself. The tobacco had an older, deeper, wiser flavor. Tobacco had character and beauty and charm. It clung to Jonah's clothes, attaching to him like a second skin. It hinted at how he lived independently, so differently from Abbie and her family. It intrigued her, and yet, it was layered underneath the deodorant and detergent that made up Jonah's socially acceptable front. Like a mask that everyone wore as they walked around Notting Hill and made nice, polite conversation. Abbie was beginning to realize that even the tobacco was not Jonah's purest scent. What did he smell like beneath that? She imagined something masculine yet warm. She knew that on some biological level, the true smell of a person was supposed to mean something.

Getting coffee with Jonah felt like a strange game. They were playing a pair of wannabe adults. Abbie kept glancing at him over the top of her menu. In Jonah's current state, Abbie got no sense of his vulnerabilities. He pinched his jumper close to the collar of his shirt to cool himself down. That unconscious tick of his. Jonah had the air of constantly being bothered by something. Perhaps it had nothing to do with her and everything to do with how he saw the world. There was a darkness behind his light brown eyes. A coldness and depth she felt incapable of truly understanding. And yet somehow, she had ended up in this well-to-do café with him. Where light streamed through the patches of clouds that had formed in the afternoon sky outside. Across the rain-drenched pavements and through the giant windows of Le Pain. Illuminating him right there in front of her.

"I'll get the Americano," Jonah said to the waitress.

Abbie stared at him blankly. An Americano. And yet that's what Jonah was: a fifteen-year-old boy who drank coffee and smoked cigarettes like a man decades wiser with life. She ordered a granola parfait, something vaguely healthy with minimal calories. The waitress left them alone together.

"How do you feel this afternoon?" Jonah asked her.

Abbie puzzled. She had been expecting a far less intrusive question.

"How do I feel? Okay, I guess. It's been a pretty normal day so far."

"What's normal to you?"

"Arguing with my mum. She still hasn't canceled my early weekend tennis lessons at the Hurlingham."

"Of course, your tennis lessons," Jonah said. "So it's her job to organize everything for you. She doesn't work, does she?"

Jonah sat back in his chair, glancing at Abbie playfully. His teeth were a greyish-white color and a little crooked along the bottom. His attempt to explain her and Charlotte away in two sentences was almost insulting. Was he flirting with her, critiquing her, or both?

"And I suppose you never ask your mum for anything? Ever?" Abbie retorted.

"I'm respectful of my mom's time, at least," Jonah said, "She's got her hands full with four boys, a husband, and a dog. Plus, she's taking on more patients in her hypnotherapy practice. She smokes weed for her anxiety. I found her stash in her sock drawer a couple of months ago."

"Aren't you worried? Weed is a gateway drug," Abbie said. That was as much as she had learned in the Drugs Prevention Program at school. Where did Jonah's mum even get her weed from? Was Jonah's mum that irresponsible? Or was Charlotte too sheltered and ignorant?

"It's not that big of a deal," Jonah said. "Smoking marijuana has a lot of medicinal benefits. Besides, this country's fear is just an extension of DuPont's misinformation campaign from the 1930s. Get hemp off the market and fill the world with plastic fibers instead. Which, by the way, are great for the environment."

"It's dangerous, though," Abbie said. "You can only buy weed from drug dealers on estates."

Jonah laughed.

"You know, you really shouldn't believe everything they teach you in school. My mom has a dealer who comes to our house, and I'm pretty sure it's safe. But you're right in the sense that it's hard to guarantee the quality of the product. That's why I believe all drugs should be legalized. The free market works best with minimal government intervention."

The waitress arrived with their orders. Abbie tucked into her granola, and she tried to dig up all the facts she could remember about US politics. She had read a long article in *The New Yorker* about Michele Bachmann and Sarah Palin and the rise of the Tea Party. Did Jonah believe in defunding the EPA and the national parks? Did he believe in abortion?

"So you're a libertarian, then?" she asked.

Jonah nodded, stirring his coffee. The metal spoon clanged irregularly against his ceramic cup.

"Then who's going to build the roads?"

"Private corporations," Jonah said, "They do things more capital efficiently and create more jobs than the government."

Abbie peered at him. Jonah said things so matter-of-factly. He was far more ready for this debate than she was. She paused for a minute and focused on her food, wondering where Jonah had gotten these insane notions about economics. She was mid-mouthful of blueberries and oats when he asked her,

"Who's your favorite artist?"

Abbie covered her mouth as she finished chewing.

"Van Gogh," she said reluctantly. Everyone liked Van Gogh. Abbie wished she could have named someone more obscure. Jonah probably thought she was simpleminded, but in all honesty, Abbie loved the bold colors of Van Gogh's paintings. Still, she felt she had to prove herself. "And I've been thinking about doing a collage inspired by Jan Brueghel."

"Ah, the seventeenth-century Dutchman. Based on his pictures of hell?"

"No, just his still life studies."

"Hell was his main deal," Jonah said confidently. "He was all about demons and the dark side of the underworld. Hades and Orpheus. The elites ate them up at the time."

"I didn't know that." His knowledge surprised her.

"But don't let me corrupt you and your pretty pictures of flowers," Jonah continued. "I'm sure painting something just because it looks nice is very fulfilling."

Abbie scoffed at him. Jonah was so uncouth, so bloody rude. She wouldn't let him get away with it.

"What's wrong with liking art for the aesthetics?"

Jonah looked at her knowingly as he took a long sip of coffee. Abbie wished she hadn't sounded so defensive and aggravated. At last, he said to her and quoted,

"Drift beautifully on the surface, and you will die unbeautifully in the depths."

"And I suppose the art you like is so much deeper, then?"

"It is, actually," Jonah said. "Take *Enter the Void*. It's incredible cinema, just teeming with symbolism. If you watch it with an untrained eye, you'll miss everything that's happening. It's not just the drug dealer in Tokyo who's shot and killed and comes back to life to haunt his sister. It's about the fact that after we die, people's lives continue endlessly and render our existence irrelevant in the first place."

"Oh, and your eyes are so much better trained?" Abbie said, this time with her mouth full. His rattling on about *Enter the Void* reminded her of her twelfth birthday party when Abbie and her friends had thought it was cool to watch scary movies. She had watched *The Amityville Horror* and been too scared to sleep for months afterwards. She would never make that mistake again.

"I won't toot my own horn," Jonah said, taking another sip of coffee. David Lynch, Darren Aronofsky, and Gaspar Noé were his favorite directors. Abbie listened, but she had no idea who any of them were. The second after Jonah said their names, she forgot them. What was an art house film, anyway? And how was she supposed to keep up with him when she hadn't even been to see *Avatar* in the cinema, the most popular film in 2009 and supposedly the best movie ever?

"Tell me about your script," she said.

Jonah paused. "I've been trying to write for a couple of years now. But I haven't been able to come up with anything good."

"Why not? Aren't you the next Steven Spielberg—"

"I'm looking for my muse," Jonah said.

Their eyes met. The light brown of Jonah's irises glistened like the color of wilting wheat chaffs, late to be harvested from an autumn field. Abbie had heard the word "muse" somewhere before. She understood at a visceral level what he was talking about, what Jonah needed. A girl, not yet a woman. Only a female human spirit could coax the creative wonders out of him.

"Why haven't you found her yet?" Abbie asked.

"I thought I had over the summer in Montauk," Jonah scowled. His cheeks flushed deep pink and blotchy. "Her parents were divorced, though. She doesn't believe in the sanctity of marriage. Nobody does these days. It's like vows don't mean anything to anyone. Anyway, I don't want to talk about it."

Jonah had a sense of desperation in his voice, as if he was troubled by people and ideas far beyond her. It made sense to Abbie. Artists were supposed to be tormented. The best artists, she had learned, lived short and painful and stunted lives, brimming with grief and anguish. Jonah understood that too. It was the curse of creativity. He relished in it, bathing in the hardship of it as a private-school-educated boy. He needed somebody to love. Somebody to be a man for. Somebody to be loyal to and take care of. Somebody to teach him how to feel things. Was that what Abbie was here to do? Had the role been designed for her?

Abbie gulped. Her nerves were getting the better of her. She focused on eating every last oat and smidge of yogurt she could scrape out of the bowl as new thoughts coursed through her. Who was Jonah's other girl? Had they kissed? Had they held hands by moonlit waters? Had they made love? No, surely not. Jonah was far too lacking in self-confidence to have lost his virginity. Maybe that was why he needed his muse. Abbie felt sorry for him in that sense. She had to say something to reassure him.

"Well, I'm sure you'll forget about her when you find someone else."

"That's exactly what Gaspar Noé said." Jonah added, "Le temps détruit tout. Time destroys everything."

"Okay, Socrates," Abbie said, dropping her spoon in the empty bowl and pushing it away from her. Jonah smirked. The sides of his neck began to redden. He gazed at her, shaking his head slowly. The intensity of his stare made Abbie giggle. He reached into his pocket and drew out a small blue box. He clicked it open, raised it to his lips, and drew out a tiny square with his tongue.

"What's that?"

"Oh, this?" he said. "Listerine. It's like a mouthwash brand, but they do these PocketPaks. Mom picks them up whenever she's in Manhattan."

Jonah closed the box and put it back in his pocket. Abbie found it very strange indeed. The gum in England was perfectly good. Why was he trying to be so alternative with everything? His foreignness had started to grate on her.

Jonah gazed at her, puzzling. "You remind me of—"

"Well, I hope she wasn't a complete twat," Abbie said.

"Far from it." He went on, "She meant more to me than anyone in the world."

The words pricked her. *She. More. Than anyone.* Who was Jonah talking about? Why was he comparing her, Abbie, to this mystery girl?

"Were you in love with her?" Abbie asked.

"With Rosalia? Oh, definitely."

The girl had a name. Rosalia. She felt older. Rosalia, whoever she was, was obviously more of a woman than Abbie. Would Abbie try to outcompete this random girl in America, who she knew nothing about? It felt like Jonah was throwing her bait, waiting to see if she would catch it. A single, detailed image had pasted itself in Abbie's mind. Jonah kissing Rosalia under that giant marble arch as the sun set over New York City. The fountains reflecting the checkered patterns of lights from the surrounding skyscrapers. The craziness of the traffic, the passersby, the skateboarders, the street dancers, the band players, and the policemen bustling about them. But their kiss and love for each other shielded them from it all. Untouchable. It was probably so much easier to fall in love in America.

"What about your art?" Jonah asked.

"What about it?"

"What are you working on?"

"Nothing at the moment," Abbie said. "But I have a lot of ideas."

"So you're an idea-ist?"

"No."

"Sounds like it," Jonah said. "You know, you actually have to make art if you want to be an artist. It doesn't have to be good art, but you've got to create something."

"I know what artists are."

"I don't doubt that you do."

Abbie folded her arms. With his little smirks, Jonah was so pedantic, and arrogant too. No wonder Rosalia had dumped him. He was far too frustrating to hold a conversation with. The biggest shame of all was that he was so interesting to talk to. Otherwise, there was really no reason to see him again.

The sky was growing darker outside. Abbie checked the time on her phone.

"I have an essay to write."

"Let me get the check," Jonah interjected, almost angrily. He reached into his pocket and pulled out some cash.

"Are you sure?"

"Of course," he said. "And I'll get the next one too."

"I-if there is a next one," Abbie said, attempting to tease him as they stood up to go. But Jonah didn't seem to have heard her.

They lingered for a moment on the street outside the café.

"Bye," Abbie said, giving him an awkward wave. Jonah waved back as he lit a cigarette. Then he turned and walked away. It started to drizzle as Abbie watched him go. Jonah's feet turned outwards slightly as he walked. She wondered what unsettling views he might surprise her with next.

7

Abbie reapplied her makeup in the bathrooms at school. She adjusted her school skirt to make it shorter, rolling it up under her jumper like she had seen the older girls do. She wore her bulky grey school jumper because it was the only layer she had. After sprucing up her hair and applying her Body Shop passion fruit lip gloss, Abbie felt hesitant to face the world. She scolded herself in the mirror. Whatever *this* was, it would have to do.

It was Friday, not even a week since she had reconnected with Jonah at Griff's house. She had barely slept on Monday or Tuesday, so she could submit a half-decent essay for Dr. Edmonton on Wednesday, even if she got most of the ideas from the summary of *Journey's End* on SparkNotes. She had caught up on sleep, but it had done nothing to help her look pretty or at least desirable. In addition to her Longchamp bag full of schoolbooks, Abbie had to lug around her art sketchbook. The book was filled with boring still life assignments and pencil sketches that Miss Hewitt had asked her to do.

Jonah called her yesterday to confirm. He kept telling her about his favorite parts of London.

"I like the art scene, the old cinemas, the video stores," he had said to her. "You never get bored because there's always a show or exhibition or installation to go see. Then you've got the signs and shops in Polish, Hindi, or Chinese. And the nutjobs at Speakers Corner, you can't forget about them."

"Don't you like Notting Hill?" Abbie had asked him.

"Sure," Jonah had replied, "But I figure there's more to life than upper-middle-class status and bullshit."

Abbie had tried to counter him,

"You're from here too, remember. Dare to include yourself in that generalization?"

But Jonah had quickly got to talking about a documentary he had watched at the French Institute. Abbie envied the fact that Jonah seemed so sure of himself.

As Abbie headed down the titanium-white corridors of Agerton Hall School, she felt like a patient escaping a psychiatric ward. The school was surrounded by a three-meter-high brick wall. It was designed in a Gothic style because, apparently, nobody thought women were worth educating before 1890. She passed under the arched entrance between groups of girls headed for Hammersmith Broadway. On the street beyond, cars and buses bobbed and swerved around potholes and puddles. Abbie tried to walk confidently, but shame wafted over her. What would Moe and Emily think if they found out she was hanging out with *Jonah Wood*? How long would it be until Amber Rutterdown and the whole of Notting Hill found out? Part of her hoped Jonah wouldn't show up.

At Hammersmith Broadway, groups of teenagers reunited all around her. Abbie looked down at the ground, hoping not to recognize anyone. But it was too late. Sure enough, she caught a glimpse of the brown buzz cut. Danny Watson. He was leaning against the mermaid of The Statue. His black trousers were baggier than she remembered and lightly stained with paint. His eyes skirted over her, clearly more interested in another girl who would arrive at any minute. Abbie tried to hide her face. She narrowly avoided tripping over a chair outside Starbucks.

"How are you?" came a rolling, New York accent.

Abbie turned around. Jonah stood in front of her, smoking. The sides of his haircut were freshly trimmed short.

"Oh, hey!" She waved sheepishly.

"How was your day?"

"It was great," she lied.

Within a second, Jonah walked towards The Statue.

"Danny!" he said before Abbie could grab him and pull him away.

"Mate!" Danny nodded. "Long time no see."

Abbie gulped, trailing behind Jonah. The boys shook hands and tapped each other on the back. Did Jonah and Danny know each other? How? Her cheeks burnt hot.

A vague sense of disgust crossed Danny's face. It brought her back to their first date when she was twelve, and Danny was thirteen, and they went to see *Ratatouille* in the cinema. But Abbie had been completely put off by the orange elastics of Danny's braces and the ginormous buttery popcorn and Cherry Pepsi he bought, which Abbie had no interest in even trying.

"Can I kiss you?" Danny had whispered to her halfway through the movie. Obviously, Abbie had said no. But the next thing she knew, Danny had left. She watched the rest of the film in the cinema alone. She got some nasty texts from him that she regretted deleting afterwards.

Fast-forward to last year. Abbie had climbed the wide staircase to the top floor of Danny's mum's house. Instead of going to Emily's room, where she had gotten ready for bops and gatherings in Chiswick, she had gone into Danny's, right next door. She remembered her hands had been shaking. She was breaking all of the rules. To this day, she was marred by guilt for being so young at the time.

Danny had had his braces off by then. Even at that age, Abbie liked that he had been so much stronger than her and on the rugby team. Strong enough to pick her up and throw her on his bed if he wanted to. It had all happened so quickly. Danny had taken off her dress. He had taken off her bra. He had sat down on his bed. Before Abbie understood what was happening, Danny had undone the zipper on his jeans. He had pulled down his trousers a little. He had gotten it all out of his underwear.

Abbie had tried not to stare, but she couldn't help it. It was, she realized, the first time she had seen an actual erect human male's penis. The organ, the thing, was thick and wide, like the torn-off branch of a small tree, except that it curved slightly upwards towards Danny's waistband. It had bobbed up and down like an animal. Abbie had seen them in 2D diagrams in school. Biology had taught her to name all its parts, the vas deferens, the scrotum, the foreskin. But a 2D black-and-white drawing, compared to seeing the entire thing in 3D, balls and all, had been like describing planet Earth in English to an alien. Danny's penis had been elongated and veiny. The base was a mass of dark brown pubic hair, which she really preferred not to touch. That's where she imagined his balls were hidden.

"Go on, babe," Danny had said to her, closing his eyes as he braced himself. "Touch it."

Abbie hated it when he called her babe, but she had known better than to bring it up. Danny's penis had continued to bob about like a buoy on a rope that separated the swimming area of the Serpentine in Hyde Park. Curiosity, more than anything, had spurred her on.

She had taken it in her hand. The head had been covered in warm, soft, folded skin as if Danny's second brain lay hidden beneath it. She had felt the girth of it. She had seen the veins along it, pulsing from the base up through its spine. It had boggled her mind to think that the human body could create such a bizarre, funny-looking thing. The tip of it was wet, as a tiny amount of silvery liquid had oozed onto her hands. The liquid, more than anything, gave her the sense that this thing was alive.

She knew it was more than a toy, but there was also a feebleness to it. Her whole life, she had heard about men's unparalleled strength. Jesus, the son of God, had been a human male. There were the men who fought in wars in Sparta, the Crusaders who jousted on horses and shot bows and arrows into the backs of the non-Christian barbarians. Yet she could not believe those grandiose visions of men only came down to this. Danny was clearly excited. He had been proud to show it to her. But the thing itself? The entirety of the human race, the center of men's power and masculinity, had come down to this? There was something savagely underwhelming about it. Deeply, paralyzingly underwhelming.

Sure, Danny's penis was large. But the thing itself was a sack of strange cells, an organ just like any other, like the liver or the pancreas. Functional, but not celestial. Useful, perhaps, but not divine. Abbie had puzzled to herself. Where had those grandiose notions of men even come from? Since when had God, the big man in the sky, come down and made man in his image? She had dismissed the idea of believing in God when she was eight. When she had learned that beyond the sun and the clouds in the blue sky were not heaven but the planets and the solar system. But that day, when she had seen Danny Watson's sizeable but ordinary erect penis for the first time, she had realized something more than that. God had not made man in his image. No, instead, man had created God in his image. And ascribed a completely overhyped holiness to a bendy, overly sensitive stick that could easily be destroyed if it was punched, bitten, or pulled too forcefully.

Still, Abbie had grabbed it firmly around the base. There had been a looseness to the skin that covered it. She had held her hand in one place and squeezed as she moved up and down along its spine. Danny sighed and closed his eyes.

"B-babe, put it in your mouth," he had said between staggered breaths. Abbie had grabbed and rubbed it with more strength, harder and faster, keeping it far away from her face. Danny may have been popular and in the year above her, but he had not been in a position to complain. About a minute later, he had lunged for a tissue on his bedside table. She heard him cry out in sweet agony, clutching over himself as he scrunched up every muscle in his face. His orgasm face, she later learned.

Abbie had laid on his bed as Danny went to the loo and cleaned himself off. She had felt exposed and dirty, lying there half-naked, looking through the slanted skylight windows at the treetops and the redbrick houses of Richmond beyond. In a moment of stillness, she heard the double, rhythmic thumping of the tube bumbling over the bridgeway. The train passed in about thirty seconds, but it was just long enough for Abbie to realize how far she felt from home. She would have to get the bus. Then she would have to somehow look Yolly in the eyes and tell her she had been out shopping at Westfield with her friends. She had put her dress back on. She had gotten out of there, somehow. One final time, she gave Danny a hand job around the back of the church near his house. That was the last time they had pretended to be together.

As she thought and felt and thought, with Jonah and Danny standing before her, Abbie's tongue felt heavy in her mouth. She couldn't speak. There was nothing to say. She just prayed it would never come up in conversation. What would Jonah think if he ever found out?

"It's been about three years," Jonah said, tapping away the ash of his cigarette.

"I'll never forget that time you made Miss Nelson cry when you said *Of Mice and Men* was shit," Danny said.

"She had it coming. I still can't believe she made us act it out. Such torture."

"Those were the days," Danny said. He pointed coolly towards Jonah's cigarette. "Mind if I bum one off you?"

"Be my guest."

Jonah reached into his pocket and pulled out his Camel Blue cigarettes. Danny stared at Abbie without smiling, as if she was a hovering mosquito he couldn't quite capture, squish, and kill. Jonah continued,

"Oh, by the way, this is A—"

"Yeah, we know each other," Danny cut him off.

Abbie smiled awkwardly. It was hard not to compare them standing next to each other. Danny was at least ten centimeters taller than Jonah. Danny's cheekbones were more chiseled than Jonah's, and his haircut was definitely hotter. Her chest tensed up as a new, more exasperating thought came to her. Danny was out of her league now, and she fit squarely next to Jonah. Jonah commanded Danny's respect, but he was still just some uncool nerd next to Danny. And she was a used, discarded plastic cup floating in a drainpipe.

Jonah lit Danny's cigarette.

"Thanks, mate."

"Anytime."

"H-how do you guys know each other?" Abbie asked sheepishly.

"Hill House," Jonah said.

It all made sense now. Jonah and Danny had attended Hill House for primary school, notorious for its horrendous school uniform of thick mustard-knitted jumpers and rust-corduroy knickerbockers. Danny seemed to relax as he took a drag of the cigarette. He waved at someone behind them. Abbie turned around to see who it was. Instantly she regretted it.

Moe and Emily arrived at The Statue. Abbie forced a semblance of posture. The last time she had been in the same space as Emily and Danny, they had watched *Hot Fuzz* on the sofa in their basement. That was before Emily found out that she and Danny were together. Before Emily had screamed at her and called her a liar and a back-stabbing bitch and a sket. The agonizing history of it all was torn open like a fresh wound. And yet, her former girl group was as solid and fortified as ever without her.

"Sup li'l sis?" Danny said.

"So good to see you, darling," Moe said, reaching over to Abbie and kissing her on both cheeks like they were best friends again.

"You too, love," Abbie managed.

Emily stared at the ground, unamused.

"So Jonah Wood's your new boy toy?" Moe said, glancing at Jonah and Danny. "What have you two been up to since you locked yourselves in Griff's room? Oh, wait, I almost forgot, this is so awkward—"

"Shut the fuck up," Abbie spat.

"And I guess Danny still remembers you," Moe continued, "from last year when you chundered on him?"

Abbie glared at her.

Emily, seeing her discomfort, began to giggle.

"Oh, sorry," Moe taunted her. "I didn't realize you'd be so sensitive in front of Jonah."

"Come off it, Moe," Danny interjected. "Jonah's chill."

Jonah took another drag of his cigarette and said nothing.

Abbie's throat ached. The viciousness of it all stoked a fire in her stomach. The words tore out of her mouth. She tapped her finger on her chin sarcastically.

"I can't decide what tastes better. Griff's dick or sloppy seconds with Horace?" Abbie snapped, looking from Moe to Emily.

Moe gasped. Emily stopped giggling, and her cheeks blushed red as she looked up at Danny.

"What's she talking about?" Danny said. "Emily?"

"See you skets at school," Abbie said, giving Moe a small sarcastic wave. She grabbed Jonah by the arm and left them stumped in their tracks. As they disappeared into the crowd heading for the tube station, Abbie thought she heard Emily say,

"What a fucking freak." But Abbie didn't look back. Her hands were shaking. Walking briskly behind Jonah, Abbie felt a sinking feeling in her chest. She wasn't better than Moe or Emily. She was a complete slag. That label was permanent. Those unspeakable acts could never be undone. She would carry the shame with her forever. Jonah deserved someone better than her, with a less-tainted, cleaner record.

"What was Moe talking about?" Jonah said over the noise of the crowd.

Abbie looked up at him, searching his eyes to try to read what he was thinking.

"Well," Abbie said, considering her words carefully, "you know when I...uh...was dancing a lot at Griff's house with Emily? Just before you stepped in?"

"Yeah."

"I...I kind of used to do stuff like that all the time."

"Abbie," Jonah said, frowning, "that was just last week."

"I know."

"If those are your true colors, I mean—"

"No, I promise. That's not who I am. I don't want to be that kind of girl anymore."

Jonah stubbed out his cigarette on the ground, seemingly unconvinced.

"I guess time will tell."

They made their way down onto the Circle line platform. Abbie needed a moment to breathe and re-center herself, but soon the low yellow beams of the train loomed towards them. The train was packed with suits, newspapers, and commuters untangling their headphones. Once the passengers got off, Jonah stayed back to let her go in front of him. They shuffled into the carriage and stood on either side of a vertical railing. Jonah seemed puzzled, away in a world of his own. He sighed and looked out of the window into the darkness of the tunnels. A couple of silent minutes passed. Then Jonah said,

"What are you drawing these days?"

He beckoned for her sketchbook.

"Tomatoes and Barbies. I fucking hate Miss Hewitt's assignments."

"Okay," Jonah said. "Why are you doing it, then?"

"I don't know."

"Aren't these things evaluated by third-party examiners? If you did what you wanted, what is she going to do? You'll never be happy if you don't make some spineless people your enemies," Jonah smirked.

"I guess you're right."

"Can I take a look anyway?" he said, already half opening her sketchbook.

"Sure."

Jonah squeezed some more room among the passengers to get a better view.

"Wow. These are insanely good."

"What, this?" Abbie said, moving to stand beside him. The arm of her jumper brushed against him. He was looking at a simple study she had done using leaves from a half-dead tree in the courtyard at Agerton Hall. "This is hardly a masterpiece."

"But you've got a personal style and talent. Seriously, Abbie, I know a teacher at Collegiate who would love your work."

Abbie imagined this teacher, whoever they were, setting her sketchbook on fire because they thought it was so terrible.

"I mean, this is crap," Abbie said, pointing to a sketch she had done of her own hand, which looked like an old man's. The prospect of anyone seeing this sketchbook made her skin crawl. "If I'm going to apply to Collegiate, I'll need to put together a whole series that takes the viewer on a journey with an actually relevant theme."

"Suit yourself," Jonah said. "I think you've got a lot of potential."

Abbie let him take his time. She watched Jonah's round fingers and thick palm turn and cherish each page of her sketchbook, taking in her work. The hairs along the back of his hand were a sandy brown, forming an upside-down L shape across the gentle redness of his knuckle. Abbie felt a tight pull in her chest, somewhere between her heart and her stomach. Jonah was so different from the kind of guys she usually liked, mostly the wave-kissed surfer dudes of *90210* and Disney Channel. But from the shape of Jonah's hands alone, she could not deny it. She wanted him to touch her somewhere in a foreign part of her body that rarely came in contact with the air. That rarely saw the sun. Then again, Jonah's calm, enigmatic look was slightly off-putting. There was little that appealed to her about the folds of his neck. His nose was slightly hooked. Perhaps it was his intelligence, his mind, that she cared about more. What could Jonah see in her work that she could not? What was he reading into it?

"What's your movie script about?" Abbie asked, uncomfortable with the amount of attention Jonah gave to her work alone.

Jonah took a deep breath, dipping into concentration. "The loneliness of this schizophrenic guy who lives with his estranged aunt in Montauk. Obviously, it's in black and white, like Darren Aronofsky did with *Pi*. And then I'm trying to film ants to symbolize the character's loneliness."

"That sounds impossible."

"Hah. Yeah, it is just about."

"But cool, though."

"Thanks."

"What are we doing tonight, anyway?"

"Oh, my bad," Jonah said, reaching into his coat pocket. He handed her a blue ticket.

"*My Purple Heart.* Screen two," Abbie read aloud. The film sounded more like a *Bratz* movie than something being shown at an independent cinema. It was probably so niche that no one would ever ask her about it at a drinks party.

"Should be interesting," Jonah said, smiling.

Up close, Abbie noticed the slight gap between his front teeth again. She gazed up at him, puzzling. She wondered precisely when he had last seen Rosalia in New York. What would Rosalia think of them seeing a movie together?

There was a moment of silence between them. Then Jonah asked her,

"Have you always wanted to be an artist?"

"No."

"What did you want to be, then?"

"A model."

Jonah laughed at her fully, uncontrollably.

Abbie frowned. "What's wrong with that?"

"I just didn't realize you were drinking the capitalist Kool-Aid."

"What do you mean?"

"Don't women have more value in society than their looks?"

"I'm allowed to have dreams, aren't I?" Abbie said. "Plus, one girl at Agerton Hall got a modeling contract with Storm, and now I always see her in *Tatler* and *Vogue*."

"So, being featured in *Tatler* and *Vogue* is your marker of success, then?" Jonah pressed her.

"It's not like society is giving me that many options," Abbie said.

"How so?"

"The only important people that have graduated from Agerton

Hall are a couple of models and Nigella Lawson, professional chef and domestic goddess extraordinaire."

"What has Nigella Lawson ever done to you?" Jonah said in a playful, defensive way.

"I just think it's a waste for my parents to pay £4,700 per term to send me to some vapid finishing school," Abbie said.

"Collegiate probably costs more," Jonah considered. "But you're right. At least I'm not sitting around, sewing in my second home on the weekends."

"Completely," Abbie said. It felt good to bury all the unacademic, unambitious girls she had surrounded herself with for the last few years. "And my parents are obsessed with Oxford."

"Well, if it's all about Oxbridge, then you definitely need to apply to Collegiate," Jonah said, "and make your parents' dreams come true. Maybe then you'll be the golden child."

Abbie sighed.

"And, of course, you'll have to vote Tory once you're of age. Because your dad went to Eton, and his dad went to Eton. Where's your gold signet ring anyway? You must have an older brother who has it. Pity that. I wonder if they'll be kind and let you inherit a shed in the village."

Jonah's words pinched her, like the time she had cut too close to the skin as she shaved against the grain of her underarms.

"Will you just shut up?" Abbie spat. "Did you get dumped or something? You'd have to be heartbroken to be so bloody horrible and insecure."

"How did you hear about that?" Jonah said. He looked at her like he knew something that she didn't. "Fine, you're right. She broke up with me. But I also wanted us to take a break."

"When?"

"It doesn't matter."

Abbie snatched her sketchbook from him. Had Rosalia broken up with him that recently? Was Jonah itching for a rebound? Or was he one of those anxious people who always had to be going out with somebody, flinging from the safety of one relationship to the next?

This news flash would take her at least half an hour to fully process. Their meeting, their conversation, and going to a film together now had a very different undertone.

"How long were you together?" Abbie asked.

"Almost a year."

"A year?" That meant Jonah had started dating Rosalia when he was fourteen. Jonah had been in a real, committed relationship.

"So you were in love with her?"

"I already told you. Yes."

Abbie's throat ached as she heard it now. Jonah spoke angrily. He had fallen for Rosalia, he told her, and had been stupid for doing so. He had wanted Rosalia to apply to fashion school and go to Parsons because she was so creative, so talented. He had filmed her in some of his scenes. He had been to a bakery with her in the West Village every day. But now Rosalia was studying AP Economics instead, doing what her parents wanted. Rosalia was no longer the girl that he had first met. Rosalia could not commit to him long-distance. Rosalia did not care about him enough to try. Clearly, Jonah's heart was somewhere else. Trapped in a glass bottle, floating in the middle of the Atlantic. Or perhaps part of it was here with Abbie, teasing her.

Abbie paused for a moment. Then she said,

"What's it like to be in love?"

"You've never been in it? Well…" Jonah said. He leaned in closer as more passengers boarded the train. "You just get the sense when you look at the person that you would do anything for them."

"Do you still feel that way?"

"No." Then Jonah said, with all the seriousness in the world, "I never want to speak to her again."

Abbie shivered. Jonah's callousness troubled her. Her life with him flashed before her eyes. If they ever became more than friends, would Jonah say the same about her one day? *I never want to see her ever again.*

"Next stop," Jonah added coolly.

The train pulled into the station, and the doors opened. They pushed their way out onto the platform. Abbie felt the rush of freezing air down the open tunnel. She read the word "Embankment" in bold blue letters on the wall.

Outside the station, the amber streetlamps glowed across the wide water of the river Thames. The silhouettes of offices and parliamentary buildings were speckled with intermittent beads of light. They combined with the red eyes of the cranes at construction sites cast out across the horizon. Together, the floating lights looked like a dot-to-dot that Abbie had tried to complete diligently in kindergarten. She wanted to connect them. They formed the lines of a rainbow, the paws of a bear cub, and the heel of a pointy shoe. But as soon as Abbie thought she had found a particular constellation, she lost it and could not find it again.

They left the traffic of the road behind them as they headed up the steps of the bridge. The black water licked the sides of the worn, stone riverbanks. She wondered how people survived the winter in London before central heating had been invented. Jonah lit a cigarette and gave her some supposedly important information about the Curzon Sea Containers. But Abbie wasn't listening. She was far too busy scanning the walkway for random passersby. Charlotte had once told her that Roma gypsies begged for money in Central London and would steal a phone right out of someone's hand if they weren't careful. Abbie gripped her phone tightly in her pocket.

Across the river, the wind subsided. They continued along the bank. They passed groups of teenagers skateboarding in the low, fluorescent lights of a skate park underneath the bridge. With each new person she saw, Abbie began to wonder who they were and why they were there on a Friday night of all times. She had followed the same routine of hanging out with her friends in Hammersmith or drinking on Turnham Green for years. Now that she thought about it, it was a pity she didn't visit new places more often. There were so many different faces of the city. And yet every night of her life blended into a blob of inextricable, unshaped memories, from Notting Hill to Chiswick, to her friends' homes in South Kensington, and back again.

"We made it," Jonah said. They reached a group of adults drinking cocktails at a candlelit bar. A sign next to the entrance said "Curzon Ticket Desk" with an arrow pointing to the right. Abbie followed him around the building to the cinema.

At the counter, Jonah bought them a salty popcorn to share. In the theatre, they sat down next to each other in the front row. Jonah insisted on front-row tickets because, he said, that was the most authentic way to experience the cinema. The air was stuffy with the red cushions of the carpeted chairs, and the smell of burnt espresso mixed with buttered popcorn wafted around them. Abbie noticed that the room was half-full, mostly with other couples who seemed to be very in love and evidently not in secondary school. As the lights dimmed, Abbie looked up at Jonah. He chewed the popcorn with his mouth slightly open. She noticed his cheekbones up close for the first time. The tip of his nose beyond its light hook was almost perfectly square. Jonah glanced back at her and grinned, motioning to ask if she wanted some popcorn, too. She gave him a cheeky smile and reached carefully into the carton. She grabbed a fistful of popcorn.

The scenes of the movie spread out before them. From the first scene alone, Abbie could tell that it was one of those movies that Yolly would have shooed her away from or shouted, "No, Miss Abbie, cover your eyes!" in a semi-state of panic when Abbie went into her room without knocking on the door. The film was rated suitable for audiences 18+ for a reason. Yet no one had even questioned why two teenagers, one in a school uniform, had come to see it.

It started with heroin needles in a drug den in Durban and a young girl forced into prostitution and pornography to fuel her addictions. Her false friends turned against her. The girl hoped each of these people would heal her, yet she was broken from the beginning. When the gangsters stormed the apartment to snatch the girl, Abbie covered her eyes and barely peeked between them. Their shouts echoed in a place deep within her. She saw what it might be like to have never had a safe home, to have to fend for yourself on the streets. Jonah seemed unfazed by it all, but something inside of

Abbie had shifted. She had never seen someone scrape the bottom of the underbelly before with no one to rescue them. No fairy godmother to swoop in and help the girl get a job or kick her crack habit. No happy ending with Prince Charming sweeping her off her feet.

8

The film ended. Abbie and Jonah left the cinema and stepped out into the brisk night air.

"What did you think?" Jonah asked her.

Abbie stood next to him, shivering. She wanted to answer Jonah's question, but all she could do was walk silently. She wanted to turn back the clocks an hour and a half and return to the time just before she had stepped into the theatre. She could not unsee those images. She could not undo the violent, tragic scenes of the girl's obliteration. The world was colder and harsher than she had imagined. In Jonah's world, there were no happy endings. In Jonah's world, there were the cruelest truths of reality, blended into stories of struggle and hardship and unsettling visual experiments. It left her feeling uprooted from the softer, cushioned core of her family's house on Clarendon Road. The safety of her childhood bedroom vanished. Safety was a mirage anyway, a falsity built to comfort fragile people. In the real world, there was so much trauma and pain.

Abbie pictured her life sliding into the misery of needing her next fix, falling apart at the seams. If she did not hold on to art, hold on to Jonah, if she didn't keep studying, she might well find herself half-naked with needles sticking out of her arm, living underneath the motorway in the industrial wasteland behind Westfield, diving into the rubbish bins of M&S to find food. All this stood before her, tall and cruel, as a real possibility. If she had stayed on the same path. If she was still trying to outperform her friends by finding the craziest things they could snort up their noses at parties. Dipping their eyes in vodka because it was quicker and faster to get drunk that way. Passing cocaine around at someone's eighteenth. Abbie couldn't remember who had told her that. She promised herself at the moment, as she shook with fear: she would never do ketamine again. Who knew what it could be laced with?

"It was difficult to watch," Abbie admitted at last. She turned to Jonah. She was hesitant to show him how much the film had scared her. Jonah was clearly accustomed to this level of destructiveness. His soul was always hungry for pain. His appetite for violence was insatiable.

They continued slowly along the riverbank towards the bridge. There was not a cloud in the gentle, light-polluted sky. A speedboat, with flashing lights around its edges, channeled across the water. The wind grasped at the loose strands of Abbie's hair. The air was damp with a slightly rotten smell of river muck and moss. Jonah found a bench for them to sit on. She sat down next to him. By now, the river was at high tide. Long ripples of waves oozed past them as if the river's edges would crystallize into ice. Jonah was sitting only an inch or two away from her. Abbie sat in the shadow of his body. He helped to block the wind. She could not figure out why or how she had ended up here with him. But she was starting to understand that many of these things were unexplainable. Part of her simply wanted to be closer to him. She was fighting with herself internally to try to ignore it.

Abbie folded her arms to try to stay warm. She was second-guessing herself. Jonah moved closer to her. Was he putting his arm around her? Was he making a move? Or did guy friends also lean in when hanging out with girls? She didn't feel that debilitating attraction towards Jonah which she had felt towards Danny or Horace, that made her knees wobble. It was a subtler glow that was growing stronger. Rosalia had loved him. Jonah was capable of being loved, it seemed. If Jonah could be loved by someone else, Abbie could love him, too. She could love the wickedness of his spirit, could love the deep bend in his brow when he frowned.

Jonah took a packet of cigarettes out of his pocket. He balanced one between his lips and tried to light it. The wind picked up. The flame of the lighter extinguished over and over. He was just about to give up when Abbie reached forwards. She took the cigarette from his lips. She kissed him.

At the touch, Jonah was calm. He had a stoic, protective presence. After a short second or two, when he did pull away, Jonah looked into her eyes like he was enraptured, drunk on a strange potion. All Abbie could do was gaze back at him, curious, nervous about what he might say next. Had he liked it? Did he think she was a good kisser? Without breaking their eye contact, she placed the cigarette on his ear, wedging it along the short-cut sides of his hair. As she balanced the cigarette, Jonah smirked. He quickly pecked her on the lips. They kissed again, with more force, more longing this time. Abbie pulled away. She put the cigarette in Jonah's mouth, half giggling. Jonah gazed at her, his breaths shorter and staggered. She could feel him craving her. She cut it short and motioned for the lighter. He handed it to her and cupped his hands as she lit it for him successfully. As he began to smoke, Jonah put his arm around her, almost cradling her.

Abbie sighed, letting the nervous energy go, allowing herself to be held. An image of Rosalia lingered in the back of her mind. Was Abbie more important to Jonah at this moment? It didn't bother her that this was not Jonah's first time. Maybe it didn't have to be for it to be unique and special. She liked that he knew where he was going, to a point. She liked that he knew where they were going together, that he existed in a world parallel to hers, and yet he had already taken her so far off-piste.

"You're so beautiful," Jonah whispered.

"Thank you." Abbie smiled. She held on to his words, ready to replay them to herself later. She could not look away from him. His pale skin, marked with light acne scars, glowed like the moon. Jonah had a heavenly quality to him that Abbie hadn't noticed before. Her stomach was tense. Had Jonah's eyes always been this piercing? Had his grin always been this cute? Why couldn't she control how she felt about him? Why couldn't she correct herself and pat her feelings down with logic?

"Are you down to walk home?" Jonah asked.

"You mean, am I up for walking home?" she corrected him.

"It's a slang term. There's no right or wrong way to say it. Gosh. You British people are so pedantic."

Abbie chuckled at his grumbling. They stood up together and set off into the darkness. The streets were peaceful at night; Jonah had been right about that. After they had walked for a few minutes, Abbie felt warmer and ready for the adventure. Jonah seemed to know everything. There were mews houses down small, cobbled alleyways that he said were used as stables in the olden days. The Romans built old horse fodders and stone signs to mark the distance from Londinium to Oxford. The old street lanterns and little crevices in the front of houses were there to help old Londoners scrape the horse muck off their shoes before they got home. There were cracked, moss-lined pavements in quiet churchyards littered with gravestones. A cyclist was biking with their flashing lights, trying not to get squished by a red double-decker night bus. Down a crescent street, a lone fox skulked along a garden square.

They arrived at an enormous church. Abbie craned her neck backwards to see the top of the bell towers. The clouds hid her view, blocking the entrance to more celestial midnight realms. Behind the church's gates were its sturdy wooden doors, needled with gold trim. The doors were closed firmly, like the entrance to an impenetrable fortress. At the doors' edges, figures of ancient worshippers dipped in bronze watched her with suspicious eyes. In the blue-and-red stained-glass windows, abstract visions whispered heroic tales of histories past.

"You know where we are, right?" Jonah said as he lit another cigarette.

She shrugged.

"Westminster Abbey?"

"Correct."

Westminster Abbey. Abbie knew what it was, but not in a way that she could say anything intelligent about. Maybe something about the Queen or that Charlotte had been invited to the prince's wedding there next summer. Obviously, the abbey was super important. She could tell that just by looking at it. Yet nothing specific came to her mind. It was as if she had been given a bowl with a giant hole. Instead of catching the details of her family's or country's history, the liquid memories had simply slipped through.

"Come on, I'll show you your future school," Jonah said, winking at her. Abbie followed him nervously. It was comforting to know that Jonah believed in her, but her future at Collegiate was far from certain. If she was set on going to Collegiate, she would have to take entrance exams in the autumn, right before her mock GCSE exams, too. Those months of studying were bound to be a nightmare. She would have to devote everything to it to have a chance of getting into the top school in the country. Still, as they passed through a cloistered walkway and came to a garden square with a perfectly manicured green at its center, Abbie got chills down her neck. She began to dream about the place. St. Peter's Collegiate School had been around since Elizabeth I and the 1500s. But Benedictine monks had been banging about there since 1042 and the coronation of Edward the Confessor, Jonah said. Ivy crept along the ancient wood carvings by the back entrance to the abbey in one corner of the square. The houses had low, small doors and speckled grey stone walls that reflected the moonlight. It was where prime ministers had had their first political discussions as schoolboys. A place of rebels and independent thinkers throughout the centuries. Authors and scientists, poets and politicians. Jonah directed her, guided her, and carried her sketchbook willingly onwards. Abbie's dreams unfolded in front of her eyes. Would she ever be able to call this place her home? Her school? What would it mean to go to school with Jonah? What more would they have done than kiss by then?

Abbie gazed at an iridescent blue clock with gold needles and painted Roman numerals perched above another cloistered tunnel. She took Jonah's hand. The tips of his fingers were cold with poor circulation.

"Maybe one day," she said. She moved in closer to him. She kissed his cheek.

Jonah paused. He had to catch his breath a little. He was both foreign and familiar, a creature she was just getting to know, just getting to explore. He reached for her hand clumsily. He interlaced their fingers. He pressed his palm to hers. He held her there for a minute. Then he pulled away and left her standing there alone.

"Hey!" she said as Jonah walked over to the porter's lodge in the cloistered tunnel.

"I'm just checking something," he called out.

There was a faint sound of creaking metal, followed by the slamming of a lid.

"Here," Jonah said, returning to her. "Got the last one. Take this—"

Jonah handed her a brochure. The paper was glossy and crisp along the edges, printed on the cold card. Abbie took it square in both hands and angled it in the light of the Victorian streetlamps.

"St. Peter's Collegiate School, Application for Sixth Form Entry in 2011," she read aloud.

"Sure is!" Jonah said. "Here, go to the Art section."

Abbie flipped through the booklet. The pristine pages made a satisfying, wobbling sound as she turned them. Ancient Greek, Athletics, Art & Design. She eagerly cracked open its spine. Beneath a band of the school's light green color were paragraphs of text. And on the other page, a picture of the grandest art studio she had ever seen, lit by studio lights across the ceiling, and paintings and creations of all shapes and sizes stretched out around the room.

"St. Peter's Collegiate offers a varied course in Art & Design at A Level. Our approach is to nurture the freedom of expression of every artist that walks through our doors, equipping them with the

sensitivities and the imagination to thrive in our increasingly abstract and digital world."

Abbie's hands were shaking with excitement.

"You won't be drawing tomatoes anymore," Jonah chuckled. "And see here. That's Mr. Grouse."

He pointed to a picture in the corner of the page. Abbie angled the brochure, and the subdued light flashed across the image. Mr. Grouse had soft eyes beneath thick, red-rimmed glasses. His hair was white, like the crop of a mop, and he wore a vibrant green-and-blue-striped suit. Beneath it, she read,

"All art is in the influences" – Sigmund Grouse, Head of Art.

"He's bonkers, in the best way possible," Jonah said. "He's trying to get me to go full Jackson Pollock but with molten copper for my final project."

Abbie's heart thumped louder in her chest. She could picture herself sprawled across one of the studio's tables, surrounded by mountains of paper debris, arranging sections of materials across a thick canvas, sowing cards and felts in places. Her abstract visions coming to life across the page.

"A portfolio and artist's statement is required to apply. Please bring your submission to the entrance exams on November 6th and be prepared to discuss your work."

"I have so much to do," Abbie said breathlessly, closing the brochure and tucking it into her schoolbag. She repositioned the bag on her shoulder.

"One step at a time."

"What if Mr. Grouse hates my work?"

"He won't," Jonah said. "I'll make sure of it."

Abbie bit her lip, only half-convinced.

Jonah took her hand. His grip was steady. He led her down an alleyway and out onto another main street. Metal grates were pulled over the front of shop windows, charmed by graffiti. The only place still open was a corner shop. Abbie's eyes, accustomed to the mellowed darkness of the streets, were stung by the white haze of the shop. The Bangladeshi owner was preparing the next day's papers for his loyal locals. There were packets of cigarettes with harsh warnings and revolting pictures that failed to dissuade a woman from counting out her pennies to buy a pack of Marlboro Reds. The refrigerators rumbled, full of fizzy drinks and beers and smoothies. Racks of sweets, chocolates, and chewing gums were built into the counter like bricks in a stone wall. These were the only familiar omens in this cold, strange world, placed in shops along their journey westward as if they were slowly walking her home.

Down another quiet, tree-lined street, Jonah randomly stopped outside a building.

"T. S. Eliot used to live here," he announced.

"How do you know that?"

He pointed. Just next to the upstairs windows, Abbie saw a round blue plaque in the glint of the streetlamps.

"'T. S. Eliot, O.M., 1888–1965, Poet, lived and died here,'" Abbie read.

"Yup," Jonah said. "I'm surprised you haven't noticed the blue plaques before. They're all over the city."

Abbie rolled her eyes. It was embarrassing how much more Jonah knew about *her* city. He was supposed to be the foreigner, the American. If only she had paid attention when she had studied London history. She might have been able to recall one simple fact that she could say to impress him.

"How do you know all this?" she asked.

"I wanted to be a flaneur last year."

"What's that?"

"A person who wanders the streets with no purpose. The French made it up."

Jonah had a whole arsenal of provocative things to say. He never mentioned shopping, or who was doing what, or who was cooler than who. Instead, Jonah delved into worlds that Abbie had yet to enter. He told her he liked to sit in the park and watch clouds move. He loved glass artists. An exhibition of Chihuly, the great glass artist from the Pacific Northwest, was taking place at the Halcyon Gallery. They should go together. And the government's cabinet could never truly represent the people of the United Kingdom because it was run by Oxford elitists who had grown up together.

"I'll walk you home," Jonah insisted.

They had walked so far already that night. A couple more streets seemed like no distance at all. They arrived in front of 173 Clarendon Road. Not even the light in Yolly's room was on in the basement. The house stood like a skeleton in front of them. Abbie looked at Jonah to see what he thought of the place. She allowed him to read whatever he wanted into its emptiness.

Jonah handed the sketchbook to her.

"Let's do this again."

Abbie nodded. Jonah gripped her arm gently. He kissed her. Abbie smelt the tobacco on his clothes. His breathing was shallow. He tasted like the cold, harsh ash of his cigarettes, but his boldness captivated her. It carried her away. It was like a catchy song she loved to dance to but didn't know the name of. Abbie pulled back, determined to keep Jonah on his toes, to save what was left of her puzzle to unlock with him later. She opened the black gate and headed down into the basement. She waved at Jonah silently. He waved back. She smiled as she found the key under the mat and let herself inside.

9

That Sunday evening, Abbie sat alone at the round table in the kitchen. Yolly was out at evening mass. Charlotte was away at Harpburgh. As she twiddled her thumbs, Abbie remembered how this time last year, with April ripening into May, she had snuck Moe and Emily around to her house one Saturday evening. They had gotten drunk in the garden before meeting up with the Barnes boys on a green in Chiswick. Those memories now seemed vapid and silly to her.

This year, Abbie had far more important things to do. She hadn't spoken to anyone that day. She had worked through her Physics revision and prepared for her French vocab test. In silence, the time passed by long and lonely. Yet somehow, with her homework done, she had finally managed to carve out these few hours before she got too tired and gave up and watched *Skins* on TV before she went to bed.

Her art sketchbook lay on the table in front of her. Beside it were the blue folder of her cutouts and scissors and a glue stick and small packets of sequins and confetti she had found, too, for the fun of it. She even had an extra set of silk samples. Charlotte had left them in the living room, and Abbie was glad to repurpose the unwanted. She had already trimmed some of them off. Silk would give her page more texture, she hoped. She had wanted to use a canvas but didn't have one. Turning the page in her sketchbook and starting afresh would have to do. But what if the examiners and Mr. Grouse were shocked by the different styles from one page to the next? Was it too much of a jolt from the old to the new? Did she have to show progression?

"Whatever," Abbie said to no one.

She opened her sketchbook and flicked through it. The vast emptiness of the next new page beamed before her. Her gaze was fixated, unnerved. She sifted through the blue folder. Most of the images were of catwalks and luxury sprawls. They were too intoxicating, too vibrant. She had to tone it down for now. Towards the back of the folder, she found a couple pages from Charlotte's copy of a magazine about old English houses. A picture of a field of lilacs. A mansion with crisscrossed Tudor windows on the hillside. It was boring, but at least Abbie could start with some color and a pattern. She stuck the circular field onto the page. She layered the house on top of it. Another cutout, and another. A patch of grass with a blue tint. A tartan oak-green quilt. A couple sequins caught her eye, glinting from within their plastic packet. As Abbie sifted through it, the seam of the plastic burst open, sending sequins everywhere. They sparkled in the subdued light of the kitchen.

"Whoops," Abbie found herself saying. The sequins had automatically stuck to the less-than-perfect, gluey edges of her composition. They lined the page like a broken frame. She scratched off the ones too jumbled together and left others sparse. Their light, even against the disappointing background of the lilacs and the Tudor house, was beginning to shine. There was no gravity in this world. Only half-contorted frozen symbols. Abbie felt as if life was being breathed into her. One inhale at a time as she pieced the colors over each other. One exhale at a time. Perhaps the color of a single image wasn't to be judged alone. Perhaps what mattered more was how the images were layered together. And yet, their amalgamation fell flat compared to Abbie's visions of what it could be. What she had wanted it to be. She folded the photo of a bushel of daises and stuck it to the page. The thickness of that added some depth. But the colors weren't enough. It needed more.

Abbie grabbed the scissors and reached for the fabric samples. If she added pieces of silk, she might have something less than terrible. She noticed that a few different sections had been stuck together. A couple crumpled sticky note labels, graced by Charlotte's slanted handwriting, fell out onto the floor as Abbie flicked through. The silk with the purple roses, hideous as it was, would work well for this piece. Abbie cut it jaggedly along the edge and stuck it over the lilac field. It gave her composition a more fantastical, wilder feel. She chopped the corners off the shades of green, sticking the triangles together like a tree line beside the Tudor house. Her creation now took up most of the page. It was a far cry from the pastel and pencil sketches of tomatoes. But at least with the multitextured levels of nature, she hadn't broken the theme. Miss Hewitt might not under-stand it. Mr. Grouse, Abbie hoped, definitely would.

As the grandfather clock on the landing struck seven o'clock, a key turned in the front door. Footsteps shuffled along the bristled carpet in the entryway.

"Hello, darling," Charlotte said as she entered the kitchen.

"Hi," Abbie said without looking up from the page. In the corner of her eye, she noticed that Charlotte rested a wicker Fortnum and Mason hamper on the countertop and quickly put something away in the fridge.

"Did you have a lovely weekend?"

"Mm."

"Abigail," Charlotte continued sternly. Abbie gritted her teeth, bracing herself for what was to come. "Are you going to ask how my weekend was?"

"How was your weekend?" Abbie said, desperate to avoid launching her mother into another of her incredibly dull stories.

"It was wonderful. The bluebells at Harpburgh are blooming ferociously, but unfortunately, Granny has a cold, so she couldn't walk around the grounds to see them."

"That is a pity," Abbie said.

"Indeed," Charlotte continued, putting the hamper away above the Aga. Abbie hoped that by acknowledging her mother momentarily, Charlotte might be satisfied enough to leave her alone. Half a minute of silence passed between them. Charlotte put her reading glasses on and walked to the sitting room. There, she flicked through a pile of magazines before stacking them neatly again.

"Darling, have you seen a set of silk samples anywhere?"

Abbie paused momentarily as she put the finishing touches on her collage. The mangled colors of her first honest attempt lay in front of her. It wasn't perfect, but it would do for now. Her fingers seemed to sing with the sense of all that had come out of her and onto the page. It felt refreshing. Or perhaps it was just the glue that had dried on her fingers, making them more sensitive to the air.

Charlotte reappeared. Her reading glasses were pushed up on her forehead, exposing more of her thin grey roots beneath.

"I could have sworn I left them here."

Abbie instinctively closed the sketchbook as her mother approached.

Charlotte gasped. Her frantic words stung Abbie's ears like molten lava. "What have you done to them?"

Abbie rolled her eyes.

"I thought you didn't need them?"

Charlotte picked up the tatters of the samples, and they came apart between her perfectly manicured fingernails. A couple of loose-cut threads drifted onto the table.

"Where are the labels, Abigail?"

Abbie glanced at the sticky notes dotted about the floor. Supposedly Charlotte's scribbles on them had actually meant something. She quickly regretted it all.

"I've spent months picking out the perfect colors with Nile for every room in Harpburgh."

"Whatever, I get it," Abbie spat at her. "It's not that big of a deal. All these stupid shades are the same, anyway."

"The samples are distinct, but that's beside the point. Please, do not use my things without asking me. How many times do I have to tell you?"

There was that dreaded, condescending phrase. Repeated to Abbie as if she was too thick to have learned any of these things the first time around. It brought her back to perhaps the most excruciating moment of her life when she had climbed up on the kitchen counter to see what was up there and accidentally dropped Charlotte's favorite tea plate, smashing it into a million pieces.

Charlotte pinched the bridge of her nose and took a couple shaking breaths.

"It's not that big of a deal—"

"Just go, please."

"Fine," Abbie said. She scraped her chair loudly along the wooden floor. She grabbed her blue folder and sketchbook and left the rest of the mess. Yolly could clean that up later. Charlotte just didn't understand how important art was to her. Charlotte was only thinking about herself and her stupid silk upholstery in the countryside. Abbie couldn't stand to be in the room with her any longer. She stomped upstairs, clutching her sketchbook and folder like a bridge into her new world. Her mother's patronizing words couldn't stop her now. If anything, they were only fueling her onwards, energizing her as she pushed herself forwards onto better things.

10

"I snorkeled with Jonah Wood," Abbie said to Julie.

They were painting in the middle of their Art lesson. All around them, their classmates worked daintily and chatted. Outside the art studio windows, clouds bumbled over the hockey pitches of Agerton Hall and the washed horizon of Hammersmith beyond. A heavier rain slashed along the windows, distorting the view outside like an impressionist painting. Julie had been diligently focused on her sketch of a Barbie in a ball gown. But as Abbie got into the details, Julie's mouth opened wide, revealing the new pink rubber bands around the train tracks of her braces.

"I just don't know if I like him that much," Abbie admitted. "Also, he's like not on any sports teams and he smokes a lot."

"I mean, you're being kind of unfair," Julie said. "You can't just go out with him if you feel like it while he's buying you tickets and things. He's probably falling in love with you."

"I guess," Abbie said. Jonah was interesting to talk to, but she definitely liked him more because he paid for things and always held the door open for her. Still, she didn't like it when his neck looked too thick and went red and blotchy when he was uncomfortable.

Abbie stopped painting. She suddenly got a surge of energy and dabbed a large spot of dark brown ink on the paper. As it dripped and became entangled with the half-arsed image of tomato stems, Abbie grabbed the edge of the page and tore it in two.

"What are you doing?" Julie said, taken aback.

Abbie tore the paper into smaller pieces.

"I'm making it into a collage."

"I'm not sure you're allowed," Julie said. She glanced over nervously at Miss Hewitt, who was inspecting another girl's sketch across the room. Miss Hewitt's long grey curls hid the distaste Abbie pictured on her face, and her long smock and crystal jewelry made her look like she was attending a yoga retreat.

"I don't care."

Abbie got up and made her way quietly across the room. She found a glue stick and returned to the table. She opened up her sketchbook and flicked through to her most recent collage. She stuck the jagged pieces of paper in an abstract form of the stems and the fruit in front of her. Julie shook her head silently. Abbie was determined to start cutting and sticking, putting together a composition in the only way she knew how.

As she elevated her next creation, Abbie's cheeks burned a little. She glanced at Julie, who was shading in the fold of the Barbie's dress with a pencil. Julie's sketch was so lifelike, so realistic. The Barbie's face, usually the most complex part of any person-like thing to draw, was perfect. In that second, Julie's future flashed before Abbie's eyes. Dressed in long robes, with her hair in a messy bun, Julie would get a standing ovation at the end of her haute couture show for Paris Fashion Week. Julie's mum, Marianne, was a slender and successful industrial designer from Geneva who had her own studio in Old Street. What made it worse was that the Loucharts had so much more money than Abbie's family did. They had renovated their London townhouse and château in Saint-Tropez years ago. Julie's life was set to be so easy. Abbie tried to reassure herself. At least she was prettier than Julie and more outgoing and social than her. At least Abbie didn't have braces anymore. At least she was in a higher set for Maths and got better marks.

"I'm applying to Collegiate for sixth form."

"Oh?" Julie said, pulling the hair of her lopsided ponytail to make it tighter. "Why?"

"I mean, let's be honest, Collegiate is a way better school than Agerton Hall."

"Surely it depends on what you mean by better?" Julie said. "Lots of people do really well at A levels and GCSEs here."

"Collegiate is way more intellectual and competitive," Abbie stated, "and more people get into Oxford there."

"Girls from Agerton Hall go to Oxford, too."

"True, but not as many," Abbie said. She had hardly expected this to be such a difficult conversation. "Look, I'm just not happy here. I'm tired of being in the same place as Moe and Emily. And everyone else here is obsessed with One Direction. I actually want to achieve something with my life."

"So that's what you honestly think about Agerton Hall? That we're a bunch of losers?"

"I don't mean it that way," Abbie said, backtracking to try not to offend her. "I just mean that Collegiate would be a better school for me."

Julie tried to keep drawing, but her hand was quivering. She put her pencil down and stared silently at the table. Julie could never get into Collegiate. And as much as she liked Julie, Abbie was not going to curtail her academic future for the sake of a single friendship. Agerton Hall was a boring cesspit of teenage girl bitchiness. Abbie had to get out while she still could and save herself.

"I'm here next year at least," Abbie said. "The exams aren't until November, and they're tough. And I need, like, a perfect portfolio if I want to do Art and everything. There's a big chance that I don't even get in."

Julie's cheeks swelled pink. Slowly she picked up her pencil and began to shade gently.

"Yeah, but you want to go," Julie said solemnly. "I get it. I mean, Agerton Hall's hardly a perfect school."

"Right."

Abbie knew Julie would understand, even though she didn't have a choice in the matter. Abbie had far greater priorities now. She could envision her future, discussing politics with Charles Barry and Griff in the Yard at Collegiate. Abbie was prepared to put every friendship at Agerton Hall on the chopping block if it meant her dreams could come true. She didn't need her Agerton Hall friends. She didn't need Julie, even. She didn't need anyone.

Abbie fixed the cutouts of her painting together, dabbing them with a glue stick. Miss Hewitt was quick to notice, and she sauntered across the room.

"Painting with a glue stick, I see?" Miss Hewitt said, peering over Abbie's shoulder.

Abbie tried to sound as confident as possible, showing her the collage. "Here, see the tomato and the stems?"

"Miss Chesterton," Miss Hewitt scoffed, "we are working on our sketchbooks for a Fine Art GCSE qualification. Not arts and crafts."

Abbie's cheeks flushed hot. A few girls at a nearby table looked up from their work.

"It's just abstract, in 3D," Abbie said.

"Indeed, I can see," Miss Hewitt said, folding her arms. "Why do you think I've assigned the class to paint and draw?"

Abbie shrugged.

"Because no artist ever succeeded in this world without exceptional classical training," Miss Hewitt said. "Art is not supposed to be fun, Miss Chesterton. In fact, it can be quite monotonous. It's about dedication and detail and skill."

"Frida Kahlo never had classical training," Abbie shouted. The classroom fell silent.

"Abbie, leave it," Julie mouthed to her.

"I do beg your pardon, Miss Chesterton," Miss Hewitt continued. "Frida Kahlo was a painter, wasn't she? That is precisely my point. Would it be too much trouble for you to pick up a brush?"

Abbie nodded, pretending to obey her teacher's baseless words. She stuck the final piece of her torn-up drawing to the page before she picked up her paintbrush.

"I'll be having a word with the examiner about this," Miss Hewitt said before quickly being distracted by another girl who had raised her hand.

Abbie sat there, raging inside. Her second composition was complete. It was far less colorful than the collage on the other side of the page, but with ripped paper, it had a far more interesting texture. And she should have been happy about it. But she had never felt so indignant and determined to prove herself.

The bell rang to sound the end of the lesson. Julie started to sweep up the wooden flakes from her pencil sharpenings that littered the table. Abbie closed her sketchbook and put the glue stick and ink palette away. It was like they were taking apart the stage at the end of a long season of performances. Their days in their Art lessons were numbered now. Their time being silly together was stunted and evolving with new currents. They gathered up their schoolbags and headed downstairs.

They stood outside the Physics lab, queuing with the other girls.

"Want to come over on Saturday?" Julie asked, "I was thinking we could rent a chick flick from Video City and have a sleepover."

Abbie tried to smile or at least appear grateful. She might have wanted to hang out with Julie, but watching a chick flick? That was such a waste of time when she had big plans to design a new collage for her portfolio for her Collegiate application that weekend. Jonah would probably text her soon and ask her out somewhere nice. On the other hand, Abbie knew how the sleepover with Julie would play out. She would go over to Julie's house, where her parents would be in the dining room three hours into their dinners that lasted for eternity. She would be forced to kiss each of Marianne's old, perfumed French-speaking friends on both cheeks. Yuck. Then Guillaume, Julie's father, would force her to try the grossest and smelliest cheese on their cheeseboard. Double yuck.

"I can't," Abbie said.

"Thought so," Julie said.

The lesson started. Julie drew a picture of a moon with all the craters and compared it to Mr. Grath's uneven, bald head. Abbie tried to giggle with Julie, but she was riddled with guilt. Julie was lucky to have her as a friend. Whoever Abbie's replacement would be, she would have a far less connected social circle.

11

Early that Saturday evening, Abbie climbed the steps of Green Park tube station and walked out onto Piccadilly. Jonah trailed a step behind her, lighting a cigarette the second they were outside. Specks of drizzle touched her face, tumbling perpetually from the washed grey sky. The buses whirred. The varied perfumes of the shops and their visitors christened the air like different notes on a harp. The ornate stone trimmings of the Ritz were dulled silver in the rain; the arches of its windows were carved with fruit and indecipherable faces. Its cloisters sheltered sheepish tourists and members of the endangered English gentry from the rain. Baubles of flowers hung on metal chains from the arches, of oranges, purples, and pinks, hinting at the magical interiors of plush pillows, dark wood paneling, grand pianos, and many-tiered chandeliers within. In a jewelry shop window were sapphire necklaces with matching rings, bracelets, and cuff links. A gentleman in a top hat and silver-buttoned overcoat stood beside the entrance to a more exclusive venue, ushering in an elderly woman in a burgundy mink-lined wrap, followed by a group of disorientated tourists, clad in cheap waterproof ponchos.

The alluring lights of the branches of boutique Middle Eastern and Chinese banks glistened across the bonnets of the rattling black taxis that waited patiently at the red traffic lights outside. In the Caviar House, fat, balding, and aged men sat between young, over-dressed women over glasses of champagne. There were shops devoted to tapestries, cheese, velvet waistcoats, and antique portrai-ture, respectively. They had passed the Wolseley, where the double-height ceiling was propped up effortlessly by great columns carrying gold-trimmed lamps. Tiered tea trays and crystal vessels for sherry and port lined the mahogany bar. Waiters wore bow ties and white aprons that were ironed to perfection. One stooped over a woman who wore sunglasses indoors, her heavy wreaths of pearls around her neck accelerating her hunchback.

Abbie held the bouquet that Jonah had bought for her. It had been a good day at the races with his dad, Clive, Jonah said. Abbie imag-ined what kind of quirky artist Jonah's dad might be. A name like Clive Wood made him sound like a pilot who flew planes in a small town she'd never heard of in America.

The sheetlike plastic around the flowers glistened in the rain. Their vibrant green stems were fresh. The tulips' light orange and pink petals shone iridescently in the grey air. They were a handful of the Dutch countryside's most pristine creations, lopped off at the base, cast into bushels, and transported in trucks to be picked out of a bunch in the urban concrete of the city. The warm, rounded petals reminded her of the wedges of fresh peaches that Yolly had prepared for her when she was a child. Yolly had brought them out on a blue plastic plate, which she laid on the picnic blanket. And Abbie had watched the pigeons plodding in the summer grass.

Abbie was enraptured by the streets they shouldered through. She thought of the thousands of proper, well-dressed people who had taken her exact steps over the centuries. Through the grand windows of the gentlemen's clubs, she saw yellowed walls covered in portraits of yesterday's Londoners and romantic landscape scenes of the English countryside. The velvet armchairs and marble fireplaces stuck out like time capsules opened in the modern day, lavish and lovely but increasingly lost. The elderly English gentlemen wore dark blue blazers, pastel-colored shirts, and burgundy corduroys. Being in public was occasion enough for finer dress.

Beyond Albemarle and Dover Street, they came to an arcade and detoured down it. The fountain pen shop offered her nibs used to mimic Anglo-Saxon scripture, the English of centuries past. They passed the soft celadon-green interior of Ladurée, whose glass counters tempted tourists with the tiny splendors of French macarons. They passed a hunting gear shop with the tweed and paisley attire, the knee-high socks, garters, and brown boots, speaking together in the absurdity of English activities. They passed a cigar shop and a cane shop with old wooden facades and boxed windows. Abbie wondered who might buy such outdated treasures. They passed a shaving shop, where sponges and brushes puffed between cologne bottles, revealing the secrets of the male beauty routine that Abbie had never considered before. There were the cheese and pâté shops, whose pungent odors wafted far down the street, advertising themselves to the suited men drinking a pint in the pub on the corner. There were the men's pajama shops for silk nightgowns, flannel undergarments, and slippers. There were the straw boater hats and blazer shops, where men could buy suits striped pink and white like candy canes, which only made appearances at the tennis at Wimbledon or the races at Ascot.

Turning the corner, they came to a redbrick palace that signified the holy grail of English tea: Fortnum and Mason. It felt a little hollowed to Abbie to visit it now. In recent years, protesters had stormed Fortnum and Mason, but she could not remember what they were advocating against. Perhaps it was low wages or that Fortnum's was not paying corporate taxes or just a general stab at inequality in the UK. Still, Charlotte remained a regular. Charlotte's hampers could have anything in them, marmalades, preserves, teacakes, or hogwash, for all she cared, as long as there was a bottle of port and a vial of sherry.

The displays in the windows were an amalgamation of teddy bears and Christmas puddings, even though it was May, jars of cranberry sauce, and fake icicles, which brought to light festive bunches of grapes in between bottles of champagne. The background was a thick white felt, which made Abbie feel like she could taste fake, powdered snow.

Inside, Abbie sat down with Jonah at a table for two. They ordered chocolate éclairs that melted in her mouth and crème brûlée that cracked like the surface of an icy pond when she tapped it with her spoon.

"How are you going to survive not smoking while we're inside?" Abbie said.

Jonah looked back at her sternly.

"I had to have two after seeing that shiny billboard with David Cameron's face on it."

"That's quite a shallow take on the election," she teased him. Jonah did not find it funny.

"Don't they shut girls like you away in boarding school? It seems like you'd be better off in the countryside, prancing around with your ponies."

Abbie laughed. Clearly, Jonah wanted to know everything about her.

"I would," she said. "But the country sucks. It's just like sheep and fields and stuff."

"So, you're a city girl at heart?"

"I think so."

"You don't know so?"

Abbie sighed, a little frustrated.

"Okay, yes. I'm a city girl at heart."

"Awesome," he said. "Well, that's good to know. I prefer cities too. But New York is a far better city than London. I want to go to film school at Columbia for university. And besides, the only thing I find vaguely interesting about Notting Hill is the magnitude of other people's problems."

Abbie gulped. Jonah knew exactly what he wanted in life. It troubled her that he was making such future-oriented statements. Why did he care to tell her where he was going in a year or two?

"What do you mean?" she asked.

"At least in America rich people think therapy is cool. In England, you all just sweep it under the rug—"

"And having no national health system is so much better?" Abbie interrupted. "But let's make sure we overmedicate everyone. Start the kids on antidepressants young."

"I believe people should have the right to make their own health decisions. This country is just a mess of paternalism. You've never lived anywhere else, so you'd never know it."

"Whatever," Abbie said. Jonah did have a point. Perhaps she would move to America with him so she could experience how terrible the private hospitals were there and finally win an argument against him. "If you hate it so much, why do you live here?"

"Mostly because I'm tied to my parents. To be clear, I don't hate it. I wish you'd just admit that Notting Hill is a bubble of rich people, which has its faults too."

"I've lived here my whole life, and it's amazing." Abbie folded her arms.

"I've lived here my whole life"—he shrugged—"but New York is a world-class city. London's heyday has come and gone. It's passé at this point."

Abbie paused. Perhaps Jonah was right? English people loved their traditions. Maybe the country had steeped like a pot of strong tea that had long gone cold, and someone had forgotten to take the tea bag out. The UK was getting left behind. China, the States, and even Russia were so much bigger and more relevant to world politics. The UK was nothing but a small country, floating somewhere off the cold Atlantic edge of continental Europe. Abbie suddenly imagined Big Ben and the Houses of Parliament and Fortnum and Mason and the old men sitting in the armchairs of the gentlemen's clubs nearby fading into dust. Westminster Abbey crumbling, brick by brick. Washed away into the sands of time. Forgotten, dust, everywhere. Piling up in dunes. Accumulating into the oceans. Gathering in the crevices and the caverns of underwater caves, the dust gradually becoming sediment, like the dinosaur bones that decayed into crude oil, bound to nothing but an unknown future of excavation to be extracted and processed and burned to fuel some civilization far off in the future. The sun, extinguishing; the universe, ending. London's heyday had been and gone. Abbie shuddered in terror.

"Well, okay, *as far as I know*, Notting Hill is the best place to live in the world," Abbie corrected herself.

"Better," Jonah said. He nodded with a smile. He seemed to care so much about her precise use of words, and frankly, she couldn't see why it mattered. Why couldn't they just talk about something less controversial, like the weather? Now she understood why Charlotte hated Americans so much.

"What I can't stand here is just how many people get divorced," Jonah said matter-of-factly. "Marriage is a vital institution that we ought to protect."

Abbie looked him directly in the eye. Jonah's gaze was solemn, enduring. She had never met a fifteen-year-old boy who was so unbelievably weird. Why did marriage, of all things, mean anything to him? Is this really what he believed? She ate the last bite of chocolate éclair, hoping the sugar would take her mind off things.

"Did you know that 66 percent of all divorces are initiated by women?" Jonah went on. "It's totally unfair to husbands. The ladies who lunch shouldn't be able to ditch their husbands just because they feel like it."

Abbie stared at him. Was Jonah trying to provoke her? She thought of Charlotte. Even though her mother had graduated with a degree in History from Oxford in the late 1980s, she hadn't had a job since she worked in a bank before Freddie was born. Charlotte's existence was frivolous. There was no purpose to it. It irked Abbie to think such damning thoughts. But a more profound question was brewing in her mind. If Charlotte stayed in bed for the day, would the world miss her? The friends Charlotte lunched with had other friends. And yet, Charlotte had often complained that Richard had never made enough money. Perhaps they were bound to get divorced if Richard ever returned from the trip with his business partner to Little Saint James.

Abbie thought back to a dinner she had attended with Charlotte and her group of lunching ladies last month at The Arts Club on Dover Street. All the whining and the mummy gossip about whoever's son was dating who. All the bitching about whoever's house renovation was in poor taste and looked terrible. All the subtly competitive comments about who was going to the fanciest ski resort in the Alps that Easter.

"We've always skied in Aspen and Park City," Abbie recalled her mother's friend, Mariam, saying, much to the irritation of the other ladies. Their teaspoons had clanged against the sides of their teacups as they stirred their tea ferociously anticlockwise. Their holidays in Verbier couldn't compete with that.

Maybe Jonah did have a point. Apart from wanting to become an artist, Abbie had never thought about having a career. Nobody had ever asked her what she wanted to be when she grew up. Nobody was there except him to take her art seriously. Still, accepting the gift of Jonah's flowers hardly seemed worth it after she had been dragged through the conversation like she was bumping up against large, jagged stones as she uncovered more of his unsettling views. He aggravated her. And yet his honesty and directness were addictive.

Jonah scraped the flat-bottomed bowl of the crème brûlée. Once he had finished, he reached for her hand at the table. Their eyes met briefly before he looked away nervously. His fingers gripped her thin wrist. His voice quavered a little.

"W-will you be my girlfriend?" he asked her.

Why? I thought you hated me, she asked him in her mind.

No, his eyes seemed to say back. I think you're quite nice. Near perfection, actually.

"Yes," Abbie said in a small voice.

Jonah smirked. He pinched her by the chin. He kissed her. His lips were cold with the dampness of the cream. Abbie could feel now that he was overheating as he got closer to her, beholding her, cherishing her. He kissed her more. Jonah closed his eyes, but Abbie kept hers open. He seemed entranced, focused, and peaceful. It was enough, she thought, for her to give him this moment together. She bit his lip tenderly. Jonah sniffled slightly. His breath caressed her cheek as he exhaled. Suddenly Abbie felt the heavy stares of the waiter, the bartender, and the other people around them. Moe, Amber Rutterdown, Yolly, Charlotte finding out. She put her hand on his shoulder and pulled away from him gently. Jonah sat back in his chair, relieved.

12

L ater that evening, in the basement of the Woods' house, Abbie sat next to Jonah on the couch. They watched a movie on the TV nestled in the center of a wall of DVDs, children's fantasy books, and board games. The ochre wooden floor was covered by a yarn carpet, its dark blue pigment threaded along pastel tones like a modern art piece. A warped, abstract lamp sculpture hung above them and lit the room with a glare that bounced off the light of the TV. The dark blue tassels on the rug looked like the old gentlemen's blazers she had seen only an hour before. The pastel tassels were like their buttoned-up shirts. With Jonah, every color she saw jogged her memory, like a snow globe that was being shaken.

On the coffee table in front of them were two glasses of red wine. Abbie had never felt like more of a grown-up. Jonah's incessant smoking was starting to irritate her, and it was not his only vice. Jonah was buried in his cynical self-hatred, accelerating his own death. And yet, she was already enjoying playing boyfriend and girlfriend with him. She loved the flowers he had bought her. She loved it when he paid the bill. He was fulfilling his role; she was fulfilling hers. She would do so dutifully.

Abbie had always wanted a boyfriend. A properly dedicated one, not someone who half-arsed it, like Danny Watson. She had always wanted to be the center of someone else's world. Yet the title of girl-friend, she knew, came with expectations. She was at a boy's house, after all. Jonah had been good to her. He probably deserved some-thing in return. Something to keep him dipping his toes in the water without revealing all of her secrets at once. It pained her to think about it that way. Weren't they supposed to be an adorable couple falling in love? Was this what love was supposed to feel like? She already knew enough about him to want to change things. To make him exercise more and smoke less. She would find him irresistible once he changed, just a little. Then they could meet in the middle. Jonah, a compromised, better version of who he was now, and herself, just as she was.

The movie played on in the background. Abbie took a large gulp of wine. Jonah kept his arms at his sides. He was far too respectful, too lacking in experience to make any moves. But she was already in his house. He had already shouted upstairs to his parents and little brother to keep out of the basement. She knew what would make this night more interesting than just finishing the movie. She leaned against his chest. Jonah put his arm around her. She felt his breaths quicken. He was patient, but he wanted it. Abbie could tell.

"Are you even following the story?" he asked. Abbie shook her head, playing dumb. A bead of sweat formed at the corner of his forehead. She reached to wipe it away, smoothly gripping the back of his head. She pulled him closer to her. She kissed him. His lips were moist. Jonah kept his hands in his lap, unsure, lacking any sense of where to touch her. He sighed as he took off his sweater. He undid the collar of his shirt. Abbie kissed him more forcefully, passion-ately. Their tongues locked. He tasted of cigarettes subdued by the mint of Listerine pockets. His cheeks were reddening, too.

Abbie wanted Jonah to be obsessed with her. She had something she needed to prove. She guided his hand up to her waist and let him run his fingers over the edges of her bra. Jonah seemed puzzled, troubled. He was captivated, like a deer caught in headlights. Had he never kissed Rosalia? Not passionately, anyway. Perhaps he had never run his hands along her body or felt her breasts or kissed the skin of her neck silently, lying on a sandy beach under the light of the moon. No. She, Abbie, would have to lead him away into the darkness.

She felt along his belly to his waistband. Jonah breathed out deeply, then seemed to skip a breath. She touched his leg, up along the gap in his crotch. The shape of his balls, smoothed over by his trousers. He was startled. Jonah fondled her bra clumsily. She felt along the hardened bulge of his crotch. Undid the round metal button of his jeans. Pulled down the zipper. Caressed the cotton of his underwear. Gauged the size of a large wet stain that had already formed there.

"Wait!" Jonah said, wincing. He closed his eyes, pinching his temples. Was he enjoying this? Maybe she shouldn't have gone straight for his crotch. Jonah fumbled for the remote and paused the movie. He kissed her on the cheek and did up his zipper. He pushed himself up from the couch. There was a transactional nature to why she was there and what they were about to do. Abbie followed him out of the room.

Up the orange-carpeted stairs, they walked along the darkened entryway of the house. Moonshine lay in a fluffy heap on the floor, stretched out in the corridor. They tiptoed past the open door of the living room. Abbie caught a blurry glimpse of horses and jockeys bundling across the screen and prayed that Jonah's father hadn't heard them. When they reached the top of the stairs, Jonah pointed right into the room on the first floor. He turned on the light. A lamp with a thin, white paper dome around it illuminated the room.

The walls of Jonah's room were painted black. His single bed was raised. A desk beside it took up most of the room. Two tall, curtainless windows looked out into the nighttime calmness of the garden that she had played in with Amber all those years ago. Clothes poured out of Jonah's closet, littering the floor. Abbie looked up at the walls, unsettled but unsurprised by what she saw. There was a large, framed movie poster of *Eraserhead*, a black-and-white picture of a man with his eyes wide open, his hair long and statically spiking upwards, staring out at her as if he was being electrocuted. Below the film's title, she read, *A film by David Lynch*. Beside the poster was a painting of a woman's open legs, the lips of her vagina from red to pink, lightening in the outer layers. She was spread, bleeding, and scarred by a bloody knife, also in the picture. The oval shapes of her insides flapping outwards were painted without precision. The drops of blood seemed to float in midair. The image concerned her, but it wasn't a masterpiece. It had been painted by this strange, rageful fifteen-year-old boy who was busy fumbling in his desk drawer. Abbie shuddered. There was nothing within herself that could understand where this terror inside of him came from.

"What are you doing?" she asked him.

"Dealing with my cigarette drawer," Jonah said proudly, stuffing it with more empty packs. There must have been hundreds in that drawer alone. Abbie stood there, her face blank, as Jonah shut the drawer and locked the bedroom door.

They faced each other. Abbie began to wonder. Perhaps Jonah, with his own take on the world, was the sane one, and she was the weird one. She liked that he was strange, that he saw the world through his own eyes. She couldn't claim to know everything about someone so complex, so preoccupied and cynical. But something about his violent, bloody painting of a woman's genitals and his incessant scowling made sense to her. She got it. She got him. And that felt important to her. Not every girl would be drawn to a boy like Jonah. There had to be some channel of darkness within her that he had merely helped to open. She wondered what, if anything, that said about her. Jonah, with his quirks. Jonah, with his nervousness and shadowed wildness. He was lovable.

Abbie wrapped her arms around him. She kissed him. His balance was off. Jonah steadied himself against his desk. He gave her small pecks at first, like he was warming up to the possibility of her body, discovering his own way of adoring her. Abbie grabbed his unkempt black hair, taking the lead and kissing his forehead, neck, and chest. Jonah kept his hands at his sides, holding himself back, confused, incapable. He had no way to tell her that she was his. That was what she craved. She leaned onto him and made him carry her weight. He grabbed her hair and attempted to pull it downwards. In that half of a second, Abbie knew what he wanted. He was so simpleminded. He had shown all his cards in this game before they had even started to play.

Abbie reached for Jonah's waistband and undid the buttons. She pulled the zip down one tiny buckle at a time. She looked up at him with a sultry pout. She was already following a script, but she didn't know why. She looked into his eyes like she had seen the porn stars do in POV videos, their sculpted breasts bulging, hungry to please. Those women gawked at whatever surprise the man had in store for them. She knelt at his feet, her knees rubbing the worn, roughened carpet. That was when she remembered that the window behind them had no curtain. Jonah did not seem to care. Anyone in the garden could have seen them there. From their silhouette alone, it was all too obvious.

Jonah's underwear was light blue cotton. The damp stain was on the center-left side. He pulled down his trousers. They gathered around his ankles. The underside of his belly was pale and hairless. He was panting already. Abbie was panting too, racing to show him what she could do, to finish this as quickly as possible. The waistband of his underwear was elastic. She pulled it down.

His penis stuck out over the top. Its red, veined, circumcised tip dipped upwards. Smaller than Danny Watson's, undoubtedly. Not excessively big, not shockingly small. It would do. His balls were red and irritated; she knew not why. All of a sudden, Jonah found the language to touch her body. But it was his language, not one they could speak together. He held her head in both hands and directed her onto him. She opened her mouth and sucked the tip. That familiar, fishy, sweat-filled taste hit her tongue. Jonah gasped. He pushed her head further down the shaft. Abbie opened her mouth wider to be sure it wouldn't catch on her teeth. His penis filled the entire length of her breath, jabbing her throat.

"D-don't do that!" she said, catching her breath and freeing herself.

"Sorry," he said, closing his eyes in deep concentration. A quick pause. A second later. "I'm coming."

Abbie picked up strength, sucked harder, moaned, and let the humming sensation in her throat send him over the edge. Jonah's entire body tensed. His temples creased. He looked upwards as he let out a short, single shout.

"Stop, stop, stop," he gasped, grasping for a tissue. Abbie pulled away just as he caught the spurt of silky liquid in his hands. It was a moment of sheer vulnerability. His trousers around his ankles. His brief seconds of ecstasy already over. She sat on the floor, fully clothed, satisfied only that she had pleased him. Jonah grimaced as he wiped himself off. He pulled up his trousers, grumbling, and shuffled to the bathroom. Abbie took a tissue and wiped the edges of her mouth. She tried to spit out what was left of him. Within a minute, Jonah returned. He headed straight for the closet. Abbie glanced over at him, but he was still frowning. He didn't even look at her.

"The bathroom is across the landing," he said to her from behind the cupboard door.

"Thanks."

She checked that the coast was clear before she crossed the landing. The toilet seat in the bathroom was up. Empty rolls of toilet paper were piled up next to the loo. Maybe Jonah's family didn't have a live-in cleaner like Yolly. The bathroom window was open, letting the night air in. Her teeth chattered. The bathroom was deathly cold, as was the water from the tap. She washed out her mouth. She wiped her chin on what she hoped was a clean towel hanging on the back of the bathroom door. Before she joined Jonah in his room again, she looked at herself in the mirror above the sink.

Her hair was a mess. Her eye makeup hung in smudged grey bags under her eyes. Her eyes were bloodshot red. She had a small wine stain on her top that she hadn't noticed before. What was she doing here? Why was she here? What had she done? She sighed deeply, uncertain. Was Jonah always going to be this clueless when it came to any kind of sex? Would he ever learn how to please her, to reach beyond the confines of his own body and touch her, let alone in the way she wanted to be touched? He would need training and a lot of it. She'd have to help him gain confidence and experience without insulting him. She had done the deed, but part of her wished he had been underwhelmed by it all. Then she might not feel so embarrassed about what she had done. And not feel so alone.

13

Abbie sat at the desk in her bedroom, diligently gluing beads onto a piece of paper. The tulips Jonah had given her and a series of half-finished collages lay beside her page. Each was trying to imitate the petals. As the flowers had wilted and hardened with age, a thin drip of crimson had appeared along the back of each petal, which was impossible to replicate on paper. The body of each flower had opened up in a pure yellowed pink, the petals circling each other like the delicately wrapped folds of a ball gown skirt she had seen in *Sleeping Beauty*. Why, she cursed to herself, did everything have to come back to fashion? She was a mixed-media artist, not a fashion designer like Julie. Fashion design was Julie's thing, not hers. And yet, it would have been so much easier to draw these flowers with watercolor pencils rather than abstract them away with beads, felt tip pens, and blobs of acrylic paint. Abbie regretted picking such a strange, unrelatable medium in the first place.

"For fuck's sake," Abbie said as she accidentally dipped her hand in a dollop of acrylic paint. The smudge of it poisoned the crisp white background of the paper. The spell had broken. Rage burst like a torrent through her body. She tore up the piece into three jagged chunks. Then she immediately regretted doing even that. She had spent over an hour on this composition for her portfolio. Now it was ruined, and she could salvage nothing from it. A great artist would work harder. A great artist would revive a composition that needed fixing. As it stood, Abbie's portfolio most certainly would not get her into Collegiate.

She noticed the mess that her desk had become. The stout acrylic paint pot, with its lid nowhere to be found. The long, tattered paint-brush resting in a glass, murky with paint-infused water. The disparate piles of beads, glues, and thick Sharpie felt tip pens she'd picked up from Ryman. There were crumpled paper shapes she had carved from *Grafik*. That design magazine presented an idyllic yet surreal world of wonder to her. She could feel the creative energy swirling into the air around her, cast out from its pages like magic dust. She had all the ingredients to create something good. And yet, all her attempts came out terrible. Even the compositions she dreamt of making wouldn't be good enough to hang in a gallery.

Over the last couple of weeks, the tulips had taken on a form of their own. At first, Abbie had kept them in water on her windowsill, as Yolly had instructed. They caught the sun as it rose over Clarendon Road in the early mornings. Yet the flowers had soon started to rot and were on the brink of turning putrid. Abbie wanted them to last forever. She had removed them from the water and left them on her desk. There they had hardened, and their color had almost faded. The green husks of their leaves had turned a muddied brown. Their bulbs had faded as if their rich peach color had been washed out with cream. They took on the shape of the desk's surface. Their leaves curled. Their stems twisted. Somehow, they were far more beautiful to her dead than alive. And yet, she was desperate to craft them onto the page.

Her imitations of them had filled pages in her sketchbook. She imagined portraits of hidden figures with a flower as their face. She detailed them in inks and paints that flowed like trickles of rain gath-ering in a gutter until she had used too much, which spoiled the medium. She had drawn their shapes in a mathematical expression, using logic and right angles. The messiness of their burgundy, the sticky tips of pollen-drenched stamens had stained one of the sleeves of her lilac cashmere cardigan. Yet she hardly cared.

Abbie looked at the flowers and thought of Jonah. She heard his voice clear in her ears,

"Think of any artist you love, and I bet you their life was mostly suffering. You liked Van Gogh, right? Well, he spent half his life in a mental hospital before he cut off his ear and killed himself. His work was the only redeeming thing he ever experienced. Yet the value of it, too, was barely realized during his lifetime. He died a pauper. Still, he has one heck of a legacy to show for it now. Making art, ultimately, is a painful and solitary pursuit. No one can help you or fully understand what you're trying to create. The more you cut yourself off from all these extraneous people, the better your work will be. Trust me."

Abbie had taken his words to heart. A new loop of thoughts was playing over again in her mind. They came to her often. She accepted them, believing them as accurate. She carried them wherever she went and stowed them away like a carry-on bag on an airplane. Jonah was helping her move in the right direction, to create more art, to have a career, and have a chance of going down in history. Maybe one day, Abbie would be as famous as Mozart. Her legacy was far more critical than hanging out with Julie. She wanted to save time and considered taking a different bus route to school. Julie always walked so slowly, and the 94 bus route through Shepherd's Bush would be far quicker for Abbie anyway. She couldn't waste any more time with friends or watching TV or going on Facebook or playing *Club Penguin* or *Neopets*. She had to secure her legacy in the history of the world. She couldn't just leave it up to chance. She was destined for a future of much greater success than any of the people she knew would ever see. They were too simple to dream of the things that she dreamt of. Awards, exhibiting her work in the Louvre, and selling her collages as the most expensive modern art pieces ever at Christie's and Sotheby's. Oh, and being invited to dinner with Tracey Emin and David Hockney, of course.

"The Next Andy Warhol." That's what the newspapers would say when she started to become famous. But she was already fifteen. How many more years did she have while she was still this anonymous? Miley Cyrus was the same age as her, and she already starred in *Hannah Montana*, the hit TV show on Disney Channel. Well, actually, she remembered that Miley Cyrus was two years old than her. So Abbie still had time to catch up and get her own TV show or win a super-impressive award or something. She had to become a star while she was young. That was the real reason she couldn't waste time at a sleepover at Julie's house. Julie was going nowhere with her life. But then again, maybe it was Julie who was destined to become as famous as Vera Wang or Vivienne Westwood. Abbie would just be her old friend, who no one had ever heard of. No, it wouldn't be so. Abbie would make sure of it. She would wake up at 5:00 a.m. just to start studying more, making more collages, and trying to be perfect at it.

Abbie didn't want to be like any of Charlotte's friends, who had never accomplished anything. Their husbands ran divisions of banks or had their own funds or investments and things. At least they had something to show for their time on Earth. But her mother? And Yolly? History was going to forget them immediately. As soon as they died, it would be like they had never existed. Abbie had to achieve more than that. And Jonah was the only person in the world who had ever understood that. He was the best thing that had ever happened to her.

Abbie found a new piece of paper. She picked up a pile of purple and blue studded sequins and a glue stick and got to work.

14

"What did you get?" Abbie asked. She pointed at the milky cocktail Jonah was drinking.

"A White Russian. It's the favorite cocktail of the Dude in *The Big Lebowski*," he said. "I think it's my favorite drink, too."

"Cool," Abbie said, pretending to get the reference.

"Want to try it?"

"Sure."

He passed her the glass. He rubbed her back as she took a sip. They were at the after-party for David's Bar Mitzvah, Jonah's younger brother. The party had descended on Hoax, a low-lit, swanky bar off Westbourne Grove. Tables and chairs were stacked against the windows as people took to the dance floor. There were the eyes of family friends and his parents again. Abbie's short black dress had a low front and deep back. She had worried all afternoon, through the ceremony that had dragged on for hours and the awkward small-talk conversation with Jonah's uncle, that it was far too revealing for the occasion. She had cast her lace blazer with gold buttons aside under a chair in the corner. She felt very exposed.

Abbie caught sight of Kat, Jonah's mother, across the room. Kat's wide, toothy smile was still visible between the bundles of her black hair. She wore a glittering turquoise chiffon dress tied by a tassel at the waist and studded heels. Her glasses covered the crow's feet around her eyes. Kat looked like a funky teacher from the 1970s, Abbie imagined, who had spent half her life growing up in a van and the other half attending art school in New York City. At least Kat seemed to be enjoying herself and not chiming in with the whispers of other friends and family members.

"…they're such an adorable couple, so in love…"

"…he's done well for himself, hasn't he? Atta boy, Jonah. Punching well above his weight…"

"…there's nothing quite like puppy love."

Abbie coughed as the vodka hit the back of her throat, hidden under the liqueur's sweetness.

Jonah looked at her, pouting. "You poor thing," he teased her. He patted her on the head.

"Fuck off."

It was a precious moment of bliss before either of them got too drunk. Abbie sipped her cocktail with Jonah at her side. She loved the feeling of being an item with him. Being Jonah's girlfriend made her feel terribly womanly, terribly grown-up. Playing couple was a game of outward projections and judgments. She gladly hid behind their smiles, their reassuring nods when she introduced herself, and their anecdotes about Jonah, how strongly they believed in him and his growth into a charming young man. Abbie almost drowned in the delight of Jonah's aunties' approving eyes.

The dance beats blared in her ears. Abbie felt the music lift her spirits and carry her towards him. They played boogie tunes. She wanted to dance with him, but Jonah shook his head. Jonah talked sternly with Hunter and Mark, his older brothers, instead. Hunter had made the special trip from Washington D.C., where he was studying. Abbie stepped away from the dance floor as David was lifted into the air on a chair and flung this way and that. She only returned to dance with Kat once she was sure David's chair was firmly on the floor again. Kat clapped and stomped her feet as she danced. Soon her curls bounded out of place and launched back like Slinkies bouncing down the stairs. She laughed, and Abbie danced along with her. Kat let herself feel things, swept up in the glee of the moment. Unlike Charlotte, Kat chose joy. Kat chose fun. Kat decided to dance like a weirdo just for the heck of it. It was such a relief.

After a couple of songs passed, Abbie looked over at Jonah. She saw the small collection of empty cocktail glasses he was harboring next to him. He knocked back another White Russian as he talked to Mark. She could tell by the glint of frustration on his face that Jonah would have been out smoking a cigarette long ago had his parents not been around. Perhaps he and Mark would head out soon.

The music stopped.

"Ladies and gentlemen, the bar is officially closed," shouted a less-than-pleased waiter.

"Honey! We'd better go!" Kat said to her.

Someone turned the lights on. Abbie's eyes reeled. The charming, freshly dressed guests were suddenly panting and excessively sweaty. She saw Jonah outside on the street with Mark, smoking. In the low light of the restaurant, his face had looked angular, his hair styled in a handsome evening silhouette. But the sides of his cheeks and his neck were flaming red. His face was podgy and pink, not to mention that his acne was getting worse. Abbie shuddered to herself. Had those spots always been there?

Kat dragged her outside.

"J, honey," she said, looking back and forth between them. Jonah stubbed out his cigarette. Abbie was unsure of what to think. Had Kat seen him smoking? Did she prefer to turn a blind eye and let him make his own choices that were slowly ruining his life?

"C-come on," Jonah said, grabbing Abbie by the shoulder, "I'll walk you home."

"Let me get my coat," she said, realizing just how inappropriate it was to have her cleavage and the entirety of her bare back on show for Jonah's brothers and Clive, his father, especially. Abbie found her blazer half-draped behind a chair, stuck under one of its legs. As she tugged it free, she felt weighed down with disappointment. Only a couple of hours before, she'd used a lint roller and shaped her outfit to perfection. Now her hair was probably a mess, and her blazer was tattered with whatever dirt and spilled liquids had been on the floor. She shook it out and put it on anyway. She took off her headband, smoothed out her hair, and put it back on, trying to leave the bar with a fresh stride in her step. She was proud of herself, at least, for limiting herself to only a couple of cocktails. Once she could find Portobello Road, she would know the exact route home.

Out on the street, she saw Jonah hunched over one of the tables. His family was around the corner, apparently searching for a taxi to get Clive home.

"There you are," Jonah said, lunging for her.

"Easy," Abbie said, catching him midstride before he toppled onto her. "I'm going home."

"I-I'll take you," Jonah said, launching down the street with all the determination in the world. He took two steps in a strong diagonal towards the bar. He steadied himself back in a straight line. "Come on!"

He grabbed her waist. Usually, she liked it when he put his arm around her, but now she had to balance him. Jonah was heavy and difficult to turn. She felt like a captain aboard a slow-moving oil tanker, trying to steer the entire ship with a single, tiny helm. His shirt was wet. Jonah didn't seem to notice. The departing guests' chatter faded away into the distance as they turned the corner.

The dim streetlamps of Portobello Road were laid out before them. The stalls and shops of the antique market were boarded up, saving their energy for the bustle of tomorrow's tourists. As Abbie steadied Jonah's body, her loafers pinched at the heels of her feet. The pain was sharp. The leather rubbed with each step, digging the blisters deeper.

Ahead of them, a couple of older men stumbled out of a gin bar in tuxedos. They toasted their glasses merrily and sang the last lines of the hymn, "Jerusalem," in slurred voices. The music at Hoax had been so fast-moving and fun, but now any sense of song or drunken dancing grated on her. The ground turned from flat to an incline on a

hill, then leveled out. She tried to keep them walking at a consistent
pace. Fresh dew cloaked the air and the pavement. The concrete
turned from a silvery grey to blackened soot. Drizzle tapped her
hair, then her forehead and face, as Abbie turned towards the wind.
The timing could not have been worse, she grumbled to herself. The
rain picked up. It trickled into the gutters, also making noise, which
also annoyed her. They passed an elderly, umbrella-less woman and
her slow, plonking Labrador. The woman stared at them coldly as
they passed. Dealing with Jonah in this drunken heap was so
humiliating.

All the while, Jonah was muttering to her on and on,

"You know, I came up with this technique. When I'm about to
come, I think about nuns throwing up. But, you know, it was so hard
today because you were so freaking cute when you were dancing
with my mom. I couldn't take my eyes off of you. Like, you are just
so adorable. My little pet—"

Abbie tried to distract herself with the scenery in the short
moments when the rain wasn't lashing across her face. Along a street
of townhouses, they passed rows of black gates that led down to
basements that scared children and up which dustbin men would haul
rubbish on Mondays and Thursdays. Abbie looked inside the living
room windows of the houses. She admired their interiors, not all
having taste, as if the residents were dolls in a dollhouse. A sitting
room was stacked high with old books. A ceiling was cluttered by a
ferociously overgrown plant. An old man shuffled through a room
with a cane, led by the light of his television. Another, clean and
modern, had a giant bulb lamp that reached across the room, illuminating the fluffy pillows of a cream-colored couch. Patchwork chairs
and tablecloths. Walls with portraits. Walls with teacups hanging
neatly in a row beside butter dishes and bread baskets. Another with
heaving curtains, reined in by belts like the potbellies of lords and
earls.

The street curved like a crescent moon. Each house was painted
in a different color. Pale pink, crimson, green, and the speckled
yellow of Easter eggs she might find on a quilted baby's blanket.

One house was lilac, another beige, another fuchsia, and another cobalt with white trim.

"I've been thinking something all day that I wanted to tell you," Jonah said proudly, almost tripping on his shoelace into a puddle.

"What?"

Abbie couldn't hold back the floodgates of her thoughts. She wished her boyfriend wasn't such a lousy, smoking, overweight drunk. None of the English boys she ever kissed would get themselves into this gross state. They had a reputation to maintain. They had football teams to play on. The collars of their shirts were even and not so lopsided all the time.

Jonah stopped walking.

"Abbie, I love you."

"Come on, let's keep going—"

"Did you hear me? I love you!" Jonah exclaimed, unwilling to walk.

"And I love you too," she forced herself to say. She hoped that might get him even a step closer to Clarendon Road.

"You do?" Jonah gasped, his face brimming with delight. "Isn't that something? Isn't that wonderful? I've never been so happy. This is the happiest day of my life. Literally, physically, metaphorically, philosophically, it is."

Jonah gave her a sloppy, sideways kiss on the cheek. Abbie let him kiss her. As long as they kept walking, she promised herself, it would all be over soon.

"Aww, that's so sweet."

"Is it the happiest moment of your life too?"

"Of course," she said, using his clunking body to shield herself from the rain. "Never been better."

"Wow. You make me so, so happy," Jonah drooled on.

As they finally turned the corner of Clarendon Road, a gloomy, sinking feeling grew in her chest. A harsh reality was dawning on her. As much as she wanted to, Abbie couldn't leave Jonah outside to drunkenly trudge home. Not in this state. Not in this weather. Not at least after he had just confessed his love for her. She would have to help him sober up first. There was only one way out that she could think of.

"We have to be very quiet," Abbie commanded him. They reached the gates of her house. All the lights were off inside. Abbie rolled her eyes, but she knew it would make no difference. Jonah made a series of childish faces and pressed his forefinger against his lips.

"Shhhhh," he said loudly.

The gate which led to the basement clanged loudly against the side railing as she opened it. Abbie winced. By the time they reached the basement door, Yolly had already turned on the lamp in her bedroom. As she dug the key out from underneath the mat, Abbie's hands were dirtied with mud. She unlocked the door and pushed Jonah inside. Inside, the house was deathly quiet. She turned on the light in the narrow warmth of the corridor.

"Miss Abbie?" came Yolly's troubled voice.

"Yes?" Abbie said. Jonah gurgled as if it was funny. Abbie glared at him. Within a moment, Yolly opened the door.

"Heavens, have mercy!"

Abbie's heart was racing. Her pulse beat in the cold tips of her fingers. She felt a single bead of rainwater inch down her forehead. Yolly stood there shivering in her long pink nightie.

"Who is this…this man?" Yolly said, gasping in horror. "I gave you the key to be home safe, not bring boys into Mr. Chesterton's house."

Abbie shook with the deep, gauging disappointment in Yolly's voice.

"I know. I'm sorry!" Abbie said. "He just got drunk after we went to dinner. I can't just leave him outside."

"He can go outside in the rain. Men need to take care of themselves."

"Hey there!" Jonah said, waving at Yolly, stumbling.

"Can we just get him some bread and water or something?"

"We only have old bread. I was going to feed the ducks in the park tomorrow," Yolly said.

"That'll have to do."

"What?" Jonah said, his eyes rolling back in his head. Abbie gathered all her might to stop him from hitting the floor. She let him droop onto the carpet, let his shoes stain it with the muck of the street outside. Yolly dodged out of the way, flicking her braid over her shoulder.

"This is the happiest, best day of my life," Jonah sang to himself.

Abbie took off her blazer in a heaping mess and left it on the floor next to the washing machine. Soon enough, Yolly returned with a glass of water and a squashed packet of Charlotte's seeded, organic bread. She placed it reluctantly on the floor next to Jonah.

"Eat the bread," Abbie said.

"I'm not h-hungry—"

"Urgh!"

Abbie got on her knees. She took a fistful of a couple pieces of the bread and thrust it into Jonah's hands. Then she yanked up the weight of his wrists and shoved the bread in his face. Jonah chewed with nowhere else to divert himself away. Then he smiled up at her, his teeth full of seeds and moistened dough. The rainwater dripped off Jonah's hair and jacket onto the carpet. The sight of him repulsed her. Abbie regretted not leaving him out on the street. He looked at Yolly gladly and said,

"It's a pleasure to meet you—"

"He's just a friend," Abbie butted in before Yolly got any more ideas. "His name is David."

"No, it isn't!"

"Miss Abbie!" Yolly said to her sternly. "Please, don't. You know it hurts me so much when you tell lies. I raised you better than that. You tell one more lie, and I will tell Mrs. Chesterton everything tomorrow."

"No!" Abbie pleaded, grabbing Jonah's arm and heaving him to stand up. He spilled some of the water before chugging it back. He started to cough as some of it went down the wrong way. Abbie forced another piece of bread into his mouth. "You were just leaving now, weren't you?"

"Of course, my sweetheart," Jonah said, his teeth still full of bread.

"Well, get home safe," Abbie insisted, lightly lashed with rain once more as she opened the basement door. She helped Jonah to his feet.

"Bye. I love you," Jonah said.

Abbie pushed him away as he tried to kiss her on the cheek. Failing, he blew her multiple kisses instead as she shut the door behind him. As she met the terror on Yolly's face again, Abbie heard Jonah's staggered, clumsy footsteps as he climbed the stairs. The gate slammed once behind him, and Abbie held her breath. Had her mother woken up upstairs? She listened intently, but the rest of the house remained quiet. Finally, Jonah had gone.

Abbie turned around. Yolly had her arms folded. She leaned against the wall, fuming.

"You are fortunate Mrs. Chesterton decided to go to the country-side today to fix the wallpaper."

Abbie stared at the ground. She was relieved, in a way, that at least her mother wasn't home. But she couldn't look Yolly in the eye. Not when she was this upset with her.

"I'm sorry. I—I promise it won't happen again."

Yolly continued, her voice harsher and louder, "I gave you the key because you said you need it so you can come home safe. And now, you bring boys to my employer's house! And you still expect me to keep a secret?"

Abbie cowered, her throat aching as tears welled in her eyes.

"I thought you were becoming a mature young lady. No, you make dangerous decisions. You only think of yourself. You never think about your actions hurting other people. Not even me. You never ask, 'Oh, maybe I will make Yolly get fired because I lied to my parents!'"

Abbie wanted to stand firm. Yolly was right, and Abbie wanted to apologize, but she was too ashamed of everything that had happened. A tear fell down her cheek. Before she could let Yolly see her breaking down, Abbie stormed upstairs. She made sure to bang her feet extra loudly on the stairs. She made sure to muddy the carpet as much as possible because Yolly would have to clean it up later, and Yolly had forced her to come face-to-face with the foolishness of what she had done. She left Yolly standing there, with her arms folded, as she disappeared into the dark silence of the house, the emptiness of it suffocating her like an oppressive force.

The spindle of the grandfather clock swung back and forth with light chimes like ticks biting her. The floor creaked, and the sound hit her between the vertebrates in her spine. Abbie wanted to punch a hole in the wall. She wanted to take two bottles of wine from her dad's cabinet, grip one neck in each hand, and smash them against the hardwood of the dining table. Glass shattering, splintering. Red wine splashing everywhere, ruining every piece of fabric and polished surface in its wake. Then she would take the jagged necks to the drawing room, slash open the upholstery on the couches, and rip the seams of the chaise longue. Tearing the curtains from their fastenings onto the floor.

How could Jonah have been such a complete idiot? And why was he so pathetic enough to have said that he loved her? He was like a dog that needed to be petted and cuddled. Boys, she had been told, were supposed to be strong. Not emotional. Not needing her to babysit him for the entire night. Her breaths quickened as she reached her room. She kicked over a pile of schoolbooks that Yolly had stacked neatly beside her desk. The books thumped as they hit the floor, but the carpet softened the blow. Abbie didn't love him back. Not even close. The image of him slurring his words as she dragged him along the street home was enough to convince her that she never would. He had done nothing but love her, and then she had lied to his face. Lied to him about the one thing he cared about most in the world. She choked on her lacking breaths between her sobs. It was too much to relive, too heartbreaking. She collapsed into a heap on her bed. She was desperate to scream, to release it. It was like she had been trying to make a perfect little birthday cake. Now the burning batter was spewing everywhere, the tin clanging, scorching everything in its path. But she couldn't bring herself to do it. Not while she was stuck in her ridiculous, unforgiving childhood bedroom. Her frustration collided with fury. Her throat seared in pain. She buried her face in her pillow and screamed into the suffocating comfort of the linens. A soul-ripping scream. She rethought the thoughts. Jonah's sweaty shirt as he reached across her back. His belly protruding.

"I love you."

Snot dripped from her nose, gushing into the pillow. Her insides were scrunched up like a stress ball, her nails digging into it so the feeble Styrofoam was torn apart. The air was crushed from her lungs. She screamed into the pillow again. She had given up everything for Jonah, for her art, and her legacy. And now Jonah loved her. They were joined at the hip. She felt like she was chained to the door of a lift as the *Titanic* was sinking. There was no way out without destroying him or herself. The alcohol on his breath still clung to her. It spewed off her dress, poisoning her clean bedsheets. What had happened to the person she was before they started going out? Who was that Abbie? Where had she gone?

"Urgh!" she sobbed. She had forgotten to take off her makeup. Now her favorite pillows from the White Company were stained with mascara. Yolly was right. A young woman, with her life together, would have remembered to use makeup remover before she got into bed. But not her. She, Abigail Mary Louise Chesterton, was nothing more than a child.

She tore herself from her bed and sprang to the bathroom. She dug through draws of lip glosses and nail polish and those stupid sparkly bracelet-making kits that she'd gotten as birthday presents years ago. She found the cotton wool and the tall bottle of makeup remover. The makeup remover was soothing to the touch. She cried more as she saw the mess of her makeup in the mirror, the mascara blackening her eyes like she'd been beaten. She rubbed her face with cotton wool and rubbed some more until every splodge of beige foundation and black mascara had been wiped away. She rinsed her face again. Her skin was red and raw. Her eyes were puffy and stinging. But she had done it.

She gathered up the stained cotton wool and threw it in the bin. A young woman, she thought, would leave a place cleaner than she found it. She turned on the tap. She washed the crusty line of dried-up toothpaste out of the sink. She saw her distorted reflection in the handle of the faucet, glistening clean and silver. The corner of her mouth curled with a hint of relief.

15

The following day, light streamed through the cracks between Abbie's curtains. She kept her eyes closed, covering her head with an extra pillow to block out the sun. Her chest relaxed. Her breaths elongated. An unsettling feeling crept over her. Time continued on all around her. Soon she would be forced to face the day. Just as she considered getting up to shower, a more sinister ache came over her. It happened only once, somewhere between her belly button and the bottom of her stomach. Her uterus was beginning to speak to her. At first, it was a calm, harmless grumbling. Hopefully, I'm just hungry, Abbie thought. She turned over. But the walls of her insides started to wobble. Squelching noises were coming from her stomach. She tried to dismiss the tiny trickles of pain from this unwelcome, irregular visitor. She hoped it had decided never to come again, and a few minutes passed. She found a colder, unused corner of her pillow. The fresh touch of it nourished her cheeks. Everything was fine. False alarm. Her body could play such evil tricks on her.

"Bloody hell," she said to herself a minute later. There was that wobbling in her stomach again, with a little more pinching than before.

"Fuck."

Her period came like a giant, squatting frog inside of her. Most of the time, the frog lay low, its eyes barely visible on the surface of a lily pad pond. Abbie would forget it was even there. But every so often, randomly, it would jump out of the water for days. It would splash around, pulling her insides in all directions. Sometimes as it started to jump, she would scoff down a couple of ibuprofen. Then other times, like this one, she would wait, dappling in the never-ending hope that it might be different this time. That the frog was not going to jump at all, and maybe her body was not trying to kill her.

Abbie drifted in and out of sleep. Then, at once, she startled awake from the pain. A more forceful wave was pulling her lower belly apart, then squashing her back together. Then calm. The walls of her uterus breathed like the lungs of an inner monster. She groaned. Since the age of eleven, she had been bleeding on and off. She was no longer a child, though her mother had been determined to treat her like one and still made her sit at the children's table at dinner parties. She could feel her insides gaining momentum as if the dial on its engine was flickering from yellow to orange to the red zone. She gasped, curling up in pain. She had less than ten minutes to spare, surely. She wrenched herself free of her blankets and darted to the bathroom. She dug frantically in the cupboard under the sink for her ibuprofen tablets. She spun the silver tap of the sink on. Ice-cold water plunged from its spout into the basin.

"Blurgh!" Abbie spluttered, swallowing four pills in a row. She chugged it down with the water, which tasted like a chilled, metallic tea. She needed eight hundred milligrams at least. Her insides were lighting on fire. She pulled down her pajama bottoms.

"Fuck!" she shouted. She gazed down at the giant, moon-shaped, brown stain along the flannel crotch. Abbie dabbed the gooey brown patch with the toilet roll. When would she learn how to stop ruining her clothes with this shit?

The stain subsided a little, but it was no use. Abbie dug in the cupboard under the sink again, this time for the inflated, spongy plastic packets. She tore open the flap of a pad. Thin strips of its paper curled away from the sticky edge, floating to the ground. She stuck the pad straight into the bottom of her pajamas, aimed at the stain. But when she pulled up her pajama bottoms, the rectangular rigidness of the pad balanced towards the right, angling itself like a skateboard about to descend along a drainpipe. The loose left edge of the pad stuck against her inner thigh as she shuffled back to bed and threw the covers over herself. She winced. She couldn't do anything right. And now she'd wasted the first hours of her day when she should have been writing her philosophy homework, so she could spend the extra time researching artists for her portfolio for Collegiate.

Her stomach seared in pain. Abbie could hardly breathe. Her lungs were like a pit of desert brush and sand catching fire. She pulled the covers up over her head, shutting the world away. No wonder she had sobbed uncontrollably yesterday and been so grumpy at Jonah. It was all her period's fault. What had Jonah ever done to her, apart from loving her unconditionally? It wasn't his fault that he loved her. A single tear fell from her left eye. It gathered speed along the bridge of her nose. It dripped onto the pillow. Abbie swallowed a small bubble of snot that had formed in the back of her throat. Did she love Jonah? She had found him so annoying yesterday. Which of her thoughts were her own, and which were her hormones screaming in her ears? Her lower belly was set alight again. She thought of Jonah's smirk as he fed her crème brûlée the night at Fortnum and Mason. The sparkling joy she felt as she looked into his light brown eyes. Him taking her hand, kissing it, smiling to reveal his teeth darkened from his triple espresso. Her spirits lifted, wanting to be wrapped up in and intertwined with his. She cried softly into the pillow,

"Jonah! I'm so sorry. How can I ever make it up to you?"

Another tear dripped across the bridge of her nose and seeped into the pillow. Jonah was perfect. She had him to thank for everything. She tucked her knees into her chest.

The anger in her uterus raged on.

16

"**A**bbie!" she heard someone call out.

Abbie stood in the cloister at school. The door to the library was closing behind her. All around her, girls rushed and dumped their bags into the cubbies of the long-reaching shelves and onto the checkered stone floor, running for the lunch hall. Abbie repositioned her bag on her shoulder. It was heavy with books she was referencing for her English coursework.

Julie panted as she caught up with her.

"Oh, hi."

"Lunch?" Julie said.

"Sure," Abbie said.

They dropped their bags and tried to overtake as many girls as possible. The lunch queue swelled in the corridor. Abbie had planned to eat lunch alone to quickly return to her schoolwork. She had finally managed to read *Journey's End* and selected it as her core text for her English Literature module. The coursework was worth 15 percent of her GCSE grade, which, Abbie tried to convince herself, could mean the difference between getting into Collegiate and not. She only had about ten minutes to eat lunch before returning to her essay.

Julie stood there, twirling her thick ponytail. "Do you want to see the Arctic Monkeys with me at the end of June? They're playing in the Albert Hall."

Abbie knew the venue well. Charlotte had dragged her there to see a full rendition of Handel's *Messiah* a couple of years ago at Christmas. What if Jonah invited her for a romantic dinner that night instead? The fact that Julie had even asked her to go to a concert concerned her. Julie relied on her so much as a friend. It was for Julie's own good for Abbie to distance herself. And sure, Abbie liked the Arctic Monkeys. But she could listen to their music alone at home on iTunes. She had to nip it in the bud before things got out of hand.

"Sorry, I can't," Abbie said. They each took a tray at the beginning of the buffet.

"Why not?"

"I'm too busy."

"Busy with what? It's in like three weeks. And, like, it's almost the summer holidays."

"I've got English coursework, my portfolio for Collegiate, and my artist's statement that I haven't even started yet," Abbie rattled on, "and Jonah's probably going to be leaving for New York around then, and I really won't be able to spend any time with him over the summer, so we'll probably have dinner."

"On a school night? The concert is on a Thursday," Julie said.

"I mean, yeah."

"I'm going to Saint-Tropez for the whole summer too, you know. You won't see me, either."

Abbie tried to nod sympathetically, but it came off as more of a shrug.

Julie sighed,

"Well, don't get too crazy with all the studying and homework."

They parted ways briefly to get some food from the pizza and salad bars. By the time Abbie had gotten what she wanted and headed out into the lunch hall, Julie had already sat alone beside a large group of the less popular but still pretty girls in the year above.

Julie's posture slumped. She seemed less than pleased. Abbie sat down across from her. They ate in silence for a while. Then, as Abbie slowly got up to return to her English coursework, Julie coughed and said,

"A-are you happy?"

"What do you mean?"

"Are you happy, like, with Jonah and everything?"

Abbie stared at her. What was Julie implying? In that second, Abbie felt determined to erase any hint of doubt in Julie's mind.

"I've never been happier," she said plainly.

"But, like, you never want to hang out—"

"Getting into Collegiate is really important to me. You have no idea how much pressure I'm under to do all this work for the entrance exams. I'm waking up at, like, five-thirty every day, and my portfolio still is nowhere near as good as it needs to be."

"You've got months to do all this, though," Julie said. "Don't you think you've changed?"

"Changed?" Abbie said. "This is who I am. I've outgrown this school and all these people here. Collegiate is, like, my only way out of here. And Jonah is helping me prioritize what actually matters to me in my life. And he loves me. A lot."

"Good for you, then, I guess," Julie said. Her expression grew sullen.

Abbie tied up her tray, ready to leave. Julie was probably just jealous that she had a boyfriend and was taking the proper steps to be more successful. There was nothing Abbie could do to help that. Julie's feelings weren't her responsibility.

"I'm headed back to the library if you want to join me."

"I'd rather not torture myself, thanks," Julie said. Abbie scoffed at her. Clearly, Julie didn't understand that torture was necessary to get anywhere in life. Now Julie was just wasting her time.

At last, Julie added,

"Will you just think about the concert? In case your plans fall through, or you change your mind?"

"Okay."

Abbie smiled at her meekly, but Julie didn't smile back. Abbie picked up her tray and walked away. As she slid it into a rack of dirty dishes by the lunch hall door, she looked over her shoulder. Julie sat alone, staring vacantly into space. The raucous of the other girls' chattering and shouting now hit her with full force, echoing all around her. She pushed the lunch hall door, and it swung open. She left the chatter, heading for the library.

17

I t was late June in the communal garden behind Jonah's house. Abbie lay beside Jonah on a picnic blanket beneath a willow tree. The straps of her orange polka-dot dress had fallen loosely over her shoulders. She pulled them up to ensure they covered her bra. Her pale legs were entirely on show. She wore Ray-Ban aviator sunglasses, a new pair Abbie had borrowed from Charlotte's closet.

Kat and Clive were out for the day, and Jonah had snuck a bottle of Clive's expensive dessert wine for them to share. The sun peeked between the clouds. Far off in the sky, a distant plane moved silently, dancing in a vaguely eastern direction. A line of bricks framed the acre of glistening, untrimmed grass they lay on. Fluttering sparrows chirped at the nearby birdbath. Up the hill beyond them, children shouted from the playground as they ascended the rope swing or descended the slide. A ginger tabby cat rubbed against the black gates of a neighbor's garden and skittered between peonies and lilacs, up a May tree, and down again before disappearing. The sound of stones came like waves crashing off the coast of Cornwall as the elderly gardener raked the gravel along the path. Beside Abbie and Jonah, at the base of the willow tree sprouted bushels of daffodils and bluebells. The long, tantalizing branches waved slowly overhead, dripping patches of shadows, forming new constellations of shade. Abbie had been watching it for an hour at least as Jonah drifted in and out of sleep. When he was awake, he held her in his arms and drew indecipherable pictures with his forefinger along her lower back.

Jonah's light blue shirt had the sleeves rolled up. Since Abbie had convinced him to become healthier, Jonah's stomach had flattened, and his skin had cleared up. With his fresh haircut, Jonah seemed to be from another era. The 1950s, perhaps, when Elvis Presley wailed ballads over a shallow moon, and girls wore skirts down to their knees. Jonah was staring up into space, quietly contemplating. He did that sometimes. Abbie always wondered what he was thinking, yet she was too afraid to ask. It might be something scarier or more painful than she wanted to know. His grandfather dying of lung cancer. His father's raging cholesterol causing concern from his doctor. Or the unavoidable fact that soon he would return to America for the summer, and they wouldn't see each other for almost two months.

Jonah hugged her. It gave her the feeling of being protected. Was he still a boy? Or was he a man? She felt the girth of his fingers and the veins along his wrist. She couldn't help but imagine him ripping off her clothes, pulling the buttons off her dress at the seams, and doing whatever he wanted to her. She swallowed in a short, silent breath of shame. The longer they had been together, the more she was haunted by violent fantasies. The more she craved him and gladly imagined him grasping at her throat as he pinned her down and fucked her. Sometimes these visions overwhelmed her. Abbie would be sitting in her English lesson, and as her class read *Journey's End* aloud, her mind would wander. The notion of the fantasies themselves was enough to cause that tightening in her chest and that dampness to form in her underwear.

Abbie pulled herself towards him. Their waists touched. Jonah's breathing was shallow. She placed her hand on his beating heart, but it wasn't enough. She wanted as much of her skin to touch his skin as possible. As she pulled him closer, he startled awake. He pinched her chin gently and kissed her on the forehead.

"I love you," Jonah said unselfconsciously.

"I love you too, Blue Jay," Abbie told him. She meant it this time.

That was her new name for him: Blue Jay. She'd called him that as a joke one night when he had walked her home in an excessively grumpy mood. It felt fitting because it was so light and free, and Jonah was such a romantic and serious old soul. Still, she knew that he loved her pet name for him, a name that only she could call him.

At the thought of making up names for boys, memories of Julie flooded Abbie's mind. Abbie had barely seen her in weeks. The only time Julie had been in her form room, she had been talking to Emily, of all people. What could they have been whispering about? Julie and Emily had never been friends.

"You know, Julie and I made virgin piña coladas in her garden last year," Abbie said. "And we got high because we put so much grenadine in them. And then we made plans for girl domination, i.e., her kissing Marco Pigatelli. Obvi, she never did it, but we had the giggles for hours. That day was so much fun."

"Isn't that your friend who you said was goofy and not very smart?"

"I mean, maybe I said that, but—"

"Why are you talking about her? When you're having fun with me instead?" Jonah said. His gaze was solemn and unwavering. Abbie pursed her lips. She hadn't laughed all day. Maybe Jonah could make her laugh, though. Maybe they just hadn't been talking about the right things. Or maybe he was teaching her to be more grown-up, and she had outgrown her days of pure silliness. Julie had always been quite childish anyway.

Jonah picked up his copy of Italo Calvino's *Invisible Cities*. Abbie buried herself in his chest as he read her another short chapter. He told her about Penthesilea, another of Italo Calvino's magical cities. Jonah's lisp rolled over his smoothed, American tones. Abbie followed along with him on the page. She wrapped her leg around him, trying not to knock over the glasses of golden wine that glowed against the wet grass. She let his words sing to her, turning into his chest, gathering as much of his scent as she could, like the slow, melting sweetness of a double bass. Yes, Jonah was very serious. But he was also honest. And he loved her so much.

The sun dipped behind the clouds. They were shrouded in cold shadows once more, and she ached with regret.

"What time's your flight tomorrow?"

"Early afternoon."

Abbie's heart sank. She hugged him tighter.

"It's good for us, though," Jonah said.

"How?"

"Absence makes the heart grow fonder."

"I disagree."

"I'm going to miss you, though. The stress of it is already getting to me."

"I miss you already," Abbie said, pulling him closer, "but this is what's right for you. You'll have so much time to work on your script and film all the scenes at the beach in Montauk. You need it. Although, I wish you'd come back a couple of weeks earlier."

"I'll try. I'll ask my mom and see if she can change the flights."

Abbie smiled, reassured. There was a long pause between them. Then she said,

"I've been writing my artist's statement."

"Oh, yeah?" Jonah said. "How's it coming along?"

"Quite well," she said. "Now that I've started making bigger collages, the idea for it became clear to me."

"You amaze me," Jonah said. "I'm so proud of you."

"Thanks."

"When can I read it?"

Abbie grinned at him.

"Now, if you want. I brought everything in case you were going to be writing your script. I left my bag in the entryway."

"Brilliant."

Jonah pulled away from her. He pushed himself to his feet and headed towards the house. Abbie lay on the picnic blanket. She smiled to herself, but once Jonah was gone, the sun hid behind the clouds. Shade covered the garden. The breeze felt cold. The emptiness of his side of the picnic blanket stretched out before her. She sat up, puzzling over what to do next. As she pushed herself to her feet, she caught a glimpse of Jonah's BlackBerry. Its silver buttons and glazed-over dark grey screen were limp and lifeless. Suddenly the screen lit up. A tiny picture of a yellow envelope appeared with a red asterisk and the number 1 next to it. Before she could stop herself, Abbie picked up the phone and typed in his password.

She clicked through to his BBMs. Her throat stung hot. She felt her entire body shake, jolting awake, ready to attack. The name was in bold, with a smiley face next to it.

Rosalia

Abbie locked the phone. Then she grabbed it and stomped inside. She couldn't believe it. Fear blackened everything in her path. Her stomach was churning like someone had taken a torpedo drill to it. They were BBMing. They were talking. Obviously, Jonah still cared about Rosalia. Maybe Rosalia let him smoke as many cigarettes as he wanted. That's why he was going back to her. She, Abbie, had only ever been a steppingstone on the course to Jonah's future with Rosalia in America, married, living in the outskirts of a city that she would mistake for a state, where Rosalia would drive their kids to baseball practice while drinking Starbucks in their minivan. How long had this been going on?

She found him in the entryway, her bag over his shoulder.

"What about Rosalia?" Abbie burst.

"What about her?"

"A-are you seeing her? In Montauk?"

"She's going to help me with the shoot."

"If you're cheating on me, just tell me already."

"Whoa, hold on," Jonah said. "What's gotten into you? You know Rosalia and I are family friends. We've been going to the same beach since we were kids. I can't just drop her like that."

"I'm not an idiot," Abbie said. "If you still love her, I'd rather know now. Tell me the truth!"

"Abbie, you are my girlfriend. I love you. I am committed to you—"

"Prove it to me, then!"

Jonah sighed. He smiled as he gazed into her eyes.

"Come with me."

"What?"

"Upstairs. Let's go. And hold your horses."

Jonah took her by the hand. He led her up the main staircase and into his bedroom. The air in Jonah's room was stuffy. The sun glared through the windows. Heat billowed off the black walls. He closed the door and dropped her bag down next to his bed. He opened the window, letting the cool summer breeze and the scents of the neighbors' lavender sweep out the thick humidity. Abbie stood there in the middle of the room.

"Close your eyes," Jonah said.

"What's going on?"

"Just close them and hold out your hands."

"This is not fair to me at all."

Abbie closed her eyes and held out her hands.

Jonah rummaged through the cigarette packages in his drawer. "Are you ready?"

"For what?"

He dropped something into her hands. It was a small box with rounded edges and a velvet finish.

"Okay. Open," Jonah said.

Abbie opened her eyes. The little black box rested in her cupped palms.

"Jonah, what is this?"

"Go on, take a look inside."

Abbie opened the box. It squeaked on its gold hinges. Inside was a gold ring with a blue square-shaped stone.

"Blue Jay!" Abbie said, leaping to hug him. "You shouldn't have. It's beautiful."

They kissed. Jonah removed the ring from the box and slid it up the ring finger on her left hand.

"A beautiful ring for a beautiful girl." He winked at her. "These last couple of months, you've made me the happiest man in the world. I know we're still a bit young, but I want to be completely clear with you about my intentions. This ring is my promise to you that one day I'd like you to be my wife."

"That's so sweet," Abbie said. Her throat tensed. She pictured them holding hands, walking down the street in winter together in New York, dipping into an old record shop for a cup of coffee. Or curling up together, with her head in Jonah's lap, as they stretched out across a worn leather couch. The ring glinted on her finger in the afternoon sun. "You mean the world to me too. I'll think of you every time I look at it."

"That would make me even happier." Jonah grinned. He hugged her. Abbie buried herself in his chest. His voice rang throughout his body as she listened to his heart. "The truth is, you're the only reason I've felt creative enough to work on my script. I couldn't have even planned this shoot if it wasn't for you. And now I have a pretty good chance of finishing my short and entering some festivals before I even apply to Columbia. All because you came into my life."

"I feel the same way," Abbie said. "I would never even have my portfolio almost ready for Collegiate if it wasn't for you."

"That's who we are," Jonah said. "Two independent creative spirits, facing the world together."

Abbie nodded, her sobs muffled into Jonah's chest.

"While you're out there having fun in New York, I'm going to be stuck at Harpburgh with my mum, who hasn't got a creative bone in her body. Working on my applications. It's not fair!"

"I know you can do it," Jonah said. "I want you in my life, now and forever. And I want you to go to the best school you can."

Over the comfort of Jonah's words came the echoes of Abbie's parents' expectations in her ears:

"We met at Oxford," Richard would say in a low, teasing tone to

any stranger who happened to be listening at a drinks party. Abbie
had to get into Collegiate. It was her best chance.

Jonah pulled a box of Listerines from his pocket. He clicked it
open and ran his forefinger inside of it. He held it out for her. Abbie
looked him in the eye. She licked the patch off his forefinger. His
skin felt rough on her tongue. The Listerine melted in her mouth.
Jonah gazed at her, mesmerized. He reached into the box for another.
He put one on his tongue this time, relishing in the taste of where she
had licked his finger. He gave her another. She bit his finger playfully. Abbie wanted him to awaken her. She wanted to know just
how special she was to him, just how exceptional she was.

Jonah tore the crumpled blankets off his bed. Abbie leaned back
against it. He pressed himself against her. The straps of her dress
skulked down her shoulders. Jonah pulled them down further,
savoring the pristine lace of her bra. She undid the buttons of his
shirt, breaking the crispness of its light blue collar. The thin patch of
hair in the middle of his chest was enough for her to imagine that it
was a man who was pinning her against the bed.

Jonah lay down on the bed clumsily. Abbie squished beside him.
She faced the wall, and her knees hit the smoothed surface of the
black paint. He was spooning her, but the mattress sank with his
weight, so she was pulled backwards on top of him. His right
shoulder was higher than hers. The tops of his feet cradled the
bottoms of hers as if she was an oil painting and he was the frame.
He struggled as her delicate, rounded buttons slipped through his
fingers. She undid them quickly, making up for lost time. The loose
fabric of the dress lapped down, off her shoulders to her hips. The
rolls of skin on her stomach were laid bare. She breathed in, holding
her stomach there to appear slimmer. He slid his forceful hands along
her thighs, grabbing the sensitive part at the base of her butt,
drinking in the smoothness of her skin like it was an elixir. He
rubbed his jeans against her at his pelvis. He threw his trousers and
his shirt aside. She hoped he hadn't noticed the chunkiness of her
love handles. She tried to ignore the dry, unevenness of the acne that
had almost healed along his shoulders.

Jonah lay on top of her. She liked it this way as he held her down with the weight of his body. She felt guilty for wanting it, for wanting more of it, for enjoying it. On the other side of control was pure, unwavering ecstasy. Their underwear was like a barrier between two oceans. The wet stain in his felt cool against her thigh. It was a brush of danger, a step into the unknown. He grabbed onto the white lace of her underwear and pulled it downwards. He struggled for her bra strap, but she couldn't stand to wait any longer. She helped unclasp it. She felt his strong fingers guide the thin fabric off of her, the last barrier to her fortress. He grunted, cupping her naked breast like it was a gift from a God. He rubbed along her nipple in a gentle, circular motion as he took in the fullness of her body. The hairlessness of her inverted triangle, the skin smoothed over after she had stooped over the toilet and frantically sculpted it off only hours earlier. Abbie closed her eyes. Jonah gripped her inner thigh. He held his breath as he chartered two fingers downwards, massaging along the fringes of her outer lips. She let out a light moan. Jonah's fingers fumbled messily. She was dripping from that sacred place in her body already. She tried to find peace as he jabbed his fingers nervously inside her. She opened her eyes, gazing up at the ceiling. How could he ever make her physically burn with pleasure? How could he ever re-create the magic of her right hand or her shower-head? Perhaps he was only useful for things she could not give herself. Perhaps all she wanted him to do was simply hold her, for them to be as close together as was humanly possible. As if somehow, if she let him hold her for long enough, their minds, souls, and skin might fuse into a strange, new, magical creature.

Jonah pulled the waistband of his underwear down, exhaling deeply. The full nakedness of his body stuck to her, sweltering in the heat. His penis was hard against the back of her leg. She wanted him to rest it there between her thighs so they were almost touching. He could feel her wetness there, too, surely. She let him. He tucked the shaft of his penis in her thigh gap. Abbie kept her legs closed. He leaned his head up off the pillow. He gazed down along her body as if to check. Was this it? Were they doing it? No, they weren't. He seemed to suddenly remember that she had breasts that he could play with, as some kind of silver medal.

Abbie was supposed to be such a nice girl. How could a nice girl want to do something so...dark? So horrendously wrong? It was the kind of thing fallen women got locked up for only a hundred years ago. Girls in the priories, witches, were burned at the stake for what she was about to do to Jonah. The promise ring, somehow, made her feel less guilty about it. Jonah wanted to spend the rest of his life with her. A thin veil of monogamy helped to make this more palatable. She was only fifteen. Surely, she should not, could not be this young and do this very grown-up thing. It was like the first time she had tried a Krispy Kreme at the doughnut factory in Harrods. Once she had taken a bite and let the delicate, buttery sugar crystals melt in her mouth, there was no turning back. She had experienced heaven on earth. But why did she have to want *this*? Why did she want *this*? Why couldn't she have stopped Jonah from taking off his underwear and never let him finger her in the way that felt jabby but ultimately good? If she had never let herself feel pleasure, never started down this slippery slope, she could have resisted all this.

Abbie kissed him, and this time, she didn't hold back. She grabbed the back of Jonah's head. She wondered what he might evolve into once they had done it. Would he change? What would it be like to kiss a man? Jonah's hands were shaking. He felt up her boobs almost instinctively, forgetting again that any other part of her body was worthy of attention. It was a thoughtless movement. Lumbering. Was this how he thought she wanted to be touched? Perhaps he was shy and nervous. Perhaps this was his way of showing her that he desired her. She would have to train him all over again. Why had she chosen this boy, of all people, to do this with? Was he simply a vessel transporting her to her destination? She would have to make do.

Abbie moved to straddle him, terrified that if she lay down, he might thrust himself into her, split her open, break her. She would be in control. The smoothness of his belly rubbed against her inner thighs. His brow was strong. His body was desperate to move now.

Desperate to try. A vein pulsed thick across his forehead. He seemed starved, hungry, and ready to take all of her. He looked away from her, up to the ceiling, tormented by something.

"Hey," Abbie said, trying to bring him back to her.

Their eyes met. She saw unease in the light brown shimmer of his eyes. She wanted to look him in the eye while they did it if she could. That was the only way she would feel that they were both there. Doing it together.

"You're so beautiful," he said, half sitting up to kiss her, then running his hands along her thighs and gripping her as if he owned her, then relaxing and lying back down on the pillow. His body was tense. He seemed so distracted, so drawn this way and that. He couldn't give a part of her attention for more than five seconds. She gently pushed his shoulder downwards back onto the bed. That was where she needed him to be. She felt the warmth and wetness of her vulva run along the coarseness, the roughness of his pubic hair. His face and neck were bright red. He was scowling, biting his tongue forcefully to try to keep his side of the deal together.

"Think of the nuns throwing up," Abbie said, smiling.

Jonah took a deep breath. His expression was solemn, as if this was far too important a moment to laugh about. Abbie wished he would smile. She wished they could share something of the silliness, playfulness, and messiness of it all. That would show her that he was there and everything would be okay. But he couldn't.

She spat on the tip of his penis. She rubbed it along the wet part of her, below where she had shaved, below the part that felt good when she angled the showerhead's water directly at it. Once they had gotten this far, she wondered, what counted as sex, anyway? Did it count when they both took off their underwear? Did it count when they both took off their underwear and then she straddled him? Did it count when they both took off their underwear, and she was straddling him, and he was quite far down, but only the tip of his penis was really touching her, but then the rim of it kind of went about a centimeter inside of her, just the tip of it, but then it was kind of uncomfortable, so she sat up on her knees and pulled out, but then

she wanted to try again, so just the tip went in again, a little further
this time, but he wasn't really inside of her, just touching?

Abbie pressed herself down onto him. Jonah inched further
inside of her. Or at least, that's what she thought was happening. Her
pelvis ached, but he slid inwards beyond the tightness at the beginning. Only when the scratchiness of his pubic hair rubbed against her
did she realize how deep he was inside her. His penis must have
disappeared, gone in there somewhere, though she couldn't feel
much. Then it hurt more, though. When she pressed her pelvis
forwards, thrusting her weight onto him, and sat back up on her
knees but kept him inside her, Jonah's face was flaming red. His
breaths heaved like he was about to explode.

"Pull out!" he said. Abbie sat up on her knees and pulled herself
off him. Jonah scrunched up his face in a distressing state of bliss.
The vein on his forehead was pulsing purple as he winced, every
muscle in his face straining, his eyes forced closed. He groaned like
she had stabbed the beast. That second of whatever had just
happened. She could never have imagined it would stir his moment
of pure, untethered weakness. Defenseless. And yet the ecstasy, the
agony of it all, lasted only a few seconds for him. Cut abruptly short
by evolution. By God or whoever had decided how long the human
male orgasm should last. It was a real pity, Abbie thought to herself.
When she *masturbated* in the shower (if she would let herself think
that word), the best part lasted at least fifteen seconds. Twenty on a
good day.

Suddenly, drops of stringy, pallid liquid gushed onto Jonah's
stomach. Instinctively, Abbie pulled herself away further, releasing
her legs and squishing into the space beside him on the bed. Only
then did she see the darkened stains along the sides of his penis and
down the sides of his legs.

"Shit!"

"Oh, fuck. What is that?" Jonah said.

Without a word, Abbie scrambled to her feet. As she hurried to
put her dress back on, the lowest part of her insides felt open and
exposed, like the tape along the bottom of a moving box had been

loosened, and everything in its contents was about to fall out. She ran to the bathroom. Her insides ached.

She grabbed the toilet paper, rubbing and rushing to inspect it. The paper shrank, soaked. Whatever had come out of her was slowly being absorbed into the wad. It was a faint, pale, reddened orange. She sat down on the toilet and peed. She straightened her hair and rubbed away the dark circles of smudged makeup under her eyes before she returned to Jonah's bedroom.

She found Jonah standing naked, scowling as he wiped his stomach and threw used tissues into the bin. The bedsheets lay crumpled, stained with the sweaty, musty result of everything. She could not have ruined the bedsheets, surely? Once he had gone to the bathroom, Abbie rushed to the edge of the bed. She turned up the pillow to inspect them.

A pale outline of the light, orangey-pink stain stood out against the crumpled whiteness of the sheets. The sheets' folded creases were the stems. The stains were the petals, peaceful and perfectly rounded like tulips. Her thinned blood was the color of shame in muted peach. A new painting of the flowers Jonah had given her. Cut straight from a Dutch field, and starting to wilt, like the innocence she had wanted to abandon for so long had finally gone.

Abbie's heart ached a little. It hadn't been anything like she expected. She spread out the bedsheets and climbed back into the bed, careful not to touch the stains. She needed the comfort of the covers, the closeness of Jonah or a hug from Julie. Or something or someone. Whatever was on the bed could not be put back inside of her. Abbie lay down. She pulled the covers over her and hugged her knees. A fearfulness, too, was creeping over her. They had so little time before Jonah left for New York. Before his parents would arrive home later that day and wonder why the picnic blanket was still out in the garden with no one around. Had she been as easy as Moe? Would Jonah be done with her now that they had done *it*?

Jonah returned to the bedroom and locked the door behind him.

"Can we cuddle?" Abbie asked.

"What?"

"I want to cuddle you."

Jonah let out a long sigh. Abbie tried not to look directly at Jonah's penis or low-hanging belly in the light. Slowly he got into bed with her, ignoring whatever mess of stains they lay in. He breathed in the scent of her hair. Now and then, he readjusted his arm as Abbie leaned on it like a pillow.

After a while, Jonah snored lightly. Abbie held up her ring, examining it. It caught the evening light as the sun glowed a deeper orange at the onset of evening. The jagged, unforgiving red numbers of Jonah's digital alarm clock flicked, one after another, as the minutes slipped away from them into memories. So much had happened so soon, Abbie thought to herself. If she and Julie had still been taking the bus together, it would have taken at least two morning bus trips to catch her up on all the details. Had Julie left for Saint-Tropez yet? Maybe there was still time. But they wouldn't be able to talk on the phone. International calls were so expensive.

Abbie hugged Jonah tighter. She wondered when they might be this close again.

18

Yolly opened the door when Abbie got home that evening. The house felt quiet and cold.

"Miss Abbie, where have you been?" Yolly said. "I was worried all day."

"Nowhere," Abbie said vaguely. She quickly pushed past her and stepped over the vacuum cleaner in the entryway. Her mind was a mess. She could not look Yolly in the eye. That would give it all away. That she had had s-e-x. But then again, Yolly knew her too well. Yolly had been able to smell when she was lying throughout her childhood, like when Abbie once stole a purple Barbie ball gown from her friend's house.

"He is watching you," Yolly had warned, pointing upwards towards the sky. She had been far too terrified to tell Yolly that she didn't believe in God. Maybe God wasn't real, but Yolly's sixth sense was. Abbie pressed on towards the back of the house. She wasn't five years old anymore, she told herself. Yolly didn't have to know everything. And there were so many things Yolly would never understand.

"Where did you get a nice ring?" Yolly called out. "Do you still have a boyfriend?"

Abbie froze.

"Not really," she admitted. It was a half-truth. Having a boyfriend surely meant Jonah would be with her, not packing for his trip and ditching her for two months.

"You deserve a very kind boy. Mrs. Chesterton's friend from her book club has a son who's very handsome," Yolly said as she picked up the vacuum cleaner and turned it back on. The sound of its whirring was deafening. It shook the house.

Abbie stormed off into the study. Her parents' filing cabinets and ring binders lined the walls. She wanted to tear them all apart. How dare Yolly? Why, after all these years, was she just Charlotte's spokesperson? Even after Charlotte had gotten mad at Yolly so many times for ruining her cashmere jumpers in the washing machine. Yolly still stood by and defended the dreaded Mrs. Charlotte Evelyn Chesterton. And to suggest that Abbie consider going out with Terrence Crowly, a vapid boy at Eton with Freddie, who dressed like an old man in blazers and corduroys and only talked about croquet because he genuinely believed it was the best game ever invented. Urgh! Yolly had no idea what she was talking about. Jonah was infinitely more interesting than Terrence. Jonah was the only person she could love in the world, and she would marry and be with him forever.

Abbie slumped into the swiveling office chair behind the wide wooden desk. She stared at the screensaver. Across the flat-screen monitor, a highlighter-green ribbon swirled in a familiar pattern, with a spell trailing from a wand against the endless darkness of the digital ether. She barely moved the dark grey mouse along the Oxford University mousepad before the screen sprang into action. She sighed to herself. There was only one person in the world she could consider discussing any of this with.

She opened up the Firefox browser. As she clicked through to check Facebook, she wondered how many exclamation marks she should use to share all the good news with Julie. But once the page loaded, Abbie's eyes were immediately drawn to the small 1 in a red speech bubble just above her Messages icon. She clicked on it. A chat window appeared. She had an unread message from "Juliette L." Julie had changed her Facebook name to that a couple of months ago after she freaked out that her Swiss uncles were going to find pictures of her on the internet, even though she didn't smoke or drink or go to parties anyway. Abbie began to read.

Juliette L: I felt sorry for you when Moe and Emily were ditching you. I've stayed your friend. And this is what I get for sticking by you? Being called a freak who's not even smart? You would literally have no friends if it wasn't for me. Emily was right about you. You think you're so much better than everyone else. Well, news flash: you're not. You're disgusting. x

Fear shot through Abbie's body. She reread the single, cold paragraph. All around her, the light singing of birds and the calmness of the summer evening carried on. But inside, everything was screaming. Set ablaze like the thin, dry brush of a valley. Winds gaining speed. Flames ripping through miles in minutes. Abbie's lip trembled. She was too exasperated to cry. She had been playing games in her head. She had plans and blueprints of her life that she had been manipulating so that everything would go her way. Was that really how Julie saw her? A conniving, selfish person who thought the sun shone out of their backside? Julie had clearly thought this for a while. Other people probably thought it, too. Moe and Emily might have kicked her out of their group because of it. No, Abbie had chosen to leave their group of her own volition. But everything else, she had calculated wrong. She had seen Julie as a feeble, senseless puppet. Abbie had just been so paralyzingly judgmental. So senselessly harsh. She had hurt Julie. But more than that, she had hurt herself. She had stranded herself and self-destructed like a beached whale that got too curious about what life was like beyond the ocean.

She wanted to log out of Facebook. She wanted to pretend like none of this had ever happened. But Julie's message cut so deep she would have trouble falling asleep that night if she didn't try to sew herself back together. She steadied herself straight in the swiveling chair. She typed her response one carefully considered letter at a time. The words crawled out of her slowly, excruciatingly, like she was trying to squeeze the water out of a splintered piece of wood.

Abbie Chesterton: You're right, okay? I thought I was too cool for everyone. But I want you to know that you should never have been friends with me if you felt sorry for me. I chose everything I have in my life right now and I live with the consequences. JESUS, you are good at insulting people when you want to. I am sorry. But you are a way more important friend to me than anything else. xxx

Julie was online. She replied within minutes.

Juliette L: I never became friends with you because I felt sorry for you. I am sorry. I am just so, so angry. x

Abbie Chesterton: I accept your apology, but you need to under-stand that even if you are really mad at someone, it's not alright to treat them like that. Calling me "disgusting" is so, so horrible and makes me feel shit about myself. What makes me feel even worse is that we've basically been best friends for ages, and you go believe Emily before me? How do I know that after all this, you don't end up bitching to Emily, or anyone really, anyway? I don't want to be friends with people who are two-faced. I think you should listen to what YOU think. If we fit into the Agerton Hall stereotype, we'd all be whores. We aren't like that and I don't. xx

By the time Abbie had typed that, Julie was offline. Would Julie respond? When? What was she planning to say? Abbie opened a tab and began to play *Neopets*. It was a short, biting, feeble attempt at softening the blows of Julie's words. She pulled up an ice cream game. Her little bear Neopet, in a turquoise matching hat and coat and booties, dodged scoops of ice cream that flew in strawberry, chocolate chip, and mint flavors.

Meanwhile, she constantly checked Facebook between rounds. Julie had to be watching JacksGap on YouTube or something. Or what if she had just left with her parents to fly to Saint-Tropez? It might be hours before she would respond. Luckily, soon, Julie was online again.

Juliette L: I am not trying to insult you or make you sad, but you continue to be a self-centered, snobbish, toxic, nasty girl. I knew that wasn't you. I was willing to let it pass. I had a chat with you about it, to tell you nicely, but you refused to admit any of it. Abbie, I love you, but please STOP obsessing over Emily. You're being so paranoid. When I talked to her, she was genuinely confused about why you don't speak anymore. I am gullible but it insults me that you think I can't draw a line between a best friend confiding me a secret. If anyone ever bitches about you again, I swear down I will come to you first. This sounds so fucking twisted, but I just wanted you to gain some perspective on who you were becoming. I knew that even if you'd despise me for a while, it was worth it in the long run. Reading this back made me realize that we both need to work on stuff. But mainly, we don't communicate properly. We should tell each other when someone isn't right so there are no misunderstandings or unhappiness. Sounds good? xx

Abbie Chesterton: I'm sorry, but I don't trust Emily. I know she has probably changed and is not a bitch anymore, but I don't believe her. I've been friends with her before, and I think you should go off and be friends with her instead. I have a lot of other stuff in my life that is more important to me now. Even if that was how you honestly felt, friends are not like that to each other. Friends support each other. I would never take every part of your life and tell you all the horrible shit you do. Don't tell me you wouldn't bitch about me to Emily if you got the chance. Don't tell me you weren't on some mission to turn the whole year against me. xx

Juliette L: Basically 1. Emily will never come close to being a special friend as you. 2. The world is not out to get you, Abbie. That's not everyone's priority. They have lives to get out on with. 3. Don't you dare lecture me on what friends should and should not do. I fucking needed you Abigail and you were too self-absorbed to realize because Jonah and getting to Collegiate are the only things you care about. I have never felt so lonely or so sad, so excuse me for not sugarcoating it. 4. Do you think you're the only one trying to find yourself, the only one wondering what the hell is the point of waking up in the morning? Because everyone does. They don't dump their friends in the process. 5. I don't know why you are closing yourself away from me. You don't laugh. You don't have fun. You concentrate on being a better person, working on your portfolio, and hanging with your boyfriend. Please don't lose yourself. Don't answer this. Just think about it: hypothetically speaking, what the fuck would you do if Jonah dumped you or you didn't get into Collegiate? What would you have left? You may go with family, but that's insubstantial, and you know it. This is not your invitation to use me as your safety net. I'm just showing you how short-term your priorities are. I get that you've changed, and whether or not I like that is irrelevant. But it's past the point where you'd actually give a shit if I told you that maybe one day you may need a friend. You would find yourself alone and unhappy. I told you this before, and it's the last time I tell you because there is nobody in this world who could get through your enormous head. xx

Abbie Chesterton: What you're saying to me is so horrible I genuinely think I'm becoming schitzo and depressed. I spend so much time being horrible to myself, how am I supposed to be nice to people now? And actually, Jonah gave me a promise ring, and he said he's committed to me forever. So there. I thought everything would be fixed, but it's tough because he's basically left for the whole summer, which is why I wanted to message you. Things with him are already shit enough, I don't need more shit from you too. And I'm tired of people getting in my way. When I look back at my life, I'm going to have achieved things that no classroom teacher or group of bitchy girls can take away from me. I've realized that people at Agerton Hall are mostly nice. We just want different things. I want to be friends with people who are interested in intellectual things and what's happening in the world. I'm tired of talking about who's done what and how boring school is and parties and drugs and that one fit guy I'm never going to talk to. Though my life may not be the one you want for yourself, it's what I want. Achievement, legacy, and the greatest intellectual institutions the world has ever seen. Goodbye. Xx

Juliette L: I am really sad that is how you see me, but I suppose there's nothing I can do now. Although you don't want my help ever, if you do, I will be here. Also, I know someone at a health center if you want to speak to them. I won't ever forget you, and you will remain one of the most strong-minded and intelligent people I have ever met. I'm sorry for blowing up at you. That's how my dad brought me up, and although it sucks at first and you hate the person, the end result works well. I genuinely thought you could handle it because you are so strong-willed, but I was so, so wrong. I hope things work out with you and Jonah. I know you don't want to ever because I'm a horrible person, but if you ever want to talk about stuff, go to an exhibition, or get coffee, call me. I'm trying hard to be nicer to people. I only hope you can give me a second chance. xx

Abbie Chesterton: Thanks. I'm glad you understand. Though your dad's method works, there are other, not as mean ways to do things. Thanks for being good to me in times when I hated myself. We laughed an awful lot like at Maria's party and all that. Maybe we could hit the gym at school in a little while. Then one day, when I am whatever I have achieved to be, and you are a stellar fashion designer, we can link and do good things. xx

Juliette L: I didn't know what else to do. Okay that sounds brilliant. I love you, Abbie. Just so you know. Ahh, fuckbungles. I'm going to miss you so much this summer! ARGH, I don't want to do GCSEs. xx

Soon, Abbie was back at the ice cream scoops after having battled the many levels of *Meerca Chase II*. An hour or more had passed since Julie's last message. The sun had set, and the study's windows that backed onto the garden were darkened with shadows of leaves. She drifted deeper and deeper into a soporific state until the room was hazy, and she finally gave up. With the endless games, she had tried to get her fix and to fix herself. The points scoring and encouraging captions had soothed her, but only to a point. She turned off the screen and forced herself out of the swiveling office chair.

19

A bbie read aloud from her artist's statement.

"'Abstracting natural forms through mixed-media is the central focus of my portfolio.' Urgh, bugger that." She crossed the phrase out and struggled to write something better in its place.

The large dining table of the Hunting Room at Harpburgh House stretched before her. On the walls hung oil paintings of fox chases, beagles, and young men in red tailcoats on steeds. The room was cold and scented with age. The gold-etched panels and the tasseled curtains were heavy with the weight of traditions. Their intensity was stifling to her, stopping her hand from moving across the page and foiling her from writing anything bold or exciting or new. On the table were stacks of her latest collages and a red pen and its corrections scribbled across a Maths paper she had attempted. Beside it, her sketchbook was thick with creations. The brochure for St. Peter's Collegiate School was open to the pages for Art & Design. The corners of the brochure's pages had been folded down and bent out of shape, and the most important sentences were underlined with a black Biro pen.

"'Natural forms are the central focus of my portfolio. In particular, I have fallen in love with abstracting tulips which I received as a gift into mixed-media.' Urgh, no! That sounds horrible." She crossed it out again.

Abbie heard a tapping sound. She looked up through the rounded windows of the veranda doors. Charlotte obstructed the grand view of the swimming pool and the vibrant hills of Northumberland. Her mother stood outside in a wide-brimmed hat and long-sleeved swimming costume, holding a glass of champagne. Charlotte beckoned to her.

"What do you want?" Abbie said.

Charlotte tapped on the window again, smiling. She found the doorknob, and the veranda doors shuddered as she opened them. Abbie noticed her legs were a horrendous shade of off-white. Charlotte had been trying to channel Kate Middleton's summer look from *Vanity Fair* magazine.

"There you are, darling," Charlotte said. "Care to join me for afternoon tea by the swimming pool? I have some plans for decorating the Green Room I'd love to share with you."

"I'm busy," Abbie said. "It's actually kind of important."

"I'm glad you are prioritizing your academics, Abigail," Charlotte said, taking a sip of champagne, "but truthfully, it's the middle of the summer. Surely your holiday homework can wait?"

"I'm not doing holiday homework," Abbie said. Her hand shook a little, and she clenched it into a fist. As much as Abbie didn't want to, it was finally time to tell her mother the truth. She had imagined her mother's reaction countless times and was already bracing herself. "I-I'm applying for Collegiate."

"Really?" Charlotte said, taken aback. "That's wonderful! St. Peter's has fantastic admittance to Oxbridge. Flora Maybell's daughter is a pupil there, and she's just won gold in the UK Chemistry Olympiad. Tell me, do the teachers at Agerton Hall think your marks will be good enough to be admitted?"

"I've been predicted all A*s in my GCSEs—"

"But I thought you loved Agerton Hall. Won't you miss all your friends?"

Abbie bit her lip. She looked up into her mother's concerned
expression and wondered how it had come to be that Charlotte knew
so little about her life. It was as if they had set off on a train to Scot-
land together, and Abbie had made it to the wilderness of the High-
lands, only to realize her mother had gotten off right outside London.

"No, I won't."

"Shall I organize a mother-daughter tea party for your leaving? I
believe I still have Sarah Watson's telephone number—"

"Don't!" Abbie said. "I haven't even gotten in yet. And I've
hated Agerton Hall for ages. Anyway, I've decided that if I don't get
into Collegiate, I won't go to school at all."

"Heavens, Abigail," Charlotte said. "Agerton Hall's a perfectly
lovely place. There's no need to be so dramatic."

"I can't stand it another year," Abbie said. "And there's another
thing."

She looked her mother directly in the eye. In the force of Abbie's
gaze, Charlotte's demeanor seemed to quiver. Charlotte tried to hide
it by readjusting the brim of her hat.

"I'm going to take Art for A level. I want to be an artist."

"An artist?" Charlotte squawked, clearing her throat of champagne. "What a terrible waste of your father's hard-earned money.
After all we've done for you, sending you to a private school for all
these years. And I was under the impression you would study Geography. You've always loved the subject, and you've been better at it
than anything else."

"For the last time, I hate Geography!" Abbie said. "And I'm still
keeping my options open. For my other subjects, I'll be taking
Maths, English, and History."

"But that's beside the point. If you truly want to be an artist, how
will you support yourself?"

"I-I'll cross that bridge when I come to it," Abbie said. "A-and I
think I'd have a better career in America. So I'm considering
studying there for university."

"In the States?" Charlotte said. "Abigail, what on earth has
gotten into you? That's simply a preposterous idea. We have no

family there and hardly any connections or friends, except perhaps Mariam and her chalet in Park City."

"I'm not saying I definitely want to do it. I might want to."

"You've always loved the idea of going to Oxford. Even since you were a child, you so thoroughly enjoyed visiting the deer at Magdalen College every Gaudy."

"Mummy, please!"

Charlotte seemed to stumble on her words.

"—I don't think you truly understand how just awful it's been for me since Richard's left. I mean, the man hardly acknowledges me on the telephone. I-I've lost count of the sleepless nights. I've wished he would just come home. And I've been left to renovate this entire stately home all on my own, which is falling apart at the seams. It's an enormous project, far greater in scope than any single person can handle—"

"I'm not saying I will," Abbie said. The fragility in her mother's voice pricked her shoulders, clawing at her with guilt. She wanted to take back her words and click undo like she did in primary school when she accidentally ruined her drawing in Microsoft Paint. "I'm just assessing all the options for my future."

"—even if we could afford university in the States, once you've left the country, I-I'll be the last one here. You haven't thought for a second of how that might affect me."

"You want me to be happy, don't you?"

"And Freddie hasn't been home for as much as a day since Christmas. He's always away with friends in Corfu or Portugal, or Zermatt. He's made it quite clear that he can't stand to be in the same room as me. It's as if I've devoted the last two decades of my life to this family, and no one seems to give a monkey's bottom whether I am indeed all right."

"Okay, okay, fine," Abbie said reluctantly. "Will you just think about it, at least?"

Charlotte's lip wobbled. She shook her head silently.

One of the mahogany doors swung open, and a maid quickly passed along the room's perimeter. Abbie was reeling with embarrassment that she could not remember her name. This maid's only job was to fetch scones and soda water for Lady Annabel, Abbie's grandmother. Lady Annabel sat alone in the East Wing, painting watercolor scenes of the countryside. She often failed to make it down for dinner because her room was a seven-minute walk from the main dining room.

"How do you do, mesdames?" the maid asked. "Shall I fetch scones for tea?"

"That's awfully kind. No, thank you," Charlotte said, forcing a smile. Her face became set like a stone as if she had never expressed a drop of distress.

"No thanks," Abbie said. Her mother's words repeated themselves to her in her mind. Her future with Jonah in New York seemed as unattainable as ever. She worried how he might react if she ever told him. What would that mean for the promise ring he had given her? She picked up her pen again, determined to write something less than dreadful.

20

Abbie arrived at the swimming pool house. The roof of the building was thatched, and its limestone walls and octagonal windows were like a newer, miniature replica of Harpburgh's main house. A long, thin lap pool stretched behind it. The pool's edges were hidden in the grassy bank as if it and a few half-broken deck chairs were baked into the hillside. She arrived at the hidden back door. A black-painted iron lamp hung over the doorway, its bulb extinguished. She turned the brass doorknob.

Abbie had taken the long way around to get there, through the apple grove, so no one would see her. Even as she made her way here every day, she could hardly admit to herself why she took this walk in the afternoon. As long as she didn't put it into words, she figured, she was never admitting fault. Admitting to things that everyone in Christianity and society had said were wrong. A sin, even. And Abbie was not a sinner, so she never had to admit it to her mother, Yolly, or anyone. If she didn't put it into words, then did it even happen? If a tree fell in a forest, but the one person who stood there to witness it wasn't really listening, did it make a sound?

Blinding visions of Jonah often came to her at this time of day.

She imagined him pulling her up close. The cushion of his arms. The irregularity of his shallow breaths, tinged with smoke from his latest cigarette. Tucking herself into the warmth of his chest. The strength of his back and the length of his shoulders forming the walls of a fortress he had built for her alone. He was the drawbridge, the spike-topped walls, the moat, the cannons. To shield her from the mockery and the harshness of the outside world. There she could breathe deeply and fully. There she could, at last, begin to open. There she could let herself be touched. There he spoke to her,

"I'll never let you go."

Yet every morning, Abbie awoke to her unmistakable aloneness. She had to close her eyes again to bring herself back. There, in her mind's eye, Jonah's body would become tense. Gearing up for some-thing more. A war within, the unmasking, the abandonment of costumes at the ball. Soft caresses turned to clutches. Tender embraces turned to grips. Abbie wanted it, too. In her imagination, she preferred to let herself be taken places by him and be acted upon. There was something less wrong about it that way.

Inside the swimming pool house, the boiler rumbled. Abbie opened the door to the changing room. She passed a small section of benches and hooks and a narrow stand of lockers. She locked the door to the shower room, pulling the little gold metal rod along and fastening it into place. She checked the lock a second time. She turned the shower on to a warm, medium temperature. Not too hot to scorch her but soothing enough for her to dip in comfortably. As she waited for the water to warm up, she checked the lock on the door for the third time. Now that she had done this quite a few times, the third lock check felt a little unnecessary, yet she did it anyway. It was becoming like clockwork to her. There was nothing wrong with each step of her self-crafted routine until this point, she assured herself. There was nothing wrong with staring at the shiny, golden fastening of a locked door.

Abbie entered the cubicle of the shower. She took off her summer dress and white lace matching padded bra and underwear. She left them hanging with a towel on the back of the door. She watched the water swirl into the gutter as she turned to face the shower. Its metallic pipe curved upwards to the clasp at the top, holding the head in place. The rings of its flexible pipe looked like smooth scales along the body of a snake. The showerhead was rounded. The water spurted out like a spout of poison-less venom. At times, this sight of the shower made her smile. She was Eve being tempted in the Garden of Eden. The more Abbie thought about it, the more she understood where Eve had been coming from. Eve was probably hungry. She had to survive somehow. God was a dude who didn't understand that girls and boys needed food at different times of the day. Her friends who were boys could go all day without eating, but Abbie would basically faint if she didn't have at least a piece of toast before noon.

Abbie unhooked the showerhead. She had to survive, just like Eve did, she assured herself as she flicked the plastic handle along the showerhead's surface. The water's pattern changed from mist to forty tiny spouts to a single, powerful surge to a small circle of intermittently beating blips. This was the only shower of its kind at Harpburgh House. The others were unforgiving. They looked like old telephone handles and treated water like a trickling fountain at a spa.

With her thoughts cast aside, her body kept going on its own, like an unmanned drone. Abbie sat down in the shallow puddle of water gathering at the drain. She spread her legs. She propped her feet up on the wall, just beyond the width of her shoulders, and relaxed as she hoped to wash herself away into the gutter. She closed her eyes, relinquishing herself to only feel. She angled the intermittent drumming of the water. She targeted it along her inner thigh, up along where the soft curls of her pubic hair gave way to dips and the asymmetrical flaps of skin, like the wings of her own mutant butterfly, more brown than pink. The bead at the top, where the butterfly's wings met, pulsed currents of light all around her body when the water hit it. Her first times, the waves had broken high and thick and fast in an instant. Yet now it was taking longer, like miles and twists and turns and obstacles had been placed along the road between her waking point and ecstasy.

Abbie exhaled softly and focused. She had only just learned that she reached the lower peaks faster when she held her breath, deep in concentration. Her toes curled. She fought herself, but gradually, she let her muscles go, losing all hope of controlling her legs. They bent outwards. The light coursed throughout her body as the foundations were quickly being laid, and someone was flicking on the switches one at a time, illuminating the palace's grandeur. Up and up, they climbed along the palace walls, higher until they reached the next lamp, ramping up over the plateau.

Abbie exhaled again to catch her breath, and reangling the water, they ascended quickly as if they had never climbed, as if the palace and the ropes of lights along its frescoes had never existed. She held her breath again. She let the light pour through her this time. She battled the random franken-statues of images that appeared in her mind. Her old pet hamster, China, who she and her father had buried in Holland Park. That embarrassing afternoon her mother had picked her up from school wearing her tennis gear after playing at the Hurlingham Club.

"Come along, darling! I've ordered a shepherd's pie from Lidgates for dinner."

"Fuck off," Abbie had to whisper to herself to banish them. She tried to focus on Jonah. Him, under the sheets in front of her. She had never let him go there. She had felt stupid and worried what he might think of her taste or that he might end up with a hair in between his teeth and be too disgusted to ever look at her again. But in her mind, things could be different.

The water went cold all of a sudden. It spurted haphazardly, as the old boiler was out of shape, and the plumbing lost pressure. Abbie waited patiently for almost a minute for it to kick back into gear again. The water blipped warm once more. Jonah reappeared in her thoughts. He was hungry for the taste of her, and that only. He popped a Listerine. He closed his eyes and put as much of her in his mouth as he could. He sucked and pulled hard.

"Mm," he sighed with pleasure, taking up the wings of her butterfly between his teeth and gently tugging. The mint in his saliva tingled. He held one of her legs in each arm. His hands fit right in place along her inner thighs, like she was a plaything he owned, a meal he had paid for. He feasted for however long it took him to be full.

"I can't get enough of you," Jonah said to her, rubbing her with his nose, his eyes closed, dipping his tongue and fingers inside of her, then sucking at her again, biting her. The image of his eyes closed beneath the white sheets, his diligence, his ceaseless hunger, sent her over the edge. It was like driving a buggy, speeding up a sand dune. She accelerated over the crest of the hill. She gazed over the top, beyond. An enormous drop stretched out before her, the steep slope of the sand nowhere to be seen. The ground gave way to nothingness. She spun, peaking in midair. The buggy drove through the air as it tumbled. Ten seconds, twenty seconds. Descending. Thirty. Until it landed back on Earth.

Abbie opened her eyes. She was sitting in a large puddle of clean water. Her legs were shaking. Her hands were shaking, too. She could breathe again. Her inside parts were pulsing, recovering, wondering if there was more to come. Would she do it again? Could she do that? She had read an incomplete guide to multiple orgasms in *Cosmopolitan* magazine in Tesco once when she was waiting for Yolly to buy vegetables for a soup. Yet the intermittent pounding of the water now seemed pointless to her. She couldn't watch the spray of the shower any longer. It was a mocking reminder. She pushed herself to her feet, wobbling a little. Her muscles were aching and tingling. She turned off the water. She hung the showerhead back on its hook.

Abbie dried herself off. She put her clothes back on and headed up the hill towards the main house. She caught sight of the little gold ring with the blue stone on her ring finger. Her posture slumped. She wanted to spend the rest of her life with Jonah, but she doubted he would ever be able to do the things with his tongue that she dreamt about. She had given him blow jobs a couple of times. But come to think of it, he had never once shown interest in reciprocating. He probably thought it was something dirty or something real gentlemen didn't do. That was the real pity. If Jonah was going to get anywhere close, he might have to spend hours with his head under the covers, practicing. And even then, it would probably take her ages to enjoy it fully. She would have to find some way to talk him into it. It would be her job to train him.

21

B ack in London, Abbie sat down in front of the computer in the study once more. She reread the last BBM from Jonah on her phone.

Jonah M. Wood: Sweet Dreams. Just got to the airport. I can't wait to kiss you and hold you in my arms again.

Her stomach clenched in excitement at the thought of him returning, running down the stairs in his house, hugging her, holding her, and whispering in her ear,

"I'll never let you go ever again." The image of it almost brought her to happy tears.

Over the summer months, Abbie had done so much work on her portfolio and had come so far. But she almost had too much material now, too many similarly colored and layered compositions based on the tulips. They were mundane to her now, yet she still couldn't tie the strings of her artist's statement together. It didn't make sense. Would Jonah think her technique was too mainstream? The prospect of his critiques riddled her nerves. There was only one way she knew to quell them.

She opened up Facebook in a new tab. Next to her News Feed, there was a flurry of red icons. The red icons signaled that even after she had spent so many months alone, at some level, other people wanted to talk to her. She needed Facebook to remind her that she was wanted, for the likes on her pictures, the comments on her BuzzFeed articles she had shared long ago, and the birthday reminders for people she hardly remembered. Yet as she scrolled, a hollowness was forming inside of her. There was a gorgeous picture of Emily on a beach with Moe, titled "Cowes Week 2k10," and the dappled sun and waters of the Isle of Wight in the background. Then there were pictures of Tilly Sorenson and Natalia Ambrosio from Wycombe Abbey jumping off a yacht into the aqua seas near Mykonos. Abbie had forgotten how model-like they were. They tanned easier, the Swedes and the Italians. Abbie's chest was ablaze with envy. Wycombe Abbey was the top boarding school in the UK. How were Tilly and Natalia both smart and beautiful? Life was so unfair. Everyone else on Facebook was leading exquisite lives, going to parties, getting into clubs, and having fun.

Abbie clicked through to her notifications. Her eyes zoomed in on the first,

"Harry Matthews has invited you to: Let's Fucking Partay 16th!"

The invitation brought her some relief, yet it was short-lived. Harry had been one of her oldest, dearest friends from The Barnes School. They met in October three years ago at the Year 7 Disco. She had not seen him in months, so he was probably aware of her plummeting popularity. He had probably only invited her out of pity. Even worse, the wave of this year's birthday parties was already in full swing, and Abbie was completely missing it. Hot fear seeped through her mind. Perhaps Harry's party was the only invitation she would receive the whole year. Perhaps this was her last opportunity to be social and have fun with the people she used to hang out with, ever.

Harry's party would take place at the Matthewses' home in Knightsbridge on Saturday, the 30th of October. Abbie had been to his party the year before; she had gotten far too drunk on tequila and danced almost topless with Moe in the basement. The party would be bundles of fun. But she didn't know how Jonah would feel about her going. And it was a week before her entrance exams for Collegiate. Would one night of destructive debauchery be enough to ruin her whole week of productivity?

Abbie would have to wear very little clothing to the party. She hated to use the word "slut," but she'd have to dress that way if she wanted all the guys at the party to talk about how fit she was, and that would make Moe and Emily look bad. That meant she definitely could not eat big meals, pasta, chocolate bars, or spring rolls for at least a week before the party if she wanted her stomach to look flat and perfect. After being a social sensation at the party, Moe and Emily would be desperate to be friends with her again. They would come crawling back; Abbie was sure of it. After all, she was the one who had built their entire social lives from the ground up. She always got the Barnes boys to join her friends at gatherings in Hyde Park or Turnham Green. She had been the social butterfly, whereas they were more like social caterpillars.

Abbie scrolled through the list to see who was invited. Griff and Charles Barry and Finlay were going already. As were Max Fritz-Galloway and Horace. She had to attend. But what on earth would she have to talk to them about after she had been so out of the loop? She was sure the last things they wanted to learn about were the causes of World War II or the trigonometry formulas she knew backwards and forwards at this point.

Absentmindedly, Abbie clicked on her message notifications. She had one from Julie a couple of days prior.

Juliette L: ABIGAILLLL. BABES. I snorkeled with Pig on the beach. It was AMAZEBALLS. Sorry I could not wait for school talkies. Can't wait to see you soon sista xxxxxxxxx

Abbie smiled to herself and wrote her a quick response.

Abbie Chesterton: I forgot to tell you, I've been snorkeling with Jonah in the deepest part of the ocean ;) Got so much to tell you xxxxxxx

She clicked through the rest of her messages. She held her breath as she opened the next one.

Ambie Rutterdown: Hey are you going out with Jonah Wood? As in...American, my neighbor Jonah Wood? Xx.

Abbie shuddered. Her secret was out. How had Amber, of all people, heard that she was going out with Jonah? Everyone in Notting Hill had probably been talking about her. Had Amber's mother also heard the news? Would she tell Charlotte? Abbie froze. No, surely not, she thought. Amber was far too off the rails to tell her mother anything. Abbie took a deep breath and attempted to write as cool a message as possible.

Abbie Chesterton: Yeah. How's your holiday? Xx

Next, she had a message from Charles Barry. She clicked on it before she could stop herself.

Charles Barry: How's Jonah Wood?

Abbie gaped at the screen. If Charles knew that she was going out with Jonah, then everyone else at Collegiate must know, too. In their minds, they had branded her as *Jonah's girlfriend.* Would they approach her about it at Harry's party? If she got into Collegiate, would they snigger at her in the cloisters when she and Jonah arrived together at school? She wrote back to Charles and immediately regretted acknowledging the truth.

Abbie Chesterton: Great, thanks.

She went back to her News Feed. The humiliation of it had already bombarded her. The study around her was calm and peaceful, but the words of the people on the internet felt like threats that would beat down her door at any moment.

Luckily, soon she had another message.

Juliette L: Way to make this about you again, lol. Anyway, the juicy deets are that Pig kissed me on the cheek and kind of slobbered on me a little, but then he put his hand on my shoulder, and like turned me towards him. And he felt so, so strong. And he has this super hairy Italian chest. It makes me weak in the knees just thinking about it xx

Abbie Chesterton: Pig is well fit, so happy for you xxx

Juliette L: I know, I'm literally on cloud 9 million. Anyway,

Abbie, what? Jonah's swordfish went swimming in your coral reef? xxx

   Abbie Chesterton: Yes xxx

   Juliette L: Freaking baby Jesus. You actually did it? xxx

   Abbie Chesterton: Yes xxxx

   Juliette L: You're using protection right? xxx

   Abbie Chesterton: What? Like condoms? Xxx

   Juliette L: Don't give me that, Abigail. You know what Mrs. Devie said. She spent like two months of Biology teaching this for a reason. If you're getting his swordfish anywhere near your coral reef, then you have to use protection xxx

   Abbie Chesterton: We've only done it like once xxx

   Juliette L: You can still get pregnant! Swordfish juice and all! And I really, really don't want to have to deal with that xxx

   Abbie Chesterton: Calm down. You're overreacting xxx

   Juliette L: No, I'm not, Abbie. You're underreacting. Have you gotten your period since? xxx

Abbie gazed out the window. Jonah would be arriving home any minute now. She was sure that if they ever had sex again, they could figure out when he needed to pull out. That was not what Julie wanted to hear. Still, using condoms made no sense. She was sure Jonah had no interest in wearing one. That would probably make the whole experience less pleasurable for him. And anyway, she loved Jonah, and maybe she did want to have a baby with him someday.

   Abbie Chesterton: I'm too busy with Collegiate exams and everything to worry about that right now xxx

   Juliette L: Oh, I forgot. Sorry schmuggums xxx

   Abbie Chesterton: That's alright xxx

Abbie exited Facebook. Julie had never been in a relationship, so she had no idea what it was like. Abbie turned off the computer and dawdled upstairs. She wanted to practice doing her makeup and hair perfectly so Jonah wouldn't be able to take his eyes off her.

22

"Hi, honey," Kat said, standing in the open doorway of the Woods' house. "So good to see you already. We just got back from vacation." Her wrinkles deepened with cheer behind the thick rims of her glasses.

"I—I hope you had a lovely time in New York," Abbie said.

"Oh, we did. Thank you."

Abbie gulped. She held up the folder of notes, a paltry excuse that anyone could see through in an instant. Her reason for being there seemed too obvious.

"I-I'm here to help Jonah with Chemistry. Got to get ready for GCSEs, you know."

"That is so sweet of you. Come in, come in. Let me get him for you," Kat said. She shouted up the stairs, "J, dear? Abbie's here."

Abbie stood there uneasily. A drop of sweat trickled down the back of her neck. Jonah was terrible at Chemistry, but she knew neither of them cared about electrons or covalent bonds. Her mind was awash with months of fantasies. She had envisaged some truly crazy things.

"Go ahead," Kat said, smiling as she ushered her up the stairs.

Abbie caught her eye in that instant. Abbie felt engulfed by the shame of what she was about to do. Did Kat know that Abbie had come to take her son's clothes off, in her own house, in the middle of the day? Did she care? It was gut-wrenching. Kat must have liked her for some unknown reason or another.

"Who's there?" came the familiar lisp of Jonah's voice.

Abbie opened the door. Before she saw him, she saw a clean brick of cigarette packets on top of his dresser. It was the kind they had on display in the duty-free aisles at Heathrow Airport.

Jonah was wearing a black Slipknot T-shirt. He looked like he was in a wannabe heavy metal punk band, about to get his eyebrow pierced. His arms were so pale, in such contrast to the redness of his face and neck. Abbie could not believe she was about to give her body away again to a boy with such a ridiculous, childish T-shirt. It was as bad as the small amount of amateur porn she had seen, back when she had thought that category on Pornhub meant a special word for romantic French lovers. But instead, amateur was the kind of sex where people wore socks and had glasses and spots on their backs and faces and did it in their bedrooms that were messy with ugly, beige-colored sheets. It was a far cry from her fantasies of them going to the opera together.

Her wearing a satin violet dress with a long slit up the sides and jewels, and Jonah wearing a slim-fitting dark blue velvet blazer with cream silk trim on the pockets and red leather boots.

"I've missed you," Jonah said. He hugged her before she had a moment to breathe. He had gained some weight back around his stomach, but his grip was comforting and firm, and he smelt clean.

"I've missed you too," Abbie said, letting herself sink deeper into his chest.

He reached for her hand as if to check. Was she still devoted to him?

"Wow, what a nice ring," he said, smirking as he kissed the back of her hand. "Who gave it to you?"

Abbie giggled.

"Oh, no one special."

Jonah grinned. He gripped the back of her head and kissed her. His lips were moist. He tasted of Listerine, fresh and minty. Abbie tried to put the brick of cigarettes out of her mind, but it was no use.

"Did you get them from duty-free?" she asked. Jonah knew precisely what she was talking about.

"You have no idea how stressful editing has been."

"You promised me you'd stop."

"I know, and I regret saying that to you," he said. "Can we please not talk about it and just enjoy being with each other right now? Please?"

He kissed her hand again, this time interlocking their fingers.

"Urgh, fine," Abbie said, though she knew it wasn't fine. But as Jonah gazed tenderly at her and the afternoon sun glowed in the caramel color of his eyes, Abbie forced herself to let it go.

"I got you a little something," he said.

"Oh?"

Jonah reached into the cigarette drawer and brought out a small paper bag. He handed it to her. The edges of its rectangular shape were straight and thick. Abbie pulled out a book of postcards. The cover showed a woman with a bleached-orange square haircut, surrounded by a multitude of her yellow-and-black pumpkin sculptures.

"Yayoi Kusama," Abbie said.

"She had an awesome exhibition at the MoMA," Jonah said. "She's pretty bold, though she came from an affluent family in Japan. I thought you'd like her work."

"I love it," Abbie said, beaming. She looked more closely at the cover. Abbie had always doubted that a typical English girl like herself could be brave enough to fully express herself as an artist, uninhibited by the fear of what other people might think. Yet the enduring strength in Kusama's expression hinted otherwise. If only she had as much courage as Kusama. She flipped through the book. Postcard after postcard doused her eyes with colors, oranges, polka dots, and blues. The postcards seemed to symbolize it all. A noble act of rebellion. A whisper of wind that was changing the course of a river.

"She's the definition of crazy," Jonah continued. "She's been a loner her whole life. Never been married. Never had any kids. She checked herself into a psych ward in Tokyo in 1977 and has been living there since."

"Are you sure?" Abbie asked. She looked again at the final post-card in the pack. Kusama was wearing a long-sleeved red frock with black shapes on it against a background of rainbow swirls, smiling as she held a paintbrush. She looked content and at ease. "I'm sure she has friends or something."

"I beg to differ. She's the definition of the lone creative genius, as far as I'm concerned," Jonah said.

"I guess," Abbie said. "Thank you, anyway. I've been struggling to finish my artist's statement. There's something about her work that might do the trick."

Jonah kissed her on the forehead. Abbie let him hold her and tried not to look again at his Slipknot T-shirt. This time, he reached for the straps of her summer dress. Everything happened so quickly. They were naked, kissing, cramped into his single bed again. She was straddling him. He was biting his lip, the sides of his neck flaming red, as she rubbed herself on top of him. His fingers gripped her waist, pressing her lower pelvis into him. He was getting carried away and panting already. She broke free of his grip.

"Can you lick me out?" Abbie asked.

"H-huh?" Jonah said. "Oh, I mean, I could. I just hadn't considered it. We haven't seen each other in months. I—I just really want to be inside of you right now."

Jonah wanted to make love to her. Abbie should have been satisfied with that answer. Why did she have to want more than that? She scolded herself. But deep down, another part of her was more than worried. Perhaps if Jonah didn't do it soon, he never would.

"Please?" Abbie said, pulling away from his kisses.

Jonah avoided her gaze.

"Fine," he grumbled. He pulled the covers off them. Abbie lay down and spread her legs apart. Jonah's chest was blotchy. He seemed to wince a little as he looked at it. He propped himself up on his elbows. He smelt it. "What if it tastes like fish?"

"It won't," Abbie said, though, in all honesty, she couldn't be sure. "Come on! I've had your ball sweat in my mouth before. Just try it."

Jonah closed his eyes. He stuck out his tongue reluctantly. The tip of it touched her, at least for half a second, but he was too far away.

"Get a bit closer," she said. Abbie closed her eyes, and Jonah inched forwards. He dabbed his tongue like he was prodding a frog with a paintbrush. He seemed to be fully concentrating, fully trying, but she hardly felt anything. His neck and back were tense. If he couldn't relax and couldn't pretend to enjoy it, there was no way she could, either. He lifted his head and took a big deep breath of fresh air beside her, then returned to work. He was being ridiculous. Why was he holding his breath? To think she had almost swallowed his semen, and he wouldn't commit to tasting her in return.

"Have I paid my dues now?" he asked a moment later.

"Yeah. That was great," Abbie lied, vowing to herself that she would instruct him how to do it better next time. Jonah lay down. She climbed on top of him again.

SOME TWENTY MINUTES LATER, they were lying in Jonah's bed together. The sheets were a little damp with his sweat, or perhaps a bit of her sweat, too; Abbie couldn't tell. They had managed to avoid too much creaking in the bed by having sex on the floor for a while. But then her knees had gotten a terrible burn from the carpet, so they stood up against the bed before he finished. Jonah's breaths were deep and heavy, as if he was about to fall asleep at a moment's notice.

"I've been thinking," he said, forcing his eyes open. "Would you ever want to get a tattoo with me?"

Tattoo, Abbie thought. The word chimed inside her like a music box crookedly out of tune. Her shoulders began to tingle. Charlotte thought people with tattoos were unworthy of respectable jobs and were destined for a life of crime and deceit. Amber Rutterdown's old nanny, Paola, had had a lot of tattoos, she remembered, including three giant stars up her arm. Charlotte could never spend more than a few seconds talking to her at a time. Her memories of the disgruntled disgust on Charlotte's face were bold and unwavering in her mind.

"They're permanent, though," Abbie said. "And a lot of them are so tacky."

"I mean, we could pick one that's not tacky," Jonah said. "I just think it would be a nice way to commemorate our love for each other."

His idea came from a pure place, Abbie tried to remind herself.

"I've never wanted a tattoo," she said bluntly.

"Well, they're kind of important to me," Jonah said. "Will you at least just consider it?"

"Okay," she said. She prayed they could avoid the topic for another six months at least.

Jonah rolled off his shoulder onto his back. He took up even more of the bed, and Abbie was squished up against the wall. She readjusted his arm to use it as a pillow and curled up in his chest.

"I've had other things on my mind," he said, staring up at the ceiling.

"What is it?"

"After we go to Collegiate, I want to go to Columbia University in New York. But your family seems dead set on you going to Oxford for college."

Abbie sighed. Part of her was relieved that Jonah was already planning a crazy amount, so she wouldn't have to break the news to him herself.

"I don't see how it will work unless we do long-distance for four years. But then again, I don't mind getting married before I graduate college. I want to have a kid by the time I'm twenty-five. And if it's a boy, he's going to be called Melchior."

Each of Jonah's words jammed her, jarred her. Abbie imagined him taking a chainsaw to the beautiful, blossoming tree of their relationship. With each sentence, he severed off a stem, a branch, the trunk. He was taking this all so seriously, so quickly. And before Abbie knew it, she would be living in America somewhere with three kids and a Bible, and one of those pickup trucks she saw in the movies. Did Jonah even know her at all?

"To be honest, I don't know what I want yet," she began. Her Collegiate exams were coming up in a couple of weeks. Why couldn't they just wait to discuss these things after that? Her head ached with the absurdity of it all.

"I'm just letting you know. That's what I want," Jonah said.

"Okay," she said, holding back the frustration in her voice. "I guess while we're bringing stuff up, I should tell you that I'm going to the doctor to get birth control."

"Don't I get a say in any of this?" he retorted.

"Well—"

"You couldn't have told me any sooner?"

"Look, it's not that big a deal," Abbie said. "Julie told me to do it. I can get one that might help my skin, and then we don't have to worry if we, you know, want to keep doing it."

"Those things can hurt your fertility if you take the wrong ones, you know? That affects me, too. That could affect us," Jonah said. "I just can't believe you wouldn't tell me about it first." He scowled.

Abbie hated to see his temper bubbling up like this. She didn't want to fight with him. She wanted to go home, to open the door to Yolly's smiling face and the smell of warm, clean laundry. "Come here, beautiful girl," Yolly would say, the gold glinting from the crowns on her back teeth as she grinned.

"Okay, fine. I'm sorry for not asking you first," Abbie said. But she knew she didn't mean it. She sat up and got off the bed.

"Where are you going?"

"Just putting my clothes back on."

"Why?" Jonah said. She didn't answer. Rather than stay in his bed alone, Jonah got up and scrambled to put his boxers on. Then he asked in a small voice, "Want to go watch a film downstairs?"

"No," Abbie said. She had to try to regain some of the ground she had lost. "You know, I don't like watching movies that much."

"Don't be ridiculous," he said to her. "You don't mean that."

"I want to go home."

"Can you just come here and kiss me? Please?"

Abbie sat on the chair next to his bed, folding her arms. The desk drawer was closed, she noticed. She could tell by the way it was stuck shut that it was still filled with cigarette packets. The drawer of death.

"Then why are you even here?"

"I'm leaving," Abbie said, heading for the door. "Don't fucking touch me. Don't text me. I can't even look at you right now."

Abbie grabbed the book of Kusama's postcards and left the room. She tiptoed downstairs. She listened for Jonah, but he didn't try to follow her. He was probably too much of a coward, too badly tempered, and too embarrassed about it. She managed to leave the house before any of his family noticed.

Outside the Woods' house, the shock waves of adrenaline hit her. Her hands quivered. Abbie wanted to cry, but she was too livid. She couldn't get the image of Jonah's repulsive, sweaty body out of her mind. How dare he probe her so much? Now she was a terrible girlfriend for not keeping him happy. The walls of her life felt like they were closing in all around her, with Jonah at the center. Like he was a shrine that had been built into the house, mixed in with the steel-reinforced concrete of the entire structure. Everything in her life had been reoriented around him. What about what *she* wanted? *Her* life? *Her* freedom? What would he do if she dressed up in her tight black dress from Primark and heels and went out without him? She could imagine the whites of his eyes pulsing red with fury.

Down the street, Abbie passed a man smoking a cigar, nodding off beside the tarp pulled over his stall on Portobello Road. She caught his eye. Her forehead felt hot with fear. She quickly looked away and continued onwards. Further up the road, she checked over her shoulder to see if he was following her. Luckily, the man was nowhere to be seen. Abbie grumbled to herself. When she walked with Jonah, she never had to worry about these things. Without him beside her, she was exposed to the elements. There was no one to shield her. The bright colors of the houses, quiet and vacant, melded together under the darkened yellow streetlamps and hinted at more sinister stories beneath. She imagined women trapped inside their homes at various points in history. They were branded as witches, held by the hair or hit by their violent, drunken husbands, and crying out in pain. She passed the black gates of a private garden square and read the plaque,

"The foundations of this square were laid in 1826…"

Abbie felt the sobs of the women of the past; their cries never heard, their agony never shared or spoken, just absorbed into the walls and the old Victorian curtains and the carpets. The darkest corners of history long forgotten. The women raped there, murdered in their own homes. The women who died in childbirth. The women who didn't have painkillers because they hadn't been invented yet. How had women even survived before ibuprofen? How had they endured the needless suffering of period cramps? Life was not some happy or cheery thing full of dandelions and daisies. The world was cruel, painting over its pain with well-intentioned dinner parties and marriage certificates and lives full of babies and child-rearing to occupy their time. Yet in all its horror, this place, London, was her home. She belonged here.

Abbie passed Notting Hill Gate tube station. She passed a trio of women, older than her, glammed up and cackling as they said sloppy, drunken goodbyes to each other at the station. They gave her an idea. There was one thing she could do. A single act. A single click she had to make on her computer to gain her power back, to regain what had rightfully been hers all along that she should never have lost. Jonah could not tell her what to do anymore.

When Abbie got home, she detoured to the study. The high-lighter-green ribbon of the screen saver flickered in tantalizing waves. She opened Facebook. She scrolled through her notifications until she came to the event page. She reread the title, scoffing to herself at how obnoxious it sounded now.

"Harry Matthews has invited you to: Let's Fucking Partay 16th!"

She clicked *"Going."*

23

Abbie bit her fingernails. She sat on a square plastic chair in the waiting room at the doctor's office. The room was drafty and sterile with the smell of Band-Aids and the alcohol of hand sanitizer. An elderly gentleman stared silently into space beside her with his walking stick tucked under his arm. It seemed he couldn't hear a thing. Stacks of pamphlets were laid out on a table. *Get your flu jab today* and *All you need to know about menopause.* The telephone rang with a smoothed-over ringtone.

"Holland Park Surgery, how can I help?" the receptionist said softly from behind the large desk.

Abbie tried not to stare at a woman sitting across from her. The woman was rocking her infant in a sheltered pram. The ends of her dyed-blond hair were frayed, and her roots were grey. Abbie's insides went cold at the sight of them. The mother's eyes looked fearful for reasons that Abbie could barely imagine. In a way, Abbie was jealous. The woman looked exhausted and stressed, but at least she was of age. At least she had enough money to buy her baby a pram, and she could drink wine whenever she wanted to. Other people probably didn't tell her what to do.

Abbie had thought that making love to Jonah would have

changed things, but somehow everything was still the same. She still had to go to Agerton Hall. She still had to prepare for her GCSEs and her Collegiate exams. And Charlotte undoubtedly would still expect her to go to Aunt Belinda's Christmas party that winter. Abbie was no closer to being an independent adult than before.

"Chesterton?" came a pinching voice from down the corridor.

Abbie stood up. Her surroundings were a blur. She stared at the ground as she walked to the open door. Could the woman with the baby guess why she was there? Why else would a teenage girl in a school uniform be there in the late afternoon for a doctor's appointment? Abbie shut the door firmly behind her.

A muddied cream carpet covered the floor beneath fading yellow walls. Along one end of the room were a medical bed and adjustable curtains. Shelves were full of syringes, pills, needles, wound dressings, black bottles of iodine, and white bottles of alcohol. It felt like the room her grandfather might die in, in a care home turned hospice in Northumberland. A bedroom that also healed sick people. Was she sick? Was there something wrong with her? Why did she have to go to a doctor at the NHS to get this?

"Gosh, you've grown, Abigail," Dr. Clark said with a smile as she typed into a loud and clunky keyboard at her desk. Abbie looked at her nervously. Dr. Clark's ginger hair was messily pinned back in a clip. Her glasses were just as nerdy, and her nose was just as pointy as Abbie had remembered.

It was all so humiliating. The last time Abbie had been to see Dr. Clark was when there had been a verruca outbreak in Year 6 when she was twelve. Dr. Clark had kindly held a heavy cylinder, like a fire extinguisher, and frozen them off for her. The awkwardness of Abbie's previous visits now paled in comparison. She wanted Dr. Clark to read her mind, but only the relevant thoughts she did not want to say aloud.

"Let's see what your reason for the visit is today," Dr. Clark said. She clicked around on her computer. Abbie said nothing. She wasn't really about to do this, was she? It wasn't too late to leave the doctor's office and pretend like none of this ever happened.

"Contraception," Dr. Clark said. Without even a murmur of suspicion, she continued, "Our meetings here are completely confidential. Mummy won't get any notices in the post or anything, so there's no need to worry about that."

Mummy, Abbie thought. Urgh! That sounded so childlike. Still, Abbie was relieved. She had barely managed the words "birth control" on the phone to the receptionist when she made the appointment last week.

Dr. Clark leaned one elbow on her desk and looked at Abbie calmly through her glasses. It was as if Abbie had dropped an egg on the floor, and the thin, delicate shell cracked instantly, and the yolk and the dangers and the shame and the uncooked whites had just spurted all over the carpet. Dr. Clark probably thought she was far too young to even consider having sex. Abbie wanted to be older, at an age where it wouldn't be a totally embarrassing, irresponsible thing to do. Why couldn't she just be seventeen or eighteen?

"So you're having intercourse, then?" Dr. Clark said.

There was silence in the room, except for the faint humming of a bus engine as it lurched down Holland Park Avenue outside. Abbie prayed that somehow Dr. Clark would forget that she had asked the question so she wouldn't be forced to answer it.

"With one partner or multiple?"

"One."

It was more than zero. Infinitely more than zero. No one else, except Julie, knew that she had had sex with Jonah or that she was having sex at all.

"Are your periods normal?"

"I think so?"

"Are you getting them regularly, every month?"

"Yes."

"And is there any chance you could be pregnant?"

Abbie paused. When had her last period been? It had been a couple of weeks at least.

"N-no," Abbie lied.

"Are you sure?"

"Yes."

"The end date of your last menstrual cycle?"

"10th of October."

A couple of weeks ago, possibly a Sunday. It was the date she had hoped to finish her portfolio. That sounded plausible, didn't it? Abbie held her breath. Her life flashed before her eyes. Like when she woke up with a large dark brown stain in her white pajama bottoms and told Yolly she might have had an accident in the night.

"You're a lady now," Yolly had said after she soaked the flannel cotton fabric in cold water. When Abbie first typed "boobs" into Google on the computer in the family study. But lying to a doctor? That was an illegal, punishable offense. There was no doubt about it. It was the kind of thing that the police would come knocking on her bedroom door late at night to investigate.

"Perfect," Dr. Clark said, typing something incomprehensible into the computer. When she spoke again, her voice was in a tone of more scripted lecturing. "Let's look at your options."

She fumbled in her desk drawer and pulled out a sheet with some pictures on it. "Which methods have you heard of before?"

"The pill," Abbie said suddenly.

"Anything else?"

Abbie shook her head. That was all that came to mind. She had gotten over 80 percent on that Biology test. Why couldn't she remember the name of just one other method?

"Well, the pill could be a good option to help with your skin as well," Dr. Clark said.

Abbie frowned. Was Dr. Clark commenting on her skin? She had a few scabs from whiteheads she had picked. Her skin wasn't that bad, was it?

Dr. Clark continued with her explanations. Abbie's whole body was still crawling with awkwardness. She couldn't get Jonah's scowl, his blotchy red skin and the creases of his eyebrows, the face he made when he orgasmed, out of her mind. There were a million things she wanted to tell Dr. Clark. Abbie wasn't sure if she wanted to be on birth control. Taking pills, or getting one of these other things, seemed like such a gigantic leap. It seemed like it would bring her relationship with Jonah to a whole different level of seriousness. Now she had to take pills? What would that do to her periods? She didn't want to gain weight or have headaches or have her vagina shrivel up from the inside out or die from a blood clot.

"You'll have to take them every day, then do a week of sugar pills, in which case you'll bleed for a couple of days, but only lightly. You must take it at the same time every day. Do you have an alarm on your phone? That would help. You might get some mood swings, but there's been no evidence of weight gain. If you don't like how this pill makes you feel, you can come back and try another instead. The coil is only for women who have had a baby—"

Why was Dr. Clark talking to her like she was a child? Giving birth, that's what it was really called.

"—and it might make sense to take some morning-after pills in case you have any accidents but be careful to only take them within seventy-two hours, not to mention if you have exams and things to prepare for. And condoms would help. The boys will sometimes complain about them, but they help, but they won't be quite as effective on their own."

Dr. Clark's words were like sirens escalating, flashing with lights. Abbie felt that she needed an ambulance, but it seemed pointless. She was already at the doctor's office. She wanted to interrupt Dr. Clark, to shake her by the shoulders and scream at her,

"I don't know how much I like my boyfriend, okay? I don't know how much sex I want to have with him anymore! Getting this birth control feels like way too much right now. Okay?"

Abbie bit her tongue, pinching it between her top and bottom teeth as hard as she could. It hurt. The throbbing seeped through her mouth, dissipating out through her jaw. Each bite was a sentence she would never say aloud. Each pinch was a feeling she was determined to flatten. At this moment, she would keep quiet. She would be a nice, polite girl.

"Do you smoke?"

Abbie shook her head.

"Any drinking or drug taking?"

An image of Julie's laughing face and the pulsing red and blue strobe lights flooded her mind. That unforgettable night of debauchery at Maria Consucla's sixteenth birthday. Abbie had downed shots of whiskey with Sam Thompkins before he did a line of ket off her boobs in the toilets. She had rubbed the white powder along her teeth like factory-grade nail polish remover. Then she found herself straddling him on the sticky bathroom floor with his tiny dick flapping outwards amongst rolls of soggy toilet paper. They were kicked out of the venue. Julie shoved her into the back of the taxi, and Abbie woke up passed out naked on her bathroom floor.

"Never."

"So, the pill seems like the best option for you, given that you know so much about it," Dr. Clark said, taking out a piece of hole-stamped paper from a tray on her desk. She scribbled something on it and handed it to Abbie. "You can pick it up from the pharmacist just across the street."

Abbie nodded, hoping that saying nothing would help her leave more quickly. She stuffed the piece of paper into her schoolbag and zipped it closed.

"You can always come back in if you don't like this pill and get another," Dr. Clark repeated.

"Thanks," Abbie managed. She stood up to signal that the conversation was over. At the door, she clutched the cold, brass door-knob. The sensation of it terrified her. She was leaving behind the possibility of asking a real adult for help. But Dr. Clark wasn't here to give relationship advice. She needed help from someone else.

Abbie twisted the doorknob to the left, but nothing happened.

"Pull the door. It's quite heavy," Dr. Clark said.

Abbie pulled the door hard, and it suddenly sprang back. She headed out into the vast emptiness of the waiting room again. She would never come back to see Dr. Clark, and she knew it. She had already made up her mind about what she was going to do.

24

A bbie repositioned her schoolbag on her shoulder as she crossed the street. The entrance to Holland Park Surgery disappeared behind her. She reached the rounded "Boots" sign in cobalt blue and clinically cursive white writing. As she stepped through the automatic doors, she was hit by a wave of heat from fans blasting overhead. She dodged between the couple of customers who milled slowly about the shop. She was trying not to dwell on the fact that her period was late. It was a most unsettling feeling. She was also feeling a little heavier than usual. But maybe that was only because she had gone to the deli in Hammersmith Broadway twice that week and ordered her favorite bagel with sausage and bacon and an egg and extra ketchup both times.

Abbie walked briskly down the aisle emboldened with the sign "Family Planning." She grabbed a box with a generic label off the shelf and headed to the pharmacist's counter, checking it afterwards. The words "Pregnancy Tests, 99% accurate in 2 minutes" were written on it in that jarringly strange writing. There was no room for her to feel. All she had was a straight shot of her pragmatism to coax her forwards.

A young female pharmacist appeared from between the shelves

stacked with medicines. Her black-cloth hijab was tucked neatly into the collar of her clean pharmacist uniform. Abbie wished she could have been there to buy foot fungus cream or a nasal drip device or laxatives. Anything that would signal that she might have an actual health problem that wasn't the result of her own reckless choices.

"Can I help you, madam?" the pharmacist asked her.

Abbie pulled out the crumpled paper of her prescription and handed it to her. Without as much of a glance, the pharmacist disappeared behind the medicine shelves again. Sure, Abbie thought to herself, this was embarrassing. But it wasn't half as awkward as when she had bought lube and condoms from Boots last year without any real hope of using them, which came in weird flavors, like blueberry. There was nothing silly or giddy about being here now. It dampened her heart. Julie was probably worried about her. But it wasn't Julie's body this was all happening to. It was hers. Abbie would have to face this leg of the journey alone. The world had decided she was sick, that she needed medicine. The world had cursed her with the apparatus to be able to get pregnant. And the world had decided that she should hide the evidence and harbor the heaviness and the secrets of it all on her shoulders alone.

Abbie paid for the tests and her prescription. She left Boots. She walked down the street and entered the Starbucks nearby. She locked the toilet door behind her. That was when it hit her. She was not one of the women in the adverts for Clearblue on TV, holding up the test that they had apparently just peed all over, with no hint of a blemish in sight. Grown women, smiling in their well-lit, perfectly decorated living rooms. Women wearing long-sleeved shirts, put-together professionals, delighted with the result, never mind whether it was positive or negative. Supposedly, these adult women were happy and empowered by their decision, delighted to have crouched down in a squat over the toilet. These adult women were evidently far too smart and sophisticated to pee on the seat accidentally or have specs of warm urine sear into their hands as they tried to angle their stream forwards, spraying off the stick and all over their tights.

Abbie smelt the faux-lavender cleaning fluids of the Starbucks bathroom. It was what made her feel furthest away from those women. The tiles were reflective black at waist height, above which was a black-painted stucco ceiling with its pipes bent out of it. There was a small white porcelain sink with long, metallic handles on the taps like levers in a woodwork shop. An open bin was full of used brown tissues, presumably pulled from the now-empty tissue dispenser. Squares of damp, disintegrating toilet paper were scattered across the floor.

Abbie saw her reflection in the water-stained, short mirror above the sink basin. Her breaths were steady and calm.

"Let's get this over with," she said to herself. She felt strangely disconnected from it all. It was her first time peeing on a pregnancy test, so she at least wanted to do it properly. She preferred to stay somewhat detached from it as if she was an angel watching over herself from a distance, from the upper corner of the room, observing without interfering. There was nothing that could be changed about the outcome anyway. She had had sex with Jonah enough times at that point. She had seen plenty of sperm. It only took one, she considered. One nasty little bugger. She imagined it like a worm, a tiny, straggly, pin-looking thing that could skulk up a drainpipe to her uterus, heading down Fallopian Way to her ovaries and eggs. At some level, she felt she deserved whatever was about to happen. It was partly, mostly, her fault.

Abbie unwrapped the pregnancy test, gripped it tightly in the middle, and pulled off the blue plastic cap. A light pink pad stuck out beneath it, like the head of a USB cable that some evil doctor might try to plug into a computer. She pulled down her tights. She sat down on the toilet. She peed on the stick. The plastic was slender and smooth, so smooth it almost slipped out of her hands into the toilet bowl.

The fan in the bathroom turned on. The loud whirring made it almost impossible for Abbie to hear her thoughts. It was better this way, distracting her from the tightness that was gathering in her stomach. Her pee splashed a little onto her nails. Its warmth made her feel even more disgusted with herself. It was that isolating kind of embarrassment, which was painful to look back on. Attached to a secret that no one else could ever know. They would think of her differently if they ever found out, and the memories of it would haunt her every time she looked in the mirror or shook hands with someone properly at a drinks party. If only Abbie could have been as girly and polite as her primary school classmates, the kinds of girls who had never farted in front of other people and had always followed the teacher's instructions in kindergarten. They had always colored neatly inside the lines. Why couldn't she be normal, like them?

Abbie placed the test on the edge of the sink. She buttoned herself up and washed her hands while she waited for the result. All this faff for Jonah had not been worth it. This stress, this embarrassment, doing this whole thing in Starbucks. This could not, would not, happen again. She had GCSE exams to study for, for Christ's sake. Jonah had been a good lover, but for all the topics he claimed to feel so strongly about, he knew nothing about them at all. It was easy for him to say that he wanted to be married and have children. And he could fight to name them whatever the fuck he wanted to. But Abbie wouldn't stand for it. No, these issues ran so much deeper for her. How much of Jonah's ideas of modesty and monogamy until death do us part had already seeped into her psyche?

She picked up the pregnancy test again. She stared at it. She noticed how it almost fit snugly in the pale palm of her hand. Her nails looked terrible, ripped, and gnawed off around the edges. Abbie caught a glimpse of the result. Her heart seemed to stop. She choked a little on her breath, stunted momentarily. A double line had appeared on the test window in red. A double line? What did that mean? Charlotte could never park on a double red line, not even for a moment. Abbie dug frantically into her schoolbag. The pens and the pennies she had accumulated at the bottom of her bag spilled out over the floor into a puddle of an unknown liquid under the sink. She grabbed the box and tore open the instructions. A double red line. A double red line. Positive? It couldn't be. How long would she have to wait until it was certain?

"Come on, come on," Abbie said, unwrapping the second pregnancy test and forcing what little pee she had left onto the stick. She sat in the bathroom for five more minutes, staring at the second test, praying that no one expected to use the loo and would knock on the door, wondering what was taking her so long. She waited patiently. Another five minutes passed. She held her breath.

"Fuck," she said, checking the double red line on the second test. She threw the first one into the open bin of used tissues, not caring if anyone found it. The hard plastic stick made a light thumping as it hit the bottom of the bin. She took the second test. She washed it off in the sink. She collapsed on the floor, holding it in her hand. She leaned against the wall, and tears streamed down her face.

25

"Anyone in there? 'Ello?" came a raspy voice. The door handle shook violently, but the door's lock held firm.

Abbie opened her eyes. Snot had hardened at the base of her nose. The salt from her tears had crystalized down her face. Her cheeks felt cracked and chapped as she wiped them. She stood up and brushed herself off, trying not to think about whatever her tights had soaked up off the floor. Her stomach was nauseous, but she ignored it. She steadied her schoolbag on her shoulder again. She opened the door.

An older man stood in front of her. He was holding a mop and pushing a yellow bucket on wheels.

"Starbucks is closed now, love," he said with sheepish concern. Abbie hadn't taken a moment to check herself in the mirror. The man probably thought she was a drug addict from the looks of her.

"Excuse me," she said, gently pushing passed him. The smooth plastic of the second pregnancy test was hidden in the sleeve of her school jumper. She headed out onto the street.

Outside, the early-evening sun was fading in the autumn air. Thick clouds with dark gray bases suffocated the sky. A fresh coldness loomed across street corners, soon to be showered with rain and swollen with puddles. The leaves from the plane trees dripped to the ground in maple brown and burnt ochre, freeing themselves from the clutches of branches with the wind. Abbie passed through a crowd of students from the local comprehensive school, who were running for buses and fighting over the best view of a magazine and arguing over a packet of crisps. The strangers around her blended into one mass of anonymous faces. Their lives, at least, continued as usual. She forced back tears at the thought of it as she headed up Holland Park Avenue towards Notting Hill Gate. She stared at the ground as she walked. She noticed the dots of darkened chewing gum cemented to the grey pavement. Each small stain was warped and tarnished now with every terrible, stupid decision she made these months past, layered upon each other. She stepped on each piece of old gum, hoping one might stick to her shoe. Perhaps then, she would have reason enough to call for help.

Drizzle started, quickly descending into rain. Abbie saw the mist of her breath between the patterning raindrops. She wondered why and how she was still alive. Her heart was being torn apart, stretched out between two lands at polar opposite ends of the world. Her dreams of creativity, her Collegiate exams, her career as an artist, her freedom at one end, filled with rainbows and lush green valleys. And then, at the other, the life-form that was half Jonah's, growing of its own accord inside her, like a desert that leeched all moisture, a dust bowl on the outskirts of some nondescript, dilapidated town. More than half of the fetus-half-egg-forming-child was Jonah's, in a way. Jonah had told her many times that life began at conception, as did its rights. And those rights truly belonged to the people who believed in them? Before, Abbie had only half believed in them. But half believing in something, she quickly discovered, was a luxury that a slap of reality couldn't afford. And all the while, her body, the thing she existed in, had been co-opted as a vessel. Perhaps her only way out was to destroy the vessel, thus destroying all its contents. The station wasn't far. The Circle line came every five minutes. She could go stand on the southbound platform and wait. Jumping would hurt less than ridding her body of whatever was growing inside of it. Jumping would hurt less than sitting down with Jonah and having the conversation. Or sitting down with Julie. Or Yolly. Or her mother. It hurt less than failing to get into Collegiate. Less than setting fire to her dreams and letting them burn for the sake of Jonah's pure notions of a family coming to life.

Abbie reached the entrance to the station. The rain was dripping across her shoulders and being batted away rigorously by the windshield wipers of the buses, taxis, and cars. She leaned against the lamppost at the top of the stairs, where she had met Finlay and Jonah less than a year ago. All around her, commuters pushed past her in a flurry of newspapers and briefcases flapping over their heads in feeble, makeshift shelters from the rain, inching towards the freedom of the weekend. Her breaths shallowed, cracking into short, hyperventilating sobs. She scrunched up her face as she thought long. Julie had been right. She should never have gone out with the Collegiate boys to Griff's house that night. None of this shitstorm would have happened if Jonah had never reconnected with her. She should have just continued on at Agerton Hall. Her life would have been boring and simple, and for the first time, she desperately wished it could be so.

"Julie," Abbie mouthed to no one, her eyes drowning in tears and lashing rain, "Julie."

She wanted to call her and tell her everything that had happened, but she couldn't. Julie had told her so many times. She had written to her point-blank on Facebook,

"I really, really don't want to have to deal with that."

Abbie had already pulled a dagger through her own life. She couldn't, she wouldn't do that to Julie too. For once, she thought, she would stop herself from spewing her pain, hurt, and suffering onto everyone else around her. Julie was probably doing her homework or studying for her mock exams. She shouldn't interrupt her. Homework? What was the point of it? Why should she even bother to do her homework if Jonah would insist that she keep their ball of cells and birth it plain out of her own vagina because an epidural would obstruct the true nature of the most beautiful moment of a woman's life?

Her stomach churned like wet clothes thumping in a washing machine. She gripped her belly, praying that the pain would go away.

"Stop!" Abbie said aloud. The rain was beating down on her, seeping through her hair, bleeding through her jumper, and soaking her to her very core. She couldn't take the weight of it another second.

She set off home. Her feet squelched in her shoes as she wrung the excess rainwater out of her hair. She turned down Clarendon Road and rang the doorbell. There was a shuffling of flip-flops inside.

"Miss Abbie?" Yolly said, hurrying her into the house and shutting the door behind her. "Mrs. Chesterton was looking for you. She just left for the countryside. Lord—"

Yolly saw Abbie's tangled hair and her mascara dripping down her chin. There was a quiver of fear in Yolly's eyes. Abbie felt the guilt tugging in her chest. Her pain and her stupid decisions were already hurting the person who had done nothing but love her and give to her for her entire life. She began to weep uncontrollably.

"Miss Abbie? Come here," Yolly said, hugging Abbie at her upper waist. Abbie rested her cheek on the top of Yolly's head, her tears dissolving into the comfort of Yolly's hair. The strength of their hug broke something inside of her. Her reality was held up to the blaring heat of a microscope. Yolly would have given her the clothes on her back, yet Abbie had been nothing but spoilt and ungrateful. After all the good that Yolly had done, this was how Abbie repaid her. This was what Yolly had gotten for it.

Yolly gripped her by both wrists as if she was about to baptize her,

"The Lord Almighty works in powerful and mysterious ways. The love of Jesus will conquer all the darkness. I free you with my full heart and my love. You will see. What is this?"

"Wait!" Abbie started as Yolly pinched the plastic rod hidden up her sleeve. She pulled out the test. Abbie could hardly see or think or feel. Yolly's expression tumbled into terror.

"Oh no, Miss Abbie!" Yolly said. She took the test with both hands. She signed the Holy Trinity.

"I—I have to keep it," Abbie wailed, "Jonah will never forgive me—"

"Don't listen to stupid boys!" Yolly insisted. "They don't know."

"You don't believe in abortion, do you?"

Yolly shook her head.

"I knew, one day, the Lord had prepared me for this," Yolly said. She hugged Abbie around her middle, and this time didn't let her go. "Remember I always try to be a good Catholic?"

"Y-yes."

"Remember I always talk a long time in confession?"

"Yes."

"It is because," Yolly said, pushing through her words with strength, "back in the Philippines, I was eighteen, and I got pregnant. I had an abortion, but it was so dangerous. They used a catheter, and I fell asleep. I almost did not wake up, and I lost so much blood. For so many years, I felt so bad and guilty. But now I understand that God put me on this Earth to keep you safe."

Yolly hugged her tighter. Abbie sniffled, shaking with her sobs. Yolly's pain seemed intractable, beyond the darkest, cruelest things Abbie could imagine.

"Your future is too important. You are not ready. It's okay. I am here to protect you. The Lord challenges me. It took me a very long time, but I forgave myself. I forgive you. I forgive every other woman pregnant in the world who doesn't want her baby. I learned that no Christian is perfect, and sometimes evil gives us no choice. But God is good. God can forgive. And you have a good NHS. You can get it safely and free. Miss Abbie, you call Dr. Clark and get help now—"

"No!" Abbie cried, "I—I can't do that. It's too late today."

"You go to A&E, then they will take you—"

"I'll go tomorrow," Abbie said, unsure when or where she meant. She'd have to find another doctor. Anyone who wasn't Dr. Clark.

"I will not leave you," Yolly said. She reached up and stroked the back of Abbie's hair. "I give you strength. You are strong. And tomorrow, I will cook your favorite spring rolls and pandan cake."

Abbie wailed quietly.

"Don't worry, Miss Abbie, don't worry," Yolly said. "Everything is going to be okay."

26

T he next day, Abbie paced outside Harry Matthews's house. The dubstep wailed from inside. She wore a purple button-up crop top with high-waisted jean shorts and black platform Converses. Tights were a must, as was her black faux-fur coat. Her hair was in a back-brushed, large, and messy ponytail. Various strands of her hair were pulled out to make herself look unkempt. Her eyes were caked in eyeliner. She had gotten a lot of looks walking from South Kensington tube station through Knightsbridge. Charlotte called it "The Arab Invasion," where Emiratis, Saudis, and others from Gulf countries set up camp in Bulgari, Armani, and Harrods. Abbie felt them staring at her and her exposed midriff, tutting to themselves about how the female youths of London were inviting sin into their lives.

It felt childish, even silly, to have her stomach on view, but part of her wanted it that way. It was an act of rebellion against whatever was forming inside of her. No one knew. No one could ever know. After all that she had found out only twenty-four hours ago, she couldn't bring herself to land back in Dr. Clark's or any medical professional's office. For one night, Abbie told herself, and one night only, she wanted to forget all the insanity.

Her phone buzzed. She declined another of Jonah's calls. He had been furious with her ever since he had found out that she had clicked *"Going"* to Harry Matthews's party on Facebook. She reread the most recent BBM he had sent her.

Jonah M. Wood: Finlay and Griff were right about you. You haven't changed at all. You're just as easy and self-centered as the rest of them.

Then two hours later:

Jonah M. Wood: Were you planning to go without asking me? How can I trust you at all after this?

Jonah's soppy, guilt-tripping texts felt so pedestrian to Abbie now. He was living on planet pea brain, not inhabiting the galaxy of philosophical ideas that she thought he had been orbiting for so long. Why couldn't she go out? Why was she tied to him like a dog on a leash? She should have taken off the promise ring before she got here. It seemed to be burning her finger. She could make her own choices. And yet, the pain of Jonah's messages bubbled up something else afresh: the shame she felt when Emily found out she had been getting with Danny.

"You complete slag."

"You're nothing but horny gash."

"You don't deserve him, or anyone for that matter."

At the time, Abbie had felt like a used tissue. Now she would do anything to switch places with her old self as Danny's side mistress. She felt like a fool for even attempting this revival of her social life. But something told her she had to be here. She had accepted Harry's invitation. Harry had remembered her after all this time. She could try to rekindle old friendships, to glue the broken pieces of her social life back together. Harry was expecting her and was probably annoyed that guests like her were taking their liberties and rocking up late.

Before she could talk herself out of it, Abbie knocked irregularly on the golden handle of one of the red double doors.

"Abbie!" Harry cried in delight, barging out the door and embracing her in one of his bear hugs. The sound of the chatter from within the house was deafening. Abbie's throat swelled up as she saw the joy on Harry's face. Here was one person at the party who still cared about her. "It's been too long, love."

"Far too long, darling," she said, trying to sound as whole as possible. "Well, you've fucking grown. How tall are you now?"

"One eighty-eight, I think," Harry said, puzzling, "or six foot two if you're American." After being tiny for years, Harry had shot up to over a head taller than her in the last year.

"So, I'm even more of a dwarf. What's changed?" she joked. Their blissful reunion lasted only a second longer. He ushered her into the dimly lit corridor. Abbie spotted Emily whispering to Moe at the bottom of the staircase just ahead of her. At the sight of them, Abbie wanted to reverse her steps and walk backwards out the front door, but Harry was hastily pushing her forwards.

"Here, let me take your coat," Harry insisted in his usual gentlemanly fashion, removing it smoothly from her shoulders.

"Oh, w-wait," Abbie stammered, shouting over the crowd. From the pocket of her faux-fur coat, she pulled out a small rectangular box decorated with a red ribbon. Emily's hawk eyes burned into her skull as Abbie gave it to him.

"A cigar!" Harry exclaimed with delight. "I've been dying for one of these. You shouldn't have!"

"Oh, it's the least I can do. Happy birthday! By the way, I'm guessing this is a good one. I swiped it from my dad's box in the cellar." Abbie winked at him.

"You cheeky one, you. Thanks a million," he said, hugging her again. Abbie glanced over towards the staircase. Emily and Moe had gone. They were probably off telling the other Agerton Hall girls that she had arrived.

"Go grab yourself a drink, food, whatever you want," Harry encouraged her. He hung back by the door to meet and greet his other guests. Abbie was left to face the mass of people on her own. She took a deep breath and pressed on through the foyer.

There were only four pieces of furniture in the Matthewses' drawing room, resembling boulders of volcanic rock found in

Iceland, which looked highly uninviting to sit on. Along the walls stood Mr. and Mrs. Matthews's peculiar marble sculptures of contorted babies. Abbie was intently counting the number of teenagers in the room. There must have been a hundred, maybe 150, in this part of the house alone. Everyone stood in perfect circles of five to nine people. The room buzzed with ponderings and postulations. She vaguely knew everyone she saw, but not well enough to scrape into their conversations.

Abbie headed over to the drinks table. The translucent glass of the alcohol bottles glinted at her wickedly. She grabbed the bottle closest to her. It was Gordon's Dry Gin. She poured herself a generous shot and knocked it back. She chugged it like it was beer at Reading Festival, rinsed the glass with more gin, and repeated.

"For fuck's sake," she grumbled. The heat of it dissipated too early in her body. She wanted to set herself on fire, or at least the part of her stomach between her belly button and her crotch. Goddamnit, why couldn't the alcohol do its job for once?

Abbie poured herself another shot when someone clapped her on the shoulder. The gin sloshed onto the glass table. She almost dropped the bottle, until she managed to steady her grip and put it back down.

"What the—"

"Ooh, careful," he muttered. It was Charles Barry. He had gotten a new haircut and shaved the sides of his head. He now looked even more attractive. The bastard. But for some reason, he was nodding at her, evidently pleased with himself. He sneered at her, "You just won me five quid."

"Excuse me?" Abbie said politely, hardly audible over the music.

"Moe bet me five quid you wouldn't show tonight. To be honest, I didn't think you would, either. But I was keen to get a fiver off of Moe anyway. She owes me so many fucking cigarettes."

"Great," Abbie snapped, giving him a sarcastic thumbs-up. Only then did she see the City girls, Alicia Foster and Hannah Vale, staring her up and down. Now they thought she was a freak, too. Perfect.

"How's life?" Abbie spat at Charles, knocking back the shot of gin.

"As social as ever. Haven't seen you in months, though. Why? Are you jealous not to be invited out?"

"No." She glared at him. She should never have challenged him. What was she thinking? She lied, "I've been going to different house parties in Hampstead."

"Oh really? Because that's not what Jo—"

Abbie had had enough. She grabbed the bottle of gin again, her only lifeline, and stomped out of the room. She had not anticipated the night going this bad so quickly. She was just about to go downstairs to dance off the humiliation when she caught sight of Harry's mum on the landing.

"Jacqueline!" Abbie called out, almost pouring the gin all over herself.

Jacqueline, Harry's mum, was about to escape from the mass of teenagers by bolting up the stairs. Abbie thought she'd take only a minute to have a harmless little catch-up chat, to get some brownie points with the parents.

"My dear, Abigail," Jacqueline said in her South African accent. "I haven't seen your mummy since book club two months ago. Tell me, how is it going with your boyfriend? Harry tells me you're seeing an American?"

Abbie gasped. She had to cover her hand with her mouth to stop herself from gaping at Jacqueline and throwing up instantly all over her. How had this gotten back to Jacqueline already? It was only a matter of time before Charlotte found out. Abbie had to put a stop to this nonsense immediately.

"He's not my *boyfriend*," Abbie said, admitting Jonah's existence. "He's just a *boy* who happens to be my *friend*."

"Well, that's exciting. You know, in life, a boy might seem like just a friend. But after a couple of years of being close, they can start to be so much more."

Jacqueline winked at her and danced around her a little with joyful jazz hands. Abbie felt sick to her stomach.

"It's been lovely to see you," Abbie said, gritting her teeth.

"You too, darling. Tell Mummy I'm looking forward to beating her socks off at the Hurlingham this week."

"Oh, I will."

Abbie hurried away. She could already picture Charlotte throwing her tennis racket onto the grass court as Jacqueline unknowingly divulged information that would set off World War III. Abbie's life would be over. There was no way around it.

She stepped cautiously down the glass staircase. The open-plan basement was lit by a strobe light, which flashed still images of the teenagers before her. They skanked out in groups, grinding to the base. The music pounded through her body. Abbie rolled her eyes at the irony of smartly dressed, private school people releasing their inner angst to dubstep. The harsh screeches of alien electronic tones, the gradual build, accelerating to a euphoric high, hit by an explosive drop. It was overwhelming. Abbie wanted it to take her away, but she still had too much control over her movements. Sobriety held her back. Later, she promised herself.

Outside, the garden was a claustrophobic concrete box surrounded by high, ivy-clad walls. The air was hazy with smoke. She felt a profound craving coming over her. She tapped someone she thought was a randomer on the shoulder.

"Could I possibly have a cig—"

"Hello there, Ab-i-gail." It was Kit Charster, the boy she had once described as the most annoying, wet, uncool Barnes boy in her year. Now he seemed like a monarch of social prowess.

"Kit!" Abbie cried in a fake, high-pitched voice. She gave him a quick, passionless hug. "How are you?"

She expected him to show some interest in her or her welfare or to at least answer her generic question. Instead, he blurted,

"I've heard the news." He did not give her a cigarette.

"What news?"

"You're banging that loser at Collegiate."

His words hit her like a slap in the face. She had to shove the gin bottle in her mouth and take a giant swig to stop herself from attacking Kit and weeping simultaneously. She took another gulp and swallowed. More gin sank into her empty stomach.

"We're not banging yet," Abbie lied as if it would save her from this one. She took another swig of gin as punishment for confirming such personal information to a scumbag.

"So, it's true? You don't deny it?" Kit gaped. He cackled to himself. Abbie stood there blankly, unable to respond. He grabbed her by the forearm and dragged her over to the corner of the garden, where four guys were reclining on deck chairs.

"Mates, get a load of this: she's banging Jonah Wood." Two of them choked on their smoke and sat up in fits of laughter.

"No fucking way!"

"She must be dying for the D. Jesus."

One of Kit's friends was a short, freckled ginger. Abbie recognized him as Rory MacFlanigan. He was from out of town, a Scot. Something compelled him to speak up in his unusual accent,

"Hey, Jonah's not a total mong, okay? My older brother plays on his older brother's football team. He's actually got some bant for a weird bloke." Had Rory had any social relevance and not given Jonah such a slighted compliment, Abbie might have appreciated him. But all she could hear was cruelty.

"Oi, fuck off," she retorted, failing to fight. "He's nicer than any of you wankers." What a pathetic comeback.

"Ooh," they chorused together, "the cat scratches back."

She wondered why they couldn't just leave her alone. Now she was embarrassed to know Jonah and guilty even for feeling that.

"Ooh, she does like him," they chimed again.

"Guys, stop it," Rory warned.

Their demonic words evaporated in the air, reaching Abbie as specks of dust. She shook her head. Then she turned around and marched away.

With a satisfactory amount of alcohol in her bloodstream, Abbie walked in what she thought was a straight line onto the dance floor. The music rang in her ears. She felt the groups of teens tighten around her like fortress walls being built around cities. The backs of

Moe, Emily and some stragglers from Agerton Hall linked arms and pulled up the drawbridge. She felt like a fly, unknowingly hitting a glass window, pounding on it over and over again, and slowly losing steam. With each attempt to wriggle in, her hopes chipped and splintered away.

She caught Harry's eye. He stood there, watching her being excluded. She crawled to him, unable to hide it any longer. The drink was doing the talking for her. She cried out to him,

"See how they treat me? Just blocking me out of the circle? They hate me, Harry. I'm a fucking punch bag!" Abbie screamed, waving the gin bottle at him, writhing.

"Calm down," he commanded her. "And for heaven's sake, stop drinking. It'll all be fine in the morning. And, Jesus, don't put yourself down like that."

Harry wrenched the bottle from her grasp.

"You hate me too!" Abbie wailed, unable to hold it in any longer.

"Don't be ridiculous," he yelled. He shook his head and walked away. Abbie watched him go, her lip trembling. Obviously, Harry had never been her real friend. After all these years, he had been lying to her, just like the rest of them. He'd always known she was a horrible person. He had waited until the night of his own birthday party to tell her. She stumbled away, too dizzy to glance back at her old friends to see what they were doing. She steadied herself against the door, searching for her next victim.

At once, Abbie happened upon a scene that made her gag. Danny Watson, the initiator of her total social eclipse, was smoking on a deck chair. Claudia Parrow, from Putney High School, was sitting on his lap. Abbie had completely forgotten that Danny was friends with Harry through rugby. She gawked at him, his aggravatingly chilled persona, his presence dominating even when he was reclining on a chair. He pinched his cigarette with his thumb and forefinger in the way that Abbie remembered. The butterflies arose from the dead in her stomach, like digested ghosts of former times. Why was he still a beacon of male beauty? Abbie wanted someone to gouge out her eyes so she would no longer feel guilty about finding him attractive and never have to see him with another girl again.

And Claudia Parrow? Before the party, Abbie had considered tagging along with Claudia for the night. Claudia was pretty, though her laugh was quite annoying. Now she looked just as stupid as Abbie had been when she was under Danny Watson's spell.

She was unsure how long she had been standing there, ogling at them. But suddenly she realized that Danny had his eyes on her. He was frowning slightly at the disheveled wreck that she was. Her conscience evaporated.

"Oh, hi, Danny. I thought your girlfriend was coming tonight?" Abbie barked at them.

Claudia looked from Danny to Abbie and back again. Then Claudia slapped Danny as hard as she could and gathered up her gin and tonic and handbag. She left. Claudia would thank her for it later.

"Clara, come on!" Danny called after her. He turned to Abbie. "What the fuck was that all about? Fucking cockblock."

But Abbie had already sauntered away, proud of herself for tearing down Danny's evil plans for girl domination. Across the box of a garden, Abbie saw someone she didn't know. He was leaning against the brick wall, intently busy on his phone. He was wearing fancy dinner attire and had a thin Afro. The chance to escape the baggage of her recent conversation overwhelmed her. She found herself cuddling up next to him, peering at his screen.

"Can I help you?"

"Is that a dinner jacket?" Abbie drooled.

"Yes."

"Isn't that a bit formal for a party?"

"I'll wear whatever I fucking want to a party," he snapped.

She shrank away from him. The boy went back to his phone. She made one final attempt to make a new best friend.

"You like Dizzee Rascal much? Like, can you rap?" she asked him.

The boy turned his head towards her slowly.

"You think I can rap cuz I'm Black?"

"I just meant—"

"Fucking racist sket," he shouted, loud enough for the entire patio to hear. "Get the fuck out of my face."

With his anger fresh in her mind, Abbie ran away as fast as her flailing limbs allowed her. She tripped on her own feet and hit the back door. Her top caught the door handle, and three buttons ripped off her purple crop top. Her head was spinning.

"Oh, my sweet baby Jesus."

Abbie looked up. Emily stood over her, tapping away the ash of her cigarette.

"Em!" Abbie said, gasping for breath.

"Stand up straight, love. You're making a right fool of yourself."

Abbie straightened her back. She stared up into the powdered foundation on Emily's face.

"H-how've you been?"

"Fine," Emily said, taking a drag. "I've been Max Fritz-Galloway's girlfriend for one month and like nine days."

"C-cool," Abbie said. "I'm glad for you."

"Mm." Emily pursed her lips.

"I-I'm really sorry about all that, by the way," Abbie said.

"About what?"

"That time I tried to get Max's BBM pin—"

Emily raised an eyebrow.

"—and you had told us for ages that you fancied him. And I—I just bulldozed all over that," Abbie said. She propped herself up against the door.

"Yeah, that was a super bitchy thing of you to do," Emily said coolly.

"L-like, hos before bros. Whatever happened to that?"

"I know." Emily nodded. "Anyway, it's okay."

"And I—I am really, really sorry about the whole Danny thing. I fucked up considerably. Wow, I mean, I'm surprised you tolerated me after that. I should have never gone behind your back. I was a right muppet."

"Thanks, Abs," Emily said. "I'm grateful you're saying this now.

Swear down I am. But it's been over a year. It took me a while, but I got over it. All of us did stupid things when we were thirteen. But we're fifteen now, so we know better."

"I—I know, but I did some ridiculously stupid things," Abbie said.

"S'alright, love. You're long forgiven." Emily winked at her.

"That's great. Thanks."

"Anytime," Emily said. "How you been, anyway?"

At once, Abbie felt her stomach heave. An inch of sick stung the back of her throat. She had to hold her breath to stop herself from retching. She looked down at her stomach and back again. Could Emily tell something was up? Oh, that's right, the buttons of her crop top had ripped open. Fuck.

"I-I've been better."

"Sorry to hear that," Emily said. "Anything you want to talk about?"

"No. Thanks, though."

"Anytime. Well, I'm here if you need. Don't be a stranger, babe."

Emily tucked the flap of Abbie's top into her bra and gave her a quick hug. Abbie's eyes welled with tears. There was too much to say. Whatever words she could try to string together, she was sure, wouldn't scratch the surface. Emily's gesture meant everything, and yet, she would never understand.

"That's a bit better," Emily said.

"Thanks," Abbie said. She was on the verge of vomiting. "Sorry, I-I've got to go."

"Bye, love."

Abbie ran into the house. Beyond the dance floor, she locked herself in the bathroom. She was panting. Her head was swaying. She plonked herself down on the toilet. The stillness of the marble and the music tucked away gave her space to think. She could barely prop her head up with her hands. She tried to catch her breath.

She saw her reflection in the curved mirror above the sink. Her skin was pale like paper against the deep purple of her ripped top. Her hair was a mess of tangled feelings. Her lipstick was faded and smudged. The drunken peeing began, a destructive amount of urine that rid her body of all fluids and left her mouth dry with an acidic sourness. Her hands were growing tired. She leaned her head against the wall, gasping for air.

Just then, Abbie looked down at her underwear. An enormous crimson stain had soaked through every inch of her white underwear, through her tights, through her shorts. It lined her inner thighs, dripping down her legs.

"Fuck!" she cried. Her favorite white pants were utterly ruined. She clutched at the fabric in horror. Her life was over.

Her insides were dripping, leaking, and lurching into the toilet bowl. She lunged for the loo roll and wound it around her hand. Within seconds it was soaked through. Abbie peered downwards. Mounds of the soaked paper oozed bright red, further plumped up with the weight of the water, floating, the blood thick like the toilet was a pot of scarlet ink, splattered along the sides, like the insides of a round red puffer fish. An animal with a beating heart of its own that was about to die. Would she hold a funeral for it? She had to flush it down.

She reached for the handle behind her and pulled with all her might. The limp mounds spun around and looked like they would sink. But nothing happened. The toilet stopped flushing. The bloody mess still stared her straight in the face. Then the musky, moldy smell of it hit her. Her stomach acid burned deep in her esophagus. The possibility of choking on her own vomit terrified her.

"Please, h-head! Stop s-spinning!" Abbie begged out loud. "You're m-making me sick."

The bile bubbled up in the back of her throat. Abbie winced. Her insides squeezed like meat mincing.

"It's coming. I—I can't stop it. Urgh," she sobbed. She dove for the sink, her shorts and tights still clinging around her ankles. The vomit sprayed from her mouth. She began to cry as the russet chunks filled the sink. Her throat stung hot with semi-digested alcohol and stomach bile. The tears from her eyes and snot from her nose combined with the remnants of vomit, forming a mixture of suffering on her chin. It dripped onto her top like sludge.

Abbie kept herself there, hunched over the sink, bawling. She forced out all the hurt into her sobs. She closed her eyes. She gasped for air. Her breaths slowed. Her wailing grew quieter.

"Abbie? Abbie, are you in there?"

The door handle rattled.

"E-Emily?"

"Are you okay?"

Abbie opened her eyes. The muffled dubstep pounded through the walls. Her face was stuck to the flat side of the sink. The arched silver faucet glistened in front of her nose. She gathered up all her energy, slipping clumsily, and lifted herself up inch by inch as if she was rousing from a sleep that had lasted for years. She turned the tap's shimmering handle. Fresh, cool water flowed into the blocked basin. She tried to wash the residue down, but it wouldn't budge. It was as if all her guilt had congealed into a clump in Harry's bathroom sink. She tried to wash out her mouth. She spat into the sink, clutching her stomach in agony. Everything hurt. Every inch of her body was shivering. She wiped her face messily on a hand towel, staining it with puke and lipstick. She improvised with a last mound of toilet paper and pulled up her pants. She tried to stand but almost toppled over. She got on her knees. She crawled to the bathroom door and thrust it open. The music tripled in volume.

Emily gasped.

"Come in. C-close the door."

"What the bugger happened to you?" Emily said, pushing her way into the bathroom.

Abbie returned to the floor, hugging her knees in a ball. The heated marble was warm and comforting against her cheek. She closed her eyes, too faint to move. With all her might, she reached into her pocket. She pulled out her BlackBerry. It was damp and covered with blood.

"C-call Julie," she managed as loud as she could.

"What?" Emily said.

"Julie!"

"I don't know your passcode, Abbie. I—"

Her head smacked down hard against the marble floor.

"HOLY FUCKBUNGLES, Abigail Chesterton. You've got yourself into a right pickle."

Abbie couldn't open her eyes.

"J-Julie? I-is that you?"

"Up you pop. We're getting you the fuck in the ambulance right now."

"I-I'm g-going to vom."

27

The midday light stung Abbie's face. Her lower abdomen was stiff, as was her left arm. She took a long, deep breath. There was a faint smell of burnt coffee and beef stew. She opened her left eye first. She was bundled up in blankets. The sterile walls of the hospital room were high and tall, as if they were weighing down on her. A giant needle had been bandaged into her arm, fixed with a plastic tube filled with a colorless liquid. She tried to move her fingers. They curled and inched flat again. She breathed a sigh of relief.

Abbie tilted her head. She could just about make out the person sitting next to her. She had a thick, messy ponytail and was curled up with her head resting on a pillow. Julie dozed with her mouth wide open and her full train-track braces on show. Julie's long-sleeved top was stained with blood.

Abbie tried to sit up. Her stomach was aching with pain, heaving and heavy.

"Ooh. Ouch."

Julie startled awake.

"Yes, she's my friend. Oh, Abbie. You're awake!"

Abbie tried to nod, but she barely made any movement at all. She tried to speak, but her voice was little more than a hoarse whisper.

"W-where are we?"

"Chelsea and Westminster Hospital. They had to operate on you immediately. They did some scans, and you were pregnant, but like an ectopic one, and you were like eight weeks along, which is super dangerous."

"What?"

"Yeah."

"Bloody hell," Abbie said. "H-how did you find me?"

"Emily called while I was watching *Buffy the Vampire Slayer*. Luckily, I had my phone on loud. I had almost turned it off. I got there just in time and got you in an ambulance."

Abbie beckoned to her, trying to sit up.

"Come here—"

"What?"

Abbie gathered her strength. Julie scooted up beside her on the bed. Abbie opened her arms and hugged Julie with all her might. She breathed in, taking in Julie's enduring warmth in a long, steady breath, emptying the darkest chambers of her heart. She hugged Julie tighter, ridding herself of toxicities that had blackened and battered her. When her tears came, she didn't know if they were happy or sad.

"Th-thank you, Julie, thank you," Abbie sobbed into her shoulder. It hurt to talk, but she knew it would hurt more not to tell Julie what she should have said to her years ago. "Y-you're the most amazing, generous friend I could have ever asked for. Ever. In the whole world. I love you, Julie L-Louchart. I—I mean, n-not in that way. But you g-get me."

"Aww, Abigail, I do get you. I love you too."

"Seriously, though, I mean it. I'm so, so sorry. I've been the most ungrateful, shitty friend ever," Abbie said, sniffling.

"It's okay," Julie said, hugging her back. "It was hard for a while there. I felt like you kept losing your way and turning everyone away. But I knew you'd come back around. And if it was me in a life-or-death situation, I know you'd do the same."

"I'd be the first one there," Abbie said, pulling back from her hug. She meant it this time. She held Julie by the shoulders. "I really owe you for this one."

"Don't see it like that," Julie said. "This is what friends are for, literally."

"I guess you're right. Can I ask you something, though?"

"Sure."

Abbie swallowed hard. Her chest was aching. It felt like the hardness in her heart was thawing and breaking open with joy simultaneously.

"W-will you be my bus buddy again?"

"Abbie!" Julie giggled. "Of course I'll be your bus buddy."

"I've been missing our chats. I mean, taking the 94 is faster, but only by fifteen minutes or whatever. It doesn't even matter."

"Aww, yay," Julie said, tapping her shoulder gently with excitement. "At least we'll have plenty of time to gossip before you go to Collegiate. Then I'll really miss you."

Abbie sighed.

"I'm not going to Collegiate anymore."

"What?"

"I'm going to have to withdraw my application."

"Why?"

"The exams are next weekend. With all of this and all the extra work I have to do on my portfolio and my artist's statement, there's literally no way I can make it in time."

"Hmm," Julie said. "I mean, the nurse did say you should be horizontal for like three weeks at least or something. But bugger that. Abbie, you've got top marks. You've wanted this for ages. You've worked way too hard for this to give up now. I'm sure we can jack you up on meds and get you there somehow."

"How, though? If I have to be horizontal, how am I even going to sit up in a chair to take the actual exams?"

"I don't know," Julie said.

"Hold on," Abbie said. She felt a bolt of energy up her spine. "Maybe we still need to figure out the exams. But God, I am such a moron. You know, I've always loved all your fashion drawings and everything. You're amazing at art. I should have asked you eons ago, but would you help me with my portfolio?"

"Hell yes!" Julie said. "I've been dying to see what you've made. And I haven't been round for tea since we watched *Kidulthood* at your house that one time."

"I know, I remember that."

"And it's okay, Abbie. You're not a moron. You're learning," Julie said, winking at her.

Abbie smiled.

"Sounds like we got a plan, then," Julie said. "The nurse is coming in a bit. Just try and convince him that you're all fine and ready to go."

"Okay," Abbie said. "Thank you for not giving up on me."

"You're welcome, schmuggums. Now, let's peace the fuck out of here."

28

The afternoon sun was fading when Julie knocked on the door at Clarendon Road. Abbie inched out of the taxi in a hospital gown, hobbling up the curb and clutching her stomach.

"Miss Julie," Yolly said. "Lovely to see you. It's been many months since you were here."

"Hi, Yolly!" Julie said. "Yes, it's great to see you too."

"My God! Did you take good care of Miss Abbie? Bless you."

"Yes, she rescued me," Abbie said. "Julie took me to the hospital."

Yolly shut the front door behind them.

"Oh, thank God. Thank you, Miss Julie. You spend the whole night there? You both look a mess. Let me run a hot bath—"

"There's no time. We have so much work to do," Abbie said, ushering Julie ahead of her into the kitchen. "But before we get started, Yolly?"

"Yes, Miss Abbie?"

"I just wanted to say I'm so grateful for everything you've done for me. You have always taken such good care of me. I don't know how to thank you enough."

"No need," Yolly said, beaming. "I love you like my own daughter. Your smile brings me enough joy. Thanks God. Now come. Let's make tea for Miss Julie."

"Okay," Abbie said, pressing on her stomach to dull the pain. Abbie entered the kitchen and headed straight for the row of mugs. She put three down on the counter and grabbed the silver-bottomed kettle. She shuffled over to the kitchen sink and began to fill it with water.

"Sit down! You need rest," Yolly said.

"No," Abbie said. "Can you both please sit down and let me make the tea?"

Yolly frowned.

"But Miss Abbie—"

"Please."

Yolly reluctantly sat down at the table next to Julie. Abbie found some tea bags and got the milk out of the fridge. Julie helped her carry the mugs to the table.

"Now, here's the plan," Abbie said. "My Collegiate portfolio is due in one week, Saturday 6th November. Half the compositions need to be finished and then stuck into my sketchbook, arranged in order of progression. Julie?"

"Yes?"

"I need your help adding details to each composition. And leave room on each page so I can write a small paragraph."

"Are you sure? I can mimic your handwriting. Pretty sure I can figure it out," Julie said.

"Would you? Okay, amazing," Abbie said, relieved. "Yolly?"

"Yes, Miss Abbie?"

"Can you go upstairs with Julie and get everything on my desk? It would be all my collages, sketchbook, cutouts, glue, and everything. Oh, and bring the tulips too."

"Of course," Yolly said, motioning to Julie. They left the room and returned within minutes. Julie had changed into Abbie's unicorn-themed pajamas and was carrying a mountain of collages and materials. Yolly balanced Abbie's favorite pajamas on top of her sketchbook.

"Here, put on clean pajamas." Yolly grinned.

"Thank you so much," Abbie said.

At the kitchen table, Julie stood with a mountain of cutouts and papers scattered around her.

"You have like fifty collages here," Julie said, pinching her temples. "How the fuck do I know which ones to go with first?"

"Well, um, start with these less colorful ones," Abbie said. "Yolly, you can help to just stick these in here in the middle. Then towards the end, these collages need more work, Julie. You can add them here and put in a couple of postcards here from Yayoi Kusama. And for the last composition, I want it to be a collage of the tulips themselves."

"Why don't I start with the tulips one, then I'll work my way backwards?" Julie asked.

"Sounds great," Abbie said. "I'll, um, get back to my artist's statement."

"Cool."

"Yolly, are you good?"

"Yes, ready," Yolly said gleefully, armed with scissors in one hand and a glue stick in the other. Once Julie and Yolly had some semblance of what they were doing, Abbie slowly walked to the sitting room. She could barely carry her pajamas, a pen, and the notepad where she had been writing her artist's statement. Abbie dropped them onto the sofa as soon as she could. She changed out of the dreaded hospital gown. Her clean pajamas were soft and comforting against her skin. She felt refreshed and sore but ready to get started.

Just then, she heard her phone buzzing from her coat pocket. Abbie rolled her eyes as she steadied herself to her feet and took out her phone. She had seven missed calls from Jonah.

Jonah M. Wood: Why won't you answer me?

Jonah M. Wood: For fuck's sake, Abbie. I knew you never loved me. You can't just ghost me like this.

Jonah M. Wood: Please, can I come over? This isn't okay. We need to talk.

She had to say something to shut him up and quick.

Abbie Chesterton: Sorry, my phone was on silent. I'm focusing on studying for the exams. Can you not wait until the week after next? Not everything is about you.

She turned off her phone. She sat down, finally able to work on her artist's statement.

"I finished the tulips collage," Julie shouted from the kitchen. "What should I do now?"

"Can you help Yolly with the progression and stick them in?" Abbie called out to her.

"Miss Abbie, I need help. There are many more drawings than pages. I don't know which ones you like more."

Abbie gritted her teeth. The notepad with the scribbles of her artist's statement seemed to mock her from the sofa. She breathed deeply through the pain and sat down next to Julie at the table.

"This is looking amazing. Okay, here, let's put the more colorful ones towards the back, and these that aren't finished, um, I guess we can just get rid of them."

Abbie felt a hollowness in her chest as she sifted through the half-finished pieces.

"Are you sure?" Julie said. "I think these work pretty well, actually, if you put them a bit earlier in the book."

"Yeah. Maybe you're right," Abbie said, smiling, "I just don't want to get rid of them."

"I get that," Julie said. She glanced at Yolly, who stared at the table.

"I feel like I've lost so much already," Abbie said, her throat cracking, "I don't know what to do. I don't want to throw away all this work I've done."

Abbie forced back tears. Yolly nodded solemnly and patted her comfortingly on the back.

"That's what I see here. Miss Abbie, you give so much effort and create many beautiful things. It's like you physically create. You put everything into it like these are your gifts to God."

"That's such a nice way to put it, Yolly," Julie said. "I agree. All these compositions are your creations, Abs. Don't worry. We're here. We can figure this out."

"Right," Abbie said. She clenched her fists, weeping reluctantly. "There has to be something to tie these all together. Creating life or death or loss or something."

"Totally," Julie said, stroking her back.

"We keep going for now," Yolly said, looking at Julie, sticking in another drawing.

"Yeah, Abs, don't worry. We got this one step at a time," Julie said.

Abbie sniveled, taking in a long deep breath in and out. Slowly she made her way back to the sofa in the living room. She lay down and tried to write something on the notepad, but her breaths became slow and heavy. She hoped that the weight of the notepad might suddenly inspire her with the thread that would sew everything in her portfolio together.

29

The key turned in the lock of the front door. Abbie awoke suddenly. The sitting room was dark and empty. The lower half of her body was throbbing in agony. Her sketchbook and a note were in front of her on the coffee table. Beside it was a plate of pork spring rolls and pandan cake. Abbie smiled to herself at the sight of them, her heart overwhelmed with gratitude. As she steadied herself to sit up, she shoved a spring roll into her mouth. She picked up the note.

Got as much done as we could. Love ya! Yolly and Julie (your #1 fan and fishmonger in crime) xx

The front door opened.

"Darling, thank God you're home," Charlotte said, slamming the front door behind her. Her arms were full of bags and trappings from her weekend at Harpburgh. She turned on the light. "Are you all right? Yolly texted me to say you've been very ill."

"Mummy, could you do me a big favor?" Abbie said.

"Anything!"

"Could you get me a glass of water from the kitchen? And the painkillers are in the pocket of my coat?" Abbie said. Her stomach felt like it was being stomped on.

"Of course," Charlotte said. She rushed to the kitchen and retrieved them both.

"Thank you," Abbie said. She chugged the water and four painkillers, praying they would start working immediately. They didn't, and her stomach once again cramped mercilessly.

"Darling, you look awful. What on earth's happened to you?"

Abbie was midway through a mouthful of spring rolls. She wanted to tell her mother everything that had happened, but it was far too raw and terrifying for her to speak. How could she put what had happened to her into words? However she put it, Charlotte was bound to start crying immediately. Charlotte cried at these kinds of things. She even cried when animal rescue commercials for the RSPCA came on television.

"Pardon the interruption while you're eating," Charlotte said, "but you know, I've been doing an awful lot of thinking. I've talked to your father. It's taken some time, but I've concluded that I think it's simply wonderful that you want to be an artist."

"W-what?"

"Please don't talk with your mouth full," Charlotte said. "One moment."

Charlotte headed to the entryway and returned with a small parcel. She tried to hand it to her, but Abbie's hands were weak and full of spring roll grease. Charlotte quickly took off the packaging.

"I found this while I was surfing the web over the weekend," Charlotte said. "To help with the inspiration and to add some more pizzazz to your colorful compositions."

Charlotte sat down daintily next to her on the sofa and handed her a copy of *Grafik* magazine. The cover was crisp, depicting a mirage of framed graphics in bright, tantalizing purples and blues.

"Oh, Mummy, thank you! That's too kind of you," Abbie said. She reached over and gave her mother a small hug.

"Do you like it?"

"I love it!" Abbie said.

"Perfect," Charlotte said. "Well, I've organized your monthly subscription so that you're highly discouraged from ever using my silk samples or interiors magazines again." She chuckled.

"I want you to know," Abbie said, swallowing hard, "I'm so sorry for ruining your samples again and for being so careless all the time. I really am so grateful for the education you've given me. I just hope you can still be proud of me, even if I want to be an artist."

Her shoulders shook with nerves. The fear of her mother's reaction felt like a dark cloud was circling her. And still, by even admitting it, the heaviness of it all seemed to dissipate a little.

"Don't dwell on that at all. You've been working so terribly hard these last few months. And now you've got this wonderful set of work to show for it. I am incredibly proud of you," Charlotte said. She sighed as she sat back and relaxed on the sofa. "I've never told you this, Abigail, but I had painted a couple of pieces of the landscape at Harpburgh and France years ago. And I can't quite remember what happened, but I simply lost account of them. Yet, the courage you've shown me in pursuing your art has been impressive, admirable even. It's giving me the itch to start painting again."

"Y-you've got to be joking," Abbie said, her eyes opening wide.

"Not in the slightest."

"You're an artist?"

"Well, that's a stretch," Charlotte said. "I haven't painted in years. But yes, I used to paint for much of my teenage years. But then I had children, and one thing led to another, and life just started to pass me by. These days I've gotten far too distracted with the renovations at Harpburgh. But your steadfastness has reminded me that I far prefer painting to interiors. I must take it up again."

"Wow." That was all that Abbie could manage to say. She leaned back next to Charlotte on the sofa. She looked up into her mother's tight-lipped but hopeful face. Above the clipped, done-up buttons of her beige blouse, Charlotte's eyes seemed to sparkle afresh. It all made sense now. Hoarding all the silk and carpet samples as if they were different shades in her paint palette. Her meticulous obsession with the interiors at Harpburgh had been her only creative outlet until now.

"The only decent paintings I ever did are in the attic here," Charlotte said. "I'll be sure to get them down."

"I'd love to see them," Abbie said.

"Now, what do we have here?" Charlotte said, pointing meekly at Abbie's sketchbook.

"Want to see?" Abbie said excitedly. "Yolly and Julie helped me put it all together this afternoon. It's my final portfolio for Collegiate."

Abbie was hit by a wave of exhaustion, but she forced herself to stay awake. She watched Charlotte flip through her sketchbook in a state of quiet contemplation. Her mother was not one for unabashed joy; her lip curved slightly into a smile. Yet Abbie could tell by the time Charlotte took to look at each composition that Abbie's work meant something to her. For her, the surprise was marred by years of confusion and disappointment. After all the times that Charlotte had shooed her away from drawing at the kitchen table and scolded her when Abbie came home from school with any remnants of creating something on her hands or in her fingernails. After all the times that Abbie had tried to make Charlotte a birthday card, only to throw it away because it wasn't perfect. Abbie had given up and given Charlotte nothing more than a quick handwritten note on a manicured card from Fortnum and Mason. The house was quiet and cold, yet, at that moment, Abbie felt a warm sense of pride coursing through her.

"How wonderful," Charlotte said, balancing the book carefully in her lap. "Darling, these compositions are simply exquisite!"

"Well, it would be exquisite," Abbie said in a low voice, "if I had time to finish it."

"Whatever do you mean?"

"Yolly and Julie did their best to help me, but it's still not done," Abbie said. Charlotte flicked through to the middle portion of the sketchbook, repositioning the loose cutouts neatly on their respective pages. "I have to bring it to my exams at Collegiate next Saturday. It's the most important part."

"Your compositions are quite *interesting* indeed," Charlotte said, eyeing her softly. "You simply must take time to finish it. You've done such an excellent job so far."

"How?" Abbie said, perplexed. "I've got school all week."

"Abigail," Charlotte said, "look at you! You're far too ill to go to school. I'll call Dr. Clark in the morning. You really must go see her—"

"No!"

"Why not?"

Abbie felt her heart pounding in her chest. She stared at her mother, her cheeks burning red hot. Her abdomen seared in pain. If Charlotte could appreciate her art, then perhaps there was more they were capable of sharing. If she didn't tell Charlotte what had happened to her now, she probably never would.

"Mummy?"

"Yes?"

"Here. Read this," Abbie said. "Just try not to freak out."

Abbie reached over. She found the slightly crumpled notepad on the floor next to the sofa. She flipped to the page where she had been writing her artist's statement. She handed it to her. Charlotte pulled her pink floral reading glasses out of her pocket and positioned them on the end of her nose. Abbie waited patiently for a grueling, drawn-out minute. Charlotte gasped. In that instant, Abbie knew that her mother's image of her had been shattered forever. As heart-wrenching as it was to see the tears form in Charlotte's eyes, Abbie tried to reassure herself. She had made the right choice. Charlotte's idea of her innocence would have to break eventually. Today was as good a day as any.

"The loss of a pregnancy? It can't be. Oh, my sweet angel," Charlotte cried, hugging her tightly. She cleared her throat and blinked back the tears, trying to distract from her weeping. "You poor thing. I simply can't imagine!"

"It's okay to cry, Mummy," Abbie said. She let her own tears swell. She let them drip down her nose and onto the soft folds of her pajamas.

"Oh heavens, my makeup will be in a state," Charlotte said. She dabbed her eyes with the palm of her hand. "For Christ's sake, where's the tissue box when you need it?"

Charlotte stood up in a huff and brought over the box of tissues from the mantelpiece. She drew one for Abbie and one for herself, blowing her nose profusely.

"On the bright side," Abbie said, "I was approved for the coil, which is a more effective birth control, so I won't have to worry about taking the pill. Once I'm better, I can go back to Dr. Clark, and she'll put it in. I just, like, don't want to go back to see her right now."

"I just wish you had never needed to go through this in the first place," Charlotte sniffled. "My dear little girl. Oh, it's too awful! I've failed as a mother. And all this to deal with right in the middle of exam season. How could I have been so negligent?"

"No!" Abbie said. "I have a boyfriend, and we were just being careless. It was my fault, really."

"You poor, poor thing," Charlotte whimpered. She stood up, gathering her composure. "Well, we must face the challenges at hand. Abigail, you should be resting in bed! You must be exhausted. Desperate times call for desperate measures. I'll write a letter to Agerton Hall saying we're going on a last-minute emergency family holiday to Sardinia. And rearrange my schedule for next Saturday. Harpburgh can wait. I'll drive you to the exams in the Mini."

"Th-that would be amazing. Thanks, Mum," Abbie said. She tried to sound earnest, but her head was heavy, and her eyes kept closing.

"You're very welcome, poppet." Charlotte smiled. "Up you get."

When Abbie tried to stand up, she almost buckled over in pain.

"Whoopsie daisies," Charlotte said, scrambling to half hoist Abbie onto her shoulders.

"H-how are you this s-strong?" Abbie said as Charlotte practically carried her up the stairs.

"My dear, I'm hardly idle during the week. Years of tennis and Pilates do come in handy from time to time," Charlotte said as they reached the landing. "Gosh, it's been about a decade since I could carry you up the stairs to the naughty corner."

Abbie sighed. Her body felt heavy and weak, relieved that those years of humiliation from her childhood were long behind her. Charlotte huffed, and her cheeks swelled pink as they reached the top floor.

"Thank you, Mum," Abbie said as Charlotte eased her onto her bed and covered her with her thick winter duvet.

"Gosh, there is a terrible draft up here. Let me turn on the heaters," Charlotte said. "Good night."

"Night," Abbie said. She relaxed into her fresh goose feather pillow.

30

That Saturday morning, Abbie sat in the passenger seat of Charlotte's Mini Cooper. They zipped hurriedly past the foggy playing fields and horse tracks of Hyde Park. The November morning was cold and blistery. In the gloom, Abbie could barely make out the great stone war memorials and the red wreaths of poppies that lined the edges of soldiers' tombs dedicated to the lives lost in WWI. They drove passed Buckingham Palace, where the Union Jacks lapped longingly against their flagpoles between the leafless branches of the trees of Green Park. Charlotte sped ahead through a light as it turned red, crossing through the tall black gates adorned with gold-painted crowns that marked the perimeter of St. James's Park. Abbie looked in the side mirror at the car door and checked that her sketchbook was safely secured in the backseat.

"How's your tummy?" Charlotte said, glancing at Abbie before she signaled left at the roundabout.

"It's okay. I took lots of painkillers. I should be fine for a few hours," Abbie said, hoping that repeating those words aloud would bring her comfort and confidence. Her hands were shaking. She had spent most of the week sleeping. The day's challenges loomed large ahead of her. She would have to muster up every ounce of her energy. So far, her fear, nervousness, and sheer terror were helping to energize her.

"Gosh, I've been so worried about you, poppet," Charlotte said. "But you can't believe how incredibly proud of you I am."

"Thank you, Mum. That's very kind of you to say," Abbie said. She glanced at her mother. The sleeves of Charlotte's light pink cardigan were folded evenly over the cuffs of her white shirt, topped with pearl cuff links to match. Her mother's limp hair was pushed back by a perfectly centered velvet headband. Charlotte was nothing what Abbie had imagined an artistic mother to be, but she was grateful for her, nonetheless. Charlotte was far from perfect, but Abbie reckoned with herself. She was lucky to have a mother at all.

"Your support means the world to me. I know it probably wasn't your first choice for me, but now I know where I got my creativity."

"Yes, it makes a good deal of sense now, doesn't it?" Charlotte smiled, assured. "Yet it's gotten me thinking. I've hatched an idea to paint a mural of Provence in the Green Room at Harpburgh. I'm sure Mama would love it. It's a slightly daunting task, as the wall is rather large. But last night, I picked up a small charcoal pencil and started sketching what it might look like. I only wish I'd had the courage at your age—"

"Or the stubbornness," Abbie corrected her.

"One might say so, yes," Charlotte said. She grinned with a twinkle in her eye.

Charlotte pulled up to a large hall across the street from St. Peter's Collegiate School. Hundreds of students were filing into the building, waving goodbye to anxious parents.

Charlotte went on,

"Now, you've simply got to focus on the task in front of you. Answer the question that they ask and nothing else. You have a tendency to wander off topic, so try to avoid veering off into la-la land as much as possible."

"I will," Abbie said. As much as Charlotte's lecturing could irritate her, there was no doubt in her mind that this time, her mother was right.

"Best of luck, darling," Charlotte said, hugging her as they got out of the car. "If you're feeling ill at all, or your tummy's upset, please just telephone me. I'll have my mobile on me all day. I'm not leaving Clarendon Road, I promise."

"Thanks, Mum," Abbie said. She let herself be hugged. She took in as much of Charlotte's frantic yet well-meaning energy as she could. Charlotte carried her sketchbook to the entrance of the building as Abbie walked slowly and calmly. Charlotte handed it to her.

"Good luck. You can do this, Abigail. I know you can."

Abbie nodded. She managed a small wave as Charlotte subtly blew her a kiss from the car.

Then she climbed the stairs into the vast exam hall alone. Inside, thousands of desks were laid out before her. She tried not to look at the endless rows upon rows of applicants taking their seats.

"You have sixty minutes for your first subject," a short, sandy-blond-haired man with a stern lip and round glasses barked across the room. Papers rustled. The odd cough, or worse, a sneeze, reverberated around the room's ocean of nerves. Abbie didn't dare look up to count how many people were in that room. She was already battling enough thoughts of worthlessness. How many of them had been reckless enough to end up in A&E only a week ago? How many of them had ever been pregnant? That thought alone made her shudder. She rushed through the Maths questions, solving unknown x's and y's. She calculated the hypotenuses of coordinates along a plane. All seemed solvable. All seemed well until she came to the last question.

Prove the volume of a sphere is $4/3pir^3$.

Abbie stalled. Heaves of stress washed away her focus. The timer ran out. Her mind was a blur. They took the first papers away. Then the pain of her two subsequent papers: History and English. She barely stumbled through them. She kicked herself repeatedly. She had not finished that last Maths question. She had not done her best. There were so many people in that exam hall. Surely, there were hundreds who were better than her. There was no hope of getting in now. Perhaps she would be better off simply dropping out and being homeschooled or going to DLD, the school for druggies, losers, and dropouts. That was where she belonged. After all this hard work, it was as if the blaring lights had been turned on at the end of a party, and Abbie was left with nowhere to hide.

After the English exam, Abbie felt defeated. She left the great hall, lugging her sketchbook along with her. She sighed in the chilled winter air as the other applicants barged far ahead of her. The cloistered entrance to the Art building was around the corner, beyond Dean's Yard. It was a worn Victorian building with a checkered stone floor. Abbie sheepishly left her sketchbook with a group of teachers for them to review before her interview.

Just as she left the building, Abbie saw a swish of white hair and round, red-rimmed glasses striding towards her. She admired his black overalls and flowing, blue linen shirt, topped with a peppermint-striped blazer. She almost swallowed her tongue; she was so nervous.

"Hello, sir," Abbie said almost instinctively.

Mr. Grouse peered at her through his glasses. Clearly, he didn't have the faintest clue who she was. Abbie immediately regretted saying anything to him at all. She bundled up warmer in her coat and headed back out into the biting November wind. She found a Pret A Manger nearby, where she popped more painkillers and ate a warm ham and cheese croissant. The food warmed her up a bit, but her nerves were still as gritty and grinding as ever. She kept checking the time on her phone. At last, bang on the dot at 1:00 p.m., she returned to the Victorian building and gently climbed the stairs.

St. Peter's Collegiate School's art studio was warm and heavenly despite the washed grey sky outside. The room was expansive and adorned with studio lights. Petals of plaster flowers christened the ceiling. They illuminated paintings and sculptures and shelves of pallets and sinks and workbenches stained with clay. Abbie smelt the pungent concoction of oil paint and turpentine, moving into the damp earthiness of the clay as if each part of the studio was its own separate universe devoted to one craft or another.

Mr. Grouse sat on a stool in the center of the room. He flipped the mop of his hair to one side as he handled the pages of her sketchbook.

"Miss Chesterton?"

"Y-yes," Abbie said.

"Please, do sit down."

He motioned to a stool on the opposite side of the table. Abbie walked as if her pace was intentionally slow. She was determined not to hobble in front of him. She took her seat. Mr. Grouse muttered away to himself as he fumbled through the pages. He had pulled out the piece of paper with her handwritten artist's statement and seemed to be comparing it to her work. Abbie waited patiently.

"Brilliant…marvelous…indeed…"

Abbie frowned.

"D-do you like it?"

"Do I *like* it?" Mr. Grouse said. The ends of his sentences trilled like the dappling of a concert piano. "What a sensationally ridiculous concept. Do I *like* Francis Bacon's paintings of the inside of a sheep spilled everywhere? Shall good art only be what we subjectively *like*?"

Abbie gulped.

"I don't know," she said.

Mr. Grouse pushed his round red frames to the bridge of his nose and clasped his hands together. A few strands of his hair got in the way, and he attempted to bat them away again. He leaned towards her.

"I'm going to be frank with you. Your portfolio is sensational. Absolutely sensational. The progression, the color pattern, your attention to subtle details, the abstraction of the forms, and the palette throughout. It's marvelous."

Abbie's heart thumped loudly in her chest. Her entire body was coursing with excitement.

"There's just one huge gaping problem I can see," Mr. Grouse sighed.

"W-what's that?" Abbie said, trying to curb her exasperation.

"Your artist's statement shows that you've missed the purpose of the assignment entirely."

Abbie stared at him blankly. She thought of all the painstaking hours she had put into perfecting her statement. Her excitement was being crookedly and drastically dismantled.

"I'm not sure I understand—"

"You say here, quite wonderfully, 'In my portfolio, I explore the fragility of life, based on my own experiences with pregnancy and miscarriage.' That part is poignant, pressing, profound even. Yet then it goes south quite quickly. 'My inspiration comes from Yayoi Kusama and her pursuit of abstract forms as a lone, creative genius. It is Kusama's isolation and depression that most inspire me.' Hello, barefaced misguidance!" Mr. Grouse said. He clapped his hand on his heart, shaking his head. "What an absolute train wreck of an idea."

"What exactly do you mean?" Abbie said, trying to be polite.

"My dear, Miss Chesterton. Have you ever researched the life of Yayoi Kusama?"

"I…um…"

"Evidently not. You see, you're off here by a factor of about 180 degrees. Have you never heard of Eva Hesse?"

Abbie shrugged.

"What about Donald Judd? Joseph Cornell? Not even Georgia O'Keeffe?"

Abbie shook her head. Her cheeks lashed hot with embarrassment.

"A simple search of a wiki, or dare I say it, a flick through an actual encyclopedia, would completely dispel the myth of the creative genius that you seem so dead set on perpetuating," Mr. Grouse explained. "Sure, Kusama is a solo artist. But do you think she has never interacted with another art-producing human? Is her art created in a vacuum? Heavens, no! Judd, Cornell, Hesse, and O'Keeffe were her closest advisors, friends, confidants, comrades, companions. Comprende?"

"I think so—" Abbie looked at him, confused.

"The point is, my dear: All art is in the influences. Not a single piece of good art was ever created alone. The myth of the creative genius is precisely that: a myth."

Mr. Grouse scratched his chin.

"So, who are your influences? Who's sunk their creative teeth into you?"

Abbie paused. Her mind dipped back to when she had accidentally spilled an entire jar of ink over one of Julie's drawings in their Art lesson. "My friend Julie and I always sit together in Art. She's super good at drawing and wants to be a fashion designer. And she helped me with the composition of the tulips at the end there."

"Indeed, that piece at the end there, of the tulips themselves, is by far the strongest," Mr. Grouse said. "A fashionista friend. Wonderful!"

"And my housekeeper, Yolly. She's the one who got me interested in Art in the first place. I used to make birthday cards for her. She loved them, and she still has a couple of them. Whenever I do art at home, she makes sure I'm wearing a smock and that I put newspaper down in the kitchen so I don't get watercolors everywhere."

"Brilliant."

"And my mother, Charlotte. She's kind of uptight and wouldn't call herself an artist, but she used to paint. She's very good at picking out interiors. And she might have a pretty cool idea for a mural soon."

"Fascinating. Fantastic."

Abbie paused another moment longer before she continued,

"And I would say the last person that influenced my art is my boyfriend. But he was the one who believes in the whole myth of the creative genius."

"It doesn't matter. The boy is wrong," Mr. Grouse said blandly, "and what troubles me more is that I don't see acknowledgments of these influences anywhere. Not even your lovely fashionista friend who assisted you in the tulip composition."

Mr. Grouse unstuck the last pages and examined the final composition once more.

"It's incredibly moving. The loss of innocence. The promise of life and then having it ripped away from you. And yet, she doesn't even get as much of a signature or a dedication."

"I'm…sorry?"

"Don't apologize to me," Mr. Grouse said. "Apologize to her! I'm simply exhausted by the prospect of these one-man, one-woman, one-human-being bands. You think Shakespeare wrote *The Complete Works* all on his own, did you? Every last word of it? God no. He had an entire army of playwrights, mostly anonymous women forgotten by the sand granules of history working for him. I simply refuse to have such self-serving narcissists as my students."

"I understand," Abbie said. "And for what it's worth, I'd be honored to be in your class. But, um, I completely understand if that's out of the question."

"Yes, it is hard to say," Mr. Grouse continued. "Talking the talk is quite a different assignment from walking the walk. In any case, Miss Chesterton, it's been a pleasure. We shall see what the future holds. And if it is not a bright one, I wish you many a silver lining in your clouds."

Mr. Grouse slipped her artist's statement back into her sketchbook. He closed it and pushed it towards her.

"Thank you," Abbie said. She gingerly took it under her arm and stood up to go. "I'm very grateful for your time and consideration."

"Indeed, I hope you are. I'll never get those minutes back," Mr. Grouse said, already flipping through another applicant's sketchbook.

Abbie nodded meekly, a little shaken. She let herself slouch as she left the room. Her belly was beginning to cramp again. Gripping her sketchbook tightly, she left the radiance of the art studio and Mr. Grouse's prying eyes behind her.

31

Abbie sat next to Jonah at the Thanksgiving table. The Woods' home smelt like cinnamon and baked apple pie. The square dining table was off-center in the rectangular room. It gave her the feeling of being unbalanced. Candles of different heights flickered along the mantelpiece, their flames reflecting in the stained mirror. The table was laid with pine branches, pomegranates, and cherries as if a tiny deer might prance across it at any moment. There was a ginormous turkey, a steaming mound of vegetables, a jar of mayonnaise the size of a jug, and unidentifiable dishes with bubbled brown surfaces that were slightly burnt on top.

Abbie was trying to use all the polished tools Charlotte had given her for society's toolbox: her politeness, her feigned interest in other people's lives, and her compliments on whatever she was about to eat. But it was no match for Jonah's biting silence. If he could just put his hand on her leg, that would remind her that everything was all right. If he could just afford her a couple of inches of comfort. The buttons of Jonah's olive-colored shirt were strained down the center of his chest. The acne on his chin was flaring up again. Sporadic patches of gingery hairs lined his cheeks, limp like those of a young billy goat. His imperfections were hers. And she loved them. He might have been scowling and grumpy, but she knew he loved her.

"Hey," Abbie whispered to him as the cranberry relish was passed around the table.

Jonah waved at her dismissively. It felt like a tiny stab, a slit in her heart.

"I was almost a professional football player," Clive said as he stuck his fork into a large triangle of brie and ate it. The thin metallic frames of Clive's glasses dug along the sides of his face.

"Dad, you haven't kicked a ball since your Little League team in 1970," Jonah said. He could talk to them, but not her, Abbie noticed. Their laughter swelled in her ears like the pounds of a deafening drum ringing through her. The conversation turned to a competition of opinions between whose Thanksgiving dishes were better: Kat's or Aunt Sarah's. Aunt Sarah lived on Long Island, and Hunter had chosen to spend the holiday with that side of their family. Abbie found herself shrinking away at the table. She didn't care for the details of people she didn't know and would probably never meet.

"Pass me your plate, honey. You gotta try these yams," Kat said to her. She took a giant spatula and shoveled stringy golden-brown lumps of sweet potato onto Abbie's plate. A sticky white texture oozed out from them between the layers. Marshmallows for dinner. Charlotte would never have allowed such a thing.

As Abbie picked at it with her fork, the metal clanged against the promise ring on her finger. The buttery sweetness of the yams hit her tongue like her mouth had been filled with a fountain of syrup. The pleasantries of Jonah's family were quietly mocking her. In a room full of people, she had never felt so stranded and separate. It was as if she was watching the dinner party play out from afar. She felt like a fool. She wanted Jonah to look at her.

Abbie put her hand on his knee. Immediately, Jonah's face sank. He was frowning again. Why was he always frowning? Why did he never make her laugh? The mess of yams in her mouth had disintegrated. She swallowed them, digesting her feelings along with them.

Next came dessert. Pecan pie with melted caramel, the very essence of the sugar globules stuck together. Abbie could only eat a small forkful at a time. She watched Clive assemble a mountain of pie and drench it in cream, his large hand fumbling with the dessert fork, his body towering over the small saucer.

"How did your Collegiate exams go?" Kat asked her.

"Okay," Abbie said. "I haven't got my hopes up."

"Well, as long as you did your best, that's something you can be proud of," Kat said, her eyes twinkling.

Abbie nodded meekly.

"J, honey, why don't you two watch a film downstairs?" Kat asked as David and Mark tied away the plates.

"I want to watch *Enter the Void*," Jonah snapped, "but Abbie won't watch it. She hates movies."

Abbie glared at him. He was digging things up, itching for her reaction so she would humiliate herself in front of his family.

"I'm fine to watch it if you want to," she said.

"It's fine," Jonah said. His negative energy spewed like poisoned vapor into the room. The room was silent. Abbie stared at the table.

"Oh, rats! I forgot to give Moonshine his dinner," Kat said. She left the room, and when she returned, she was wearing her feathered turquoise cleaning gloves up to her elbows.

"Lookee, the pecan went quick this year," Kat said cheerfully.

Jonah smiled briefly at his mother. Then he turned to Abbie and said,

"I guess you want to go home, then?"

"Jonah, I—"

"Just stop pretending that you want to be here."

"Fine."

Abbie stood up, and what was left of the cutlery clanged lightly on the table. Jonah stared at her sullenly. It seemed that part of him wanted her to fight for them. But he also wanted her to fall apart in front of him.

"Thank you for a wonderful dinner, Kat," Abbie said, heading for the door.

"You're welcome, sweetie. So great to have you, as usual," Kat replied.

Abbie found her coat in the entryway.

Jonah grabbed his jacket next to hers. "You know I love movies. I thought you could just do this one thing for me. But I guess I was wrong."

Abbie's chest tightened, yet she had to admit it to herself. She liked Jonah's brown lambskin overcoat. She liked his smell. They stood in the darkened hallway. The door to the TV room was open. Clive was already watching the horse racing. The weight of the house seemed to suffocate her. She had to get out. She had to leave.

Outside on the street, the Victorian streetlamps glowed orange in the coldness of the winter evening. Abbie could see the water vapor in her breath. It was like she was a dragon, breathing out hateful words that neutralized as they hit the air. The street was quiet and empty, except for a brisk-looking man in a suit walking his dog. Once they had passed him silently, Jonah said,

"I can't believe you just sat through the whole of dinner with my parents like everything is fine."

"Why are you being so mean to me?" Abbie cried, walking ahead of him. "You literally have no idea what I've been through these last few weeks. And you're behaving like a fucking five-year-old. I am so sick of you. Get away from me." Her throat swelled up. She tried to blink back the angry tears.

"Shouldn't I be able to walk you home? As your boyfriend?" Jonah protested. He trudged behind her, his pace slower and more deliberate than usual. His black suede boots clicked along the pavement.

"Come here," he said. He grabbed her by the wrist. Abbie stopped walking. She wept to herself quietly, gently, as she let herself be taken back in by him. They stood face-to-face. He took both her hands.

"Can I kiss you?" he asked her.

Abbie nodded.

Jonah steadied her. He gripped her waist. He pressed his lips to hers. He breathed out childishly like he had never kissed her before. Abbie let herself be kissed. Suddenly things felt so easy. They could love each other.

Abbie pulled away from him. She looked searchingly into his light brown eyes. In their reflection, she wanted to see their future together. But she could hardly breathe through the pain. Her tears came ceaselessly. She imagined them walking hand in hand down an alleyway in New York, Jonah holding a bag of baked goodies from an upscale market, some fresh breads and pâtés, and the kinds of spreads that adults ate along with their coffee on the weekends. She imagined them making love in the endless pillows of their shared bed in a high-reaching Manhattan apartment, the dappled lights of the city sprinkled out below them. She imagined herself crafting her next masterpiece as Jonah sat across the room from her at his writing desk, typing out his new screenplay on a typewriter, which he preferred, he said, because the serif font and the repetitive noise of the keys inspired him to feel like he was in Hollywood in the 1950s, postwar when all the best movies were made. She imagined standing beside him and his parents as he wore that American-style cap and gown on the day of his graduation from Columbia. She imagined herself running her fingers along dusty covers in a secondhand bookstore in Manhattan as he handed her a copy of Karl Marx's biography. She imagined them dressed up, finding their seats along the red-cushioned rows in the opera, Jonah whispering something in her ear, and her grinning. She imagined him pouring her a shot glass of floral-smelling sake at a Japanese bar, the pale woodwork, the wall of brightly colored bottles of alcohol, and the surrounding crowds jumbled up all around them in the tiny room. Yet they were so enraptured by each other that they wouldn't notice. Their life together, she could feel, was there, right in front of her. If he could just, if she could just, if they could just…

But when Abbie looked more closely, there was no hint of her in Jonah's eyes. There was just the boy, the man he was becoming, staring back at her. With his clammy palms and his endless temper and his smoking and his stubbornness and his biting opinions about

everything. With his lack of laughter and his condemnation of her
control of her own body. The withdrawn, isolated, depressed life he
wanted them to live together, and all the sobering conversations planning their future that he wanted them to have. Their future together
appeared to her beautiful and bright. But, somehow, it was only a
dream. No matter how much she wanted it to be.

"Let's go," Jonah said.

He took her hand and led her around the corner of Clarendon
Road. He lit a cigarette. Jonah smiled as he smoked, seemingly satisfied that he was trampling on something that mattered to her, yet she
was still here with him. He must have thought he was gaining
ground.

They stopped outside Abbie's house. The lights were on in the
basement. Abbie peered more closely inside. Yolly was watching a
Korean drama as she did her ironing. Abbie was slowly, gently
flooded with warmth at the sight of her. Within a moment, her heart
felt full. She leaned her head on Jonah's shoulder, breathing in the
fumes of his cigarette, trying one last time to find that comfort in
him. The clinging ash heaved in her chest. It spoke to her. It said
what she had seemingly known all along. She had to get out of her
own way. She looked up at him. The thought, the feeling, was on the
tip of her tongue. She took the promise ring off her finger. She
placed it in the palm of his hand.

"I can't do this anymore," Abbie said, fighting back the tears.
"I'm sick of pushing everyone away from me so we can chase some
messed-up, tormented idea of being creative geniuses together."

"What the hell are you talking about?" Jonah said.

"I hate who I am when I'm with you," Abbie said. "I hate
feeling so isolated from everyone. Like I'm better than them. Did
you know that I've treated the people who love and care about me
like shit for most of my life? Maybe they're not the most intellectual people ever. Maybe they're not the most creative. But they
care about me, whether or not I'm the next Mozart or Van Gogh.
They deserve a lot more from me, and I've got a lot to do to give
them that. But every day with you, it's like we have to turn

everyone away and go be hermits in Walden, like Henry David Thoreau. You know that's a fucking myth, right? I read about it on Wikipedia. Thoreau completely made up this whole image of being alone in the woods. Did you know his mum and his sister came to give him doughnuts on the weekend? And he was living on his friend's land? And his aunt paid his taxes for him? But no, you believe that shit. Every day with you, it's like us against the fucking world. This last month with you has been nothing but hell."

"Is this about the tattoos thing? Or am I somehow failing for being honest with you about the life that I want for us?" Jonah said, stubbing out his cigarette. "Finlay and Griff were right. You don't love me. If you did, you'd be willing to make sacrifices. That is what people who love each other do."

"Finlay and Griff?" Abbie spat at him. "Oh, and I guess if they told you to jump off a cliff, you'd do that, too? I did love you. I kind of still do. But you've been nothing but a selfish, stupid prick. And you have no idea what the fuck my body has been through because you wouldn't wear a condom."

Jonah lit another cigarette.

"Will you just calm down? The entire of Notting Hill will hear you!"

"I will not just fucking calm down," Abbie said, her fury ripping through her like a storm. "I got fucking pregnant, okay? A fucking ectopic pregnancy. And I almost fucking died. And all you can do is stand there smoking, folding your stupid fucking arms, and throwing a tantrum. And then kiss me after treating me like shit and pretending everything is going to be magically better. Your libertarian view of the world is complete bollocks. The things you've done have really, really hurt me, and you can't even acknowledge it."

"I can't believe you're throwing this all in my face like it's my fault. Are you even telling the truth? How can I know?" Jonah said.

"You think I'd make something like that up? How sick and twisted are you? I will never forgive you for that. We are never having sex again. Ever."

Jonah opened the pocket of his coat. He slipped the promise ring inside of it and patted it sarcastically.

"It's over," he said.

The basement door opened. Yolly called worriedly up the stairs,

"Miss Abbie? Are you in trouble? I will call the police—"

"Thank you, Yolly. He's just leaving," Abbie said. She glanced at Jonah. She was shaking. But her breaths were steady.

Jonah threw his half-smoked cigarette onto the pavement. He turned around and walked away. Abbie opened the gate and headed down into the basement. She didn't care to stay to watch Jonah fade away from her, trailing off into the distance. As she descended the stone steps, she caught sight of his cigarette. A trail of grey smoke rose from its tip, burning amber and umber against the dampness of the pavement.

"Come in, Miss Abbie. It's so cold," Yolly said. She shut the door behind her.

32

A couple of days later, Abbie arrived home from school. Charlotte opened the door.

"Hello, darling," Charlotte said.

Abbie hung up her coat and hugged her mother.

"Hello, Mummy. How was your day?"

They made their way into the living room. Charlotte had transformed the side table next to the fireplace into a makeshift studio. Balancing against the wall on top of the table was a crisp, neat canvas. Charlotte had pulled it out of the attic. Abbie smiled at the perfectly manicured clouds, rolling hillsides, and sheep fleeces that Charlotte had painted. She expected nothing less than her mother's immaculate attention to detail, even when painting something as wild as the English countryside. On the table were wide pieces of paper and a single mechanical pencil.

"Wonderful, my dear," Charlotte said. "Thank you for asking. I quite lost track of time after I began to sketch. It's almost time for tea!"

Abbie surprised Yolly in the kitchen, hugging her from behind.

"Gosh, Miss Abbie! You give me such a fright. I almost spilled all the chicken soup. Please go wash your hands."

"Okay," Abbie said.

She washed her hands at the kitchen sink and began to set the table.

"D-darling?"

"Yes?"

"A letter arrived for you in the mail," Charlotte said, coming to stand beside the Aga stove.

Abbie turned around. Charlotte glanced over her floral reading glasses at a thin, white envelope resting on the countertop. It was thick enough to only contain a single sheet of paper. Yolly had salvaged it before it got lost in the mountain of Richard's post by the front door. Abbie dried her hands on a tea towel and picked up the letter. As she examined it, her fingers felt disconnected from her body. On the top right-hand corner of the envelope was a red first-class stamp of the Queen's silhouette, interrupted by a smudged scribble with the date. It was addressed to:

Abigail Chesterton
173 Clarendon Road
W11 4HK
London

Her heart sped up as she read the return address. All the hours Abbie had poured into her portfolio and her exams had culminated at this moment. Her efforts had dripped like mortar binding bricks in a wall built months ago. It felt like they were from another lifetime.

Charlotte stared at her vacantly. Yolly stood calmly just over Abbie's shoulder.

"Whatever happens," Charlotte said, sighing nervously, "there'll be no putting your talent to waste. You've found your passion. You'll have to work very hard, but your father and I are behind your success completely. There's nothing to worry about."

"Thanks, Mum," Abbie said.

"The Lord is watching over you," Yolly said, signing the Holy Trinity, "I know it."

"Thank you, Yolly."

Abbie took a deep breath. Her fingers slipped easily between the glued folds of the paper, revealing the blue checkered office pattern on the inside of the envelope beneath. The paper inside was a cream-colored card that could have been used as an invitation to a wedding or a banquet. She began to read,

"'Dear Abigail Chesterton, After a highly selective application process, we are delighted to offer you a place at St. Peter's Collegiate School for sixth form beginning September 2011'—I got in!" Abbie exclaimed, her hands shaking.

"Well done, fabulous girl!" Yolly said.

"Heavens!" Charlotte shot up straight, rubbing her on the back. "That is really well done, Abigail. Congratulations. You'll be only a stone's throw away from Oxford now. Simply marvelous!" She repositioned her reading glasses on her nose, then said, "Excuse me," taking the letter absentmindedly as she got up from the table. "I'll just call Richard to tell him the good news. We'll have to have dinner at the Ledbury to celebrate!"

Abbie smiled as she pictured herself fashioning a new collage from a copy of *Grafik* magazine. Mr. Grouse's wide-eyed smile. She imagined herself studying late in the library, being challenged in the classes that were more like ongoing political debates, and walking the cloisters to the abbey, where she would decipher the gravestones of admirals and scientists and prime ministers and poets of the past. But how would she face seeing Jonah every day at school? Not to mention Finlay and Griff and Charles Barry? Was Collegiate really where she belonged?

As her future at Collegiate emerged, her other future crumbled to the ground. The future she had planned with Jonah, she was only just beginning to let herself feel, was being broken down into ruins. She typed out a longer BBM and shortened it before she sent it to him.

Abbie Chesterton: I got into Collegiate. Thank you for all your help.

He responded a couple of minutes later.

Jonah M. Wood: I knew you could do it. Congrats.

Abbie Chesterton: Will it be awkward? Seeing you at school?

Jonah M. Wood: It won't be. I'll make sure of it :)

It was a sweet thing for him to say. It was as if they were still together, as if he still cared about her. She had been trying not to think about Jonah every day, but she did care about how he was. She had loved rolling up into his arms while they were in bed together. She was strong enough, she thought to herself, to admit that she missed him.

Abbie Chesterton: How are you?

Jonah M. Wood: Not too bad.

Another minute passed before his next message.

Jonah M. Wood: I'm sorry for not believing you. I should have trusted you.

Abbie Chesterton: Apology accepted. I'm sorry too, for not telling you sooner.

Jonah M. Wood: I'll never forget what we had together. And I miss your kisses already.

Abbie Chesterton: I'll never forget you either.

33

Abbie made it to Holland Park station on a Saturday morning. The turnstile made a familiar string of beeps as she swiped her Oyster card, and the grey barriers briefly opened. She slipped through them in a daze. Light peeked through the Victorian windows of the station. Abbie descended the long staircase to the train, passing a wall of hundreds of sea-green and brown-glazed tiles. The station was humid and suffocating. As she breathed it in, Abbie felt light-headed.

Down the spiral staircase she went. She heard pipes dripping and the low rumbling of the train as it sped towards the station. She broke into a run. She could not miss this train. Not after she had seen pictures of Jonah on Facebook, of all places, a platform whose existence he had always denied, in pictures with Moriah Shepherd. She had stalked Moriah on Facebook, then tried to suppress her feelings by playing two hours of *Brick Breaker* on her phone. Abbie turned the corner at the base of the stairs and heard the whooshing of the train doors opening. She stumbled down the last flight. The doors whooshed again. She boarded the train, the doors slamming shut behind her. She caught her breath in a quiet personal moment of glory before she sat down amongst the indifferent faces of the other passengers.

Jonah would have wanted to go to this exhibition with her. They would have held hands on the platform. He would have said,

"The surrealists were just sadomasochists on acid, but nobody wants to admit it," or something as ridiculous and controversial as that. When Abbie played over her memories with him, it felt like every inch of air was being punched out of her. Then when she thought she had no breath left, it was like she had been hit in the chest again. She had been emptied and hollowed out, thin and fragile. Slowly, in her own time, she had begun to heal. Still, Abbie sniffled. She looked up at the people around her. Their silence haunted her. She drew a long, deep breath in.

As the tube stations passed her, Abbie was desperate to go back to that time when she was younger, when the worst thing that could happen to her was scraping her knee or not being able to bring Bluey, her cuddly bear toy, to school with her. She would pick physical pain over pain like this any day. But that was years ago now. Now it was the destruction of her future and the images in her mind of the boy she had loved cradling his new girlfriend, kissing her, smiling, caressing her body.

A couple sat across from her. Abbie tried not to look at them. The man had his feet firmly on the floor, whereas the woman leaned on him slightly. They seemed to be friendly, simply sitting next to each other. It was only at the next stop, when new passengers boarded the train at Marble Arch, that Abbie saw the man slip his hand behind the woman's back and gently pull her closer to him.

The wind was knocked out of her lungs again. She closed her eyes and focused hard, trying to catch her sobs like bubbles as they flew away from her into the air before the other passengers noticed. She did her best to breathe through the tears.

"You're an artist," Jonah had said to her while they lay spooning together in his single bed. "You're going to create things that this world has never seen." He had seen the beautiful, honest side of her. The daring side that the world of Oxford academics and parents' expectations and GCSE exams had tried to remove from her. He'd seen in her what she had never been able to see in herself. Talent. Boldness. Love. Well, at least now she knew that those parts of her existed. Perhaps they had always been there. Perhaps Jonah had helped them to emerge. But now that they were hers to keep and nurture.

Abbie changed trains at Bond Street and got off at Green Park. She passed under the awnings of the shops as it started to drizzle. She passed the old-fashioned hunting gear shops with the plaid, tweed, and paisley attire, the knee-high socks, garters, and brown boots. There were the cigar shops and the cane shops, with old wooden facades and boxes of straw and fine cheese in the windows. There were the shaving shops, where sponges and brushes puffed between bottles of cologne. There was a shoe shop that had existed, it said, since 1546. It was the same view of Piccadilly, the luxury and pomp she had visited so many months ago with Jonah. But her experience of it, and seeing it through her eyes only, made the feeling of being there completely different.

Abbie had come to Piccadilly alone. She was walking down the street, making her own way. She felt like the captain of a ship, with her own vast, billowing sails. Except that, well, as she passed Fortnum and Mason and saw the familiar, opulent berry and biscuit arrangements in the windows, she felt that tug in her body again, down the middle next to her heart.

She had hoped to have buttoned up her feelings by now, to have wrapped it all up in a neat little package and shipped it off, far away for someone else to receive in the post and have to open and deal with. But she was still here in London, accidentally retracing the steps they had taken together when they were so in love. Or perhaps it was because Abbie had found out that Moriah Shepherd went to Francis Holland School near Baker Street, and Moriah was from Wales and was definitely heavier and less pretty than her. Perhaps Moriah would fulfill Jonah's dreams of early marriage, of moving to New York, of having kids. She wondered if he had brought Moriah around to watch *Enter the Void* with him. She wondered if Moriah had met David, Mark, Clive, Kat, Moonshine, Hunter or Aunt Sarah. Abbie wondered when Moriah would meet Jonah's old Jewish aunties in North London. She wondered how long they would stay together. If Moriah, Jonah's new girlfriend, was the permanent one who would be with him until the end of their lives. Would love Jonah. Would care for him. It was a bitter pill to swallow. But a girl from Wales? How did that fit into his picture of living in New York?

Abbie sent Julie a BBM.

Abbie Chesterton: CODE RED. Jonah's got a new girl. I want to die xxx

Julie messaged her back immediately.

Julie Louchart: Holy fuckbungles. Phish food in the freezer. Come over at 7:30 and bring anything that reminds you of him. It's bonfire time xxx

Abbie Chesterton: Sounds brilliant. You're the bestest, Julie xxx

Abbie sighed, relieved. She found a new spring in her step. She would reclaim these streets as her own. She would come here again, many times if she had to, on her own or with friends or with new lovers. To paint over any hint of Jonah in her life with new memories. Lather over the trodden earth with a new civilization until the old ruins of their relationship had been washed to sediment. Until there was no trace of him left in her. That was the only way to wash away something that still felt so permanent and stuck to her.

At least, Abbie thought, it wasn't all bad. As she entered the Royal Academy, she placed her hand softly on her lower belly. She had gotten her coil put in a couple of weeks earlier, and Dr. Clark had promised that it would last for five years. It was Abbie's small way of commanding the direction of the universe, of controlling her own life. She could look concerned teachers and adults in the eye and know that she had a secret up her sleeve. Especially in case some new boy came along, walking down the street or bumping into her at a party. And they were to romantically embrace and fall into the best sex of her life. That was a real possibility, she imagined. Abbie smiled to herself at the idea of it.

She reached the gallery. She passed under the arches of the Royal

Academy, with complex patterns carved into the limestone facades, and through black-painted wrought iron doors decorated with gold-painted flowers. Inside the quieter, cobbled courtyard, groups of drifting pilgrims loyal to the arts gathered under the cloisters to shelter from the rain. Abbie looked up at the building. Something new stood out to her. It gave her the most unsettling feeling. It was the first time she had noticed that the stone figures along the front of the gallery were all men. She vaguely recognized the era of their clothing. She read the names at the bases of each plinth. Rousseau, Epicurus, Wren, and Locke. The statue in the middle of the square was of a man in a wig and a buttoned-up shirt, with a slight potbelly, his right hand raised, holding a long sticklike thing as if he was painting in the air. Abbie frowned. Where were the statues of women? Where were the female artists and philosophers and astronomers and theorists? And those from other parts of the world, beyond England? She didn't know.

Abbie bought a ticket from a smiling receptionist. She climbed the carpeted stairs to the entrance of the Salvador Dalí exhibition. An attendant opened a wooden door with glass panes and a silver handle. Abbie stepped into the dimly lit gallery. The room was quiet. The air was fresh with varnished wood and the fashioned leather of the flattened benches in the center of the room. A low fan rumbled, circulating the inspired thoughts and pauses of curiosity of those who passed through the room like polite ghosts. Still, the floorboards creaked. A brass-fashioned lamp illuminated each painting, like the lights of an anglerfish, as if the paintings themselves were skulking through the darkness on the ocean floor.

Abbie admired Dalí's attention to detail in his oil paintings on wood, yet she felt that they were too small to fully enjoy. She passed between canvases of repulsive limbs and distorted bodies in a vague state of indifference. The questionable human body parts alienated her because, firstly, she was not sure what they were, and secondly, she did not know what she was supposed to feel when she looked at them. She dawdled between rooms, more interested in how the color of the walls changed from navy to maroon to navy than in the paintings themselves. She had only been there some fifteen minutes before she got the feeling that she was ready to leave.

Just as she headed for the exit, Abbie noticed a much larger painting in the corner of the room. She hesitated. Okay, fine, she thought. She had come all this way. She might as well make the effort to walk across the room to see it. Its size, more than anything, intrigued her. Once she reached it, the image instantly captivated her.

It was a portrait of a woman. She was the central focus of the painting, behind which unfolded a tumultuous background of windswept mountains, dry earth, and smooth white horses, hollow like phantoms below a vibrant blue sky kissed intermittently by clouds. Yet Abbie gazed directly at the woman. She was, perhaps, in her early sixties. She wore a yellow floral calico dress with a light pink cardigan and a pearl necklace. She was sitting calmly with her hands in her lap. Her hair was brown but greying, tied up in a loose bun. Her pale skin was wrinkled as if it spoke of years of her experiences. Perhaps the extremes of pain and loss, but also joy that she had witnessed.

Abbie focused on her expression. Her subtle smile and blue eyes reflected the sky, staring out enduringly at something above Abbie's head. It was an expression of constancy, generosity, of a loving mother, of an honest, independent character, as if all the shallows and depths of her life had been stenciled into her cheekbones. They made up the face that was aging gradually.

Abbie's heart sped up as she stepped closer to the painting. Her eyes zoomed in to take in every brushstroke of the woman's face. Her thoughts were racing. All that she could see and think and feel was that the image of this woman: it was her. Abbie. It was her future self, staring back at her. Her eyes carried the years of life between them. An empowering and entrancing window into her own soul. Her older, wiser self. A reminder. A warning. A bridge. A life-changing connection between the distracting present and the certain future. It was the curse that she would only have one life. It was the relief that she could diverge in a different direction, yet she would only take one path. Her path. It was the promise of liberation from teenage anxieties, the control of her fate, and the inevitability of her destiny. After so much fear and discomfort, she could finally picture her future self. She heard the constant part of herself clear in her ears,

"Abbie, this is you. You will live to be in a time when everything around you is different, and you will see many things over the years, and one day you will be her. You will grow old. But you get to live."

Of course, Abbie knew that she might never wear a yellow floral dress, or a pink cardigan, or have blue eyes. But the woman in the portrait resembled her enough to tell her of the years ahead of her and the potential for her life to change. It signaled to a world where all her current worries and issues and setbacks would be forgotten. And when she would have different focuses and problems. It was exciting to think of all the things that would happen to her between now and then. The weddings, the news stories, the changing faces, the discoveries, the lessons she would have to learn. Tears of ecstasy. More tears of heartbreak. And the choice to love or hate. Seeing that woman in the painting renewed her. It gave her the energy to live because Abbie began to wonder in which direction each moment would take her. Her life could go anywhere. She could be anyone. She could do anything. All she knew for sure was that one day, she would be the exact age of the woman in the portrait and that if she didn't take control, those years of her life would happen to her. And she would leave the steering of her life, the only thing she would ever be responsible for, to someone or something else.

Abbie stood there in the gallery. The other museumgoers passed by her, fuzzy in her peripheral vision. She felt their gazes skirt over her, puzzling, as she stood with her arms folded, leaning to her right side, her gaze never breaking from the woman's face. She stared deeper. She felt the energies come to her gleaming and profound. She felt the calm, the collectedness, and the peace of her realization drip over her like treacle. It saturated her, dripping from the top of her head, and seeped down through her body. She could be alone. She could thrive alone. Before she realized what had come over her, everything suddenly made sense. It spoke to her of all she had ever wanted. Freedom. To be free.

Sure, Jonah had inspired her. He had taken her places. He had shared books and ideas that brought magic into her life. Perhaps one day, she would thank him for that. He had upturned her beliefs about her life like flowerpots in her mind and examined the ugly roots below the surface. Jonah might have planted the seeds. But she was the earth, the soil, there long before him. Something, her spirit or her energy, must have always been there. Nothing comes from nothing. Nothing ever could. She was a self-contained entity. And from the enduring eyes of the portrait, she knew the truth. All she needed was already within her.

"Nothing is missing in me," Abbie said to herself under her breath.

ACKNOWLEDGMENTS

It has taken me 14 years to write this book and get it out into the world. It might take another year to thank everyone who helped me with that process.

Firstly, to my outstanding beta readers, my wonderful friends, and everyone who read the book: Kailey Chew (who read it multiple times!), Abena Anim-Somuah, Janelle Batiste, Eloise Dupee, Madison Collins, Kristina Cahojova, Ana Rancic, Holly Li, Clay Vickers, Carolina Weinberg and Serena Bian. It's been two years since most of you sent me edits, which is crazy! Your efforts helped give this book life and made the story substantially better. Your support gave me the momentum I needed to keep going. Thank you!

To my writing teachers and communities: Ann Randolph and my friends in Unmute; Joshua Townshend, Adam Lesser and my friends in Notes On Your Notes; Matt Trinetti, Parul Bavishi, and all the hosts and fellow writers of London Writers' Salon and Writers' Hour. You helped me find my tribe, express myself, and put in the time to work on my craft. I have learned so much from you all. I am eternally grateful to you. Thank you also to Marko Ayling for supporting my creative growth and introducing me to most of those people!

To my enthusiastic readers, my friends who I love, and my Misseducated supporters: Amy Zhuo, Nikolas Baron, Soren Christian, Angelique von Halle, Tiffany Yue, Madeline Penn, Archie Hall, Dr. Diane Sandler, Betel Sánchez Villar, Eza Koch, Emily Paszkiewicz, Alex Golub, Jacqueline Korren, Itzel Garrido, Alara Gebes, Tina Greene, Chery Owens, David Webster, Gayle Ulrich, and Andru Lemon. I am so grateful to have met you and had you in my life. You are patrons in the modern day. You are stars on Earth. Thank you for helping me reach my biggest dream of all: becoming a living, breathing, financially-stable artist. Also, a huge thank you to Wanda Wen, my first patron, for your bounds of support and for inspiring me to create more TikToks!

To my editors, Caroline Kessler, Makena Onjerika, and Tricia Callahan, for bringing the same wit, insights, and professionalism to my book as you would have done for a book at a major publisher. Also, thank you, Lilly Dancyger, for helping me with my query letters when traditional publishing was something I dreamed of.

To my fellow writers and creators: Adam Smiley Poswolsky, Janet Frishberg, Laura Gao, Emi Nietfeld, Steph Smith, and Saleema Vellani. Thank you for answering my questions and quelling my anxieties when I had no idea what to do next. You helped me get unstuck and keep going. You are my living proof, my guiding forces, that being an author is possible. Also, shoutout to Smiley's Author Support community and the Connection Builders that sprung out of that: Rory Gerberg, Ashira Prossack, Elana Gurney, and Jim Kleiber. Thank you for being my ride-or-die friends during the pandemic when I was entertaining the prospect of writing my novel again.

Not to mention my English teachers back at The Godolphin and Latymer School, Miss Fryer, Mr. Bell, and Dr. Stevens, who read early drafts of this book around 2009 (Wow, we are all so ancient!) and believed in me from the beginning. Mr. Pyatt and Mr. Griffiths at Westminster School and whoever chose me for the Fred D'Arcy award for my manuscript back in 2013. Also, Mrs. Marsden and Miss MacDonald at Pembridge Hall (sorry, everyone else, my memory fails me). Thank you all for encouraging me and for teaching me how to read and write. That's no small feat. Dr. Orkan Telhan, thank you for helping me keep my creative spirit alive in your design classes while I was at Wharton. Sandi Hunt, thank you for opening doors and always supporting everything I wanted to do. Kendal Barbee, for ensuring that I could keep exploring a wide and wild curriculum and stay inspired in business school.

To my therapist, Barbara Fazio-McGrory, for helping me heal

and rediscover what I wanted to do. I can't thank you enough for the new quality of life that our sessions have given me. And, well, I have finally finished my novel!

To the people who have put up with me over family holidays or generously given me space and time to write: George, Georgene, Harrison, Triana, and Michael Mitsanas; Maria, Doug, Alexander, Juliana, and Timothy Farrow; Steve, Joanna and Alexandra Demetriou; Rosalind Hyde and Torsten Christian; Jon and Susan Brandler and John Cummins. You gave me many precious moments over the years when I could sit at my laptop in a peaceful setting. When you add up all those moments, that's how the book got done! Thank you!

To everyone on Instagram who helped me change the title at the last minute as I set sail to birth my book into the YA Literature Market. To everyone in ITAA (Internet and Technology Addicts Anonymous) who helped me rediscover a better, sober life away from reality TV and YouTube so that I get to live my dream. To everyone at the St. Elmo Club of Philadelphia for being my home away from home, across the pond, and back again.

To my first real audience: Sarah Pledger, Sydney Crowe, Caroline Roper, Tamar Nahir, and Kal Kini-Davis. You reminded me who I was writing this book for. I hope you liked it!

To my friends who have stuck with me over the years. Juan Sebastián Pinto, who once called me "prolific" when it came to my writing. Your belief in me means more than you know. Daniella Gruenspecht, thank you for taking me on the trip of a lifetime that helped me quit my job and realign. Amel Abid, for being an endless and inspiring force of nature. Katka Sabo, for constantly encouraging me and asking when the book would be out (well, it's out now!). Caroline Wallis, for being someone I could share the challenges of becoming an author with along the way. Diana Hawk, thank you for your self-publishing inspiration and mentorship as a friend. Emilia Barrosse, for being a partner in creative crime. Morgan Snyder, for getting me to pick up The Artist's Way and warming my heart and mind. Summer Yue, for supporting me through my perpetual lack of stable employment and believing I could make it big in the creative world. Josephine Fauchier, thank you for letting me write the first words of this book at your house in France. Terilyn Steverson, for bringing more fun and joy into my life. Katya Christian, thank you for your willing feedback on the book and attention to detail that has saved me multiple times. Julia Christian, for inspiring me to build a life of my own and helping me get into university, lol. Rose Cummins, Cecilia Weissbein, and Pepe Molina, thank you for your help designing the book cover. Kashish Hora, thank you for giving me the promo code of a lifetime! María Isabel Cole, thank you so much for being such a fierce champion of my work. Ashna Yakoob, thank you for your honest feedback and efforts to help me get my book out there in the world.

Thank you to my family: Karen, Peter, Anya, Cían, Dandy, and our latest addition, Mariia Masliuk. I'm so grateful to have grown up in a stable and academically rigorous home and to have such rad younger siblings that I can look up to. I love you all, and I'm sorry if you end up reading the awkward parts of the book. As well as my fabulous grandmother, Patricia Weinberg, an artist herself, for faithfully asking me every Sunday, "How's your writing going?" To my other grandparents, Neal Doherty, Josephine Doherty, and James Weinberg. You are loved. You are missed.

Lastly, if you've made it this far, I would like to thank you also! This whole creative experience would not have been possible without your interest lingering until the very end. I hope you liked the book and will share it with a friend or two to spread the word. Or ping me on social media, demanding I write the next one.

See you on the internet!

@misseducated_

ABOUT THE AUTHOR

Tash Doherty is a British-Irish-American writer and author. She is the creator of *Misseducated*, a blog and podcast about unlearning and the female experience. Tash started writing her first novel, *These Perfectly Careless Things*, at age 14. She graduated from the Wharton School, University of Pennsylvania, and lives in Mexico City.

ALSO BY TASH DOHERTY

Misseducated Substack

Misseducated Podcast

Articles